PRAISE FOR CLARE FURNISS

'Lingers in the mind long after the final word has been read'
Malorie Blackman, author of *Noughts & Crosses*

'Absolutely gorgeous, heartfelt and incredibly enjoyable'
Robin Stevens, author of the Murder Most Unladylike series

'Funny, moving and packed with characters that jump off the page'
Lisa Williamson, author of *The Art of Being Normal*

'Funny, sharply observed, shocking and wonderful'
Sunday Times

'A beautifully executed story . . .
gloriously funny, deeply emotional and a triumph'
Daily Mail

'Beautifully written'
Stylist

T0316106

ALSO BY CLARE FURNISS

The Year of the Rat
How Not to Disappear

CLARE FURNISS

THE THINGS WE LEAVE BEHIND

SIMON & SCHUSTER

First published in Great Britain in 2024 by Simon & Schuster UK Ltd

1 3 5 7 9 10 8 6 4 2

Simon & Schuster UK Ltd
1st Floor, 222 Gray's Inn Road
London WC1X 8HB

www.simonandschuster.co.uk
www.simonandschuster.com.au
www.simonandschuster.co.in

Simon & Schuster Australia, Sydney
Simon & Schuster India, New Delhi

A CIP catalogue record for this book
is available from the British Library.

PB ISBN 978-1-4711-6981-6
eBook ISBN 978-1-4711-6982-3

Typeset in Times by M Rules
Printed and bound in the UK using 100% renewable
electricity at CPI Group (UK) Ltd

MIX
Paper | Supporting
responsible forestry
FSC® C171272

'Just for today,' Dad said. 'Forget everything else. Just let today be perfect.'

So we did. We forgot that at fifteen I was really too old for a birthday picnic that had become a family tradition when I was three. We forgot that the weather forecast had said light to moderate showers and a strong breeze were likely in the southeast by mid-afternoon. We forgot that society may or may not have been collapsing around us. Dad cast a spell, we allowed ourselves to fall under it. And my birthday was perfect.

He invited the same old family friends every year and, when I was a kid, half my classmates. Now the only schoolfriends to make the invite list were Mischa and Danny, my oldest friends. Most years the picnic wasn't perfect, not quite. There'd be arguments. Or a kid went missing, or was sick, or injured themselves. Or the weather was wrong, because despite humanity's best efforts to set the planet on fire, somehow London on a holiday weekend in May is often rainy, or the wind turns out to be colder than you expected, and everyone has to try to pretend they're not wishing they'd worn at least one sweater.

This day was magical. The sun shone in defiance of the forecast, and we stretched ourselves out like cats, lazy and happy in its warmth. We ate iced gems and cocktail sausages on sticks and a squashed chocolate cake I'd watched being carefully covered in Smarties by Billie in our kitchen that morning, acting like I didn't notice she was eating half of them.

Mischa sneaked paper cups of wine for us while Dad and his friends were too busy dozing or having boring conversations to notice, and Danny played football and rounders with Billie and the other little kids, organizing them into teams, cheering them on, resolving their arguments, until their shadows grew long. I felt a pang of happiness watching him and I knew Mischa did too. She'd never have admitted it but she'd worried like I had that he was drifting away from us, that everything was changing. It was a relief to see the old Danny, like he always had been. It was right. Everything was right.

Claudia almost broke the spell. She arrived at the picnic very late, and there was a forced brightness about her, a kind of distracted sadness when she thought no one was looking. She laughed and said she was just tired but it was obviously more than that. Dad put his arm round her, looked concerned.

She waved a dismissive hand. 'Something at work,' she said. 'Boring. Now let's enjoy this bloody picnic. Have you lot left me any booze?' There was plenty left for Claudia despite Mischa having placed herself strategically next to whichever bottle had just been opened.

Billie spotted her and waved.

'Mum! You missed my goal!'

She turned away to chase after the ball, but Claudia kept watching her with an expression that didn't belong at my perfect, sunlit birthday. I felt a pinprick of irritation. Why did she always have to worry? What happened to you when you were a grown-up that made you serious all the time, just under the surface, even when you were supposed to be having fun? Nothing could really be wrong on this enchanted, golden day.

Eventually people started to drift off, slow and reluctant. I feel now like we sensed what was coming and that was why no one wanted to leave. But probably it was just the sun and the wine. Dad and Claudia packed up and persuaded Billie and her friends it was time to go home, their howls of protest quietened by encouragement from Danny and promises of popcorn and a movie from Dad. Billie didn't want to leave me and hung on to my hand till I promised I'd see her at home later and tell her a story.

It was early evening, no curfew patrols out yet. Mischa and Danny and I wandered down to the boating lake and sat and talked till the sky turned orange and pink in front of us, deepening blue above. We argued about whether the first star was really a plane but made a wish on it anyway. *Star light, star bright.* I wished that ... I don't know. What was it that I wished for, back then? When I was a little kid it was that Mum would come back or even that she had never left in the first place. By fifteen I knew there was no point wishing for the impossible. But I can't imagine now – that day, my birthday, with my friends there with me, my home round the corner, my family waiting for me, what could I possibly have wished for?

'I've got to go,' Danny said suddenly, awkward. 'My dad needs me to . . .'

Something. I don't remember what. He always was a bad liar. He goes red under his freckles and looks at the floor, has done ever since he was a little kid in trouble with a teacher.

But our spell was too strong for even that to break it. We wouldn't let it.

'Just you and me then, babe,' Mischa said as we watched him disappear. 'Like it should be, right?'

She pulled a bottle half-full of warm wine out of her bag like she was pulling a rabbit out of a hat, and I got the giggles and laughed so hard it made my belly hurt and I had to lie down, so Mischa lay down too and we propped ourselves up on our elbows and drank the wine. We invented backstories for all the people who walked past and wondered what it would be like to be them and laughed some more because everything was funny and because we were so happy not to be any one else but us.

And then we walked home through the dusty London summer streets, arm in arm, sun-dazed, wine-dizzy, singing loudly and out of tune as the first drops of the light to moderate showers fell. We turned our faces up to the sky and the thick summer smell of rain on warm pavements rose around us and Mischa held her arms out and grabbed my hand as thunder rumbled.

As we spun and whooped and splashed our way home, I

told myself I would *never* forget, not even when I'm ninety years old, what it feels like to be fifteen and right on the edge of everything exciting and real, and have the best friend in the world, and to walk together in a summer rainstorm through the streets we grew up in.

That's how I remember it.

Mischa told me once that when you're remembering something you're actually just remembering the last time you remembered it. So it's like a whispered message passed along a line. Who knows how close the end result is to how it started out? You get things wrong and cut things out and add things without even realizing, and over time the tiny changes get bigger. So all memories are stories really. *Based on real events*, like they say about movies.

But whatever. That's how I remember it.

My fifteenth birthday was the last perfect day.

STORY

Shortening of Latin *historia* meaning 'history, inquiry, account, narrative, story'. An account of imaginary or real people and events told for entertainment. A description, either true or imagined, of a connected series of events. A particular person's representation of the facts of a matter. A lie.

The woman doesn't notice the girl at first, though her outside café table is only a few feet away from where the girl is standing. Dusk is falling and the woman is cold, despite the canopy hung with fairy lights and the heaters. She tries in vain to attract the waiter's attention and watches with irritation as he hurries instead to a much younger woman with sleek blonde hair just behind her.

When you're used to being seen you can't imagine being invisible, the woman thinks, and looks away, out to the square where tourists and Christmas shoppers are getting in the way of those heading home from work.

And now she notices the girl hovering nearby, lank-haired, an unwashed look about her clothes, her limbs too thin inside them.

The woman stiffens. There have always been beggars in Edinburgh of course, as there are in all big cities. Like overpriced coffee, it's an inconvenience she accepts as part of city life. But there are more and more of them every day now: mothers, children, old men – hands held out to people like

9

her, sitting in cafés and restaurants with their lipstick-marked coffee cups, empty wine glasses, remains of abandoned meals on their plates. She is resentful of the prickle of guilt she feels. *These people ought to leave us in peace*, she tells herself. *We're doing no harm. We're luckier than they are. That doesn't make us bad people, does it?*

This girl doesn't hold out her hand though. She watches. The woman watches back and is reminded unexpectedly of her own daughter, of a book they used to read together at bedtime. There was one story in particular Anna would ask her to read over and over, even though it made her cry. 'The Little Match Girl', about a child who saw comforting visions in the light of the matches she lit as she froze on the streets. The woman had never liked it herself. Children's stories ought not to have sad endings. She had changed the ending until Anna was old enough to decipher the words herself. Was the little match girl an angel in that last picture? No! She had simply grown wings and flown away. *The poor girl*, Anna had said with tears in her eyes when she finally pieced the real story together, her fingers stroking the picture of the frozen little match seller. *It's not fair*. She'd say the same now, no doubt, if she was here.

'Are you all right?' the woman finds herself calling out to the girl. She feels the couple at the next table turn to stare at her with surprise that echoes her own.

The girl moves closer. The woman instinctively leans back in her chair, already regretting speaking to her.

'He came here,' the girl says.

The woman, who is never unnerved, is unnerved. By the

girl; by herself. She smiles at the girl in the brisk, dismissive way she always smiles at people when she wants them to go away. But the girl doesn't notice. She barely seems to look at her at all.

'Grandpa. He came here.'

'Your grandfather?' The woman looks around for him. 'Here?'

'Not now,' the girl says. 'Before.'

The woman says nothing. She shouldn't have spoken to the girl. She is missing Anna, that's all. Not a good reason to strike up conversation with beggar girls, especially ones who talk in unsettling riddles instead of just asking for money and going away when you don't give it to them.

'With my granny,' the girl who isn't Anna says. 'This is their place.'

Her eyes are glassy, her face a little flushed. She has a fever, the woman thinks. She isn't well. When Anna was ill as a child, she would make her chicken soup.

'Is anyone with you? Family?'

'My sister.'

'Your parents . . . ?'

The girl shakes her head. 'Just us.'

'No one to take care of you? You don't look well.'

The girl doesn't seem to be listening now, or rather she seems to be listening to something the woman can't hear.

'Where do you sleep?' the woman persists, not knowing why. She knows about the camps that grow up like weeds in the grey, unloved cracks in the city. Small, tented towns, ripped down by the police from time to time only to bloom again somewhere else.

'*Psshht*,' a waiter says loudly, flicking a cloth at the girl as if he's scaring off a mangy pigeon pecking at leftover crumbs. 'No begging here. *Go!*' He gestures dismissively to her.

'Fucking cockroaches,' he mutters as he turns away and the woman flinches despite herself. The waiter is young, not much older than the girl who isn't Anna. His face is handsome and – the woman had thought – kind.

And now the girl has turned and is walking away. The woman wants to call after her but doesn't know what to say, what to tell her that would help. Her sister would know. But the thought of asking Polly for help ... Anyway, they're so different these days.

She feels panic – why? – as the girl gets further from her. She remembers the picture of the little match girl flying off to heaven, and it seems to her for a moment that as she walks away the girl begins to float. She imagines she sees wings unfurling from the thin, dirty coat the girl is wearing, not warm enough for the Edinburgh winter.

But Clem does not fly.

Instead, she sways and drops to the pavement. The woman runs to her.

'Hey,' the waiter calls. 'Your bill!' *Now* he pays her attention.

'Are you okay? Can you hear me?' The girl's eyelids flutter. 'Stay awake, little match girl,' the woman mutters as she reaches for her phone. 'Polly?' she says, trying to sound businesslike. 'It's me ... Yes, yes, I'm fine. Look, there's a girl. You need to help her. I'm with her now. She was begging and ... I think she's ill. Or maybe just hungry, I don't know. No parents, she says, just a sister—'

The woman scans the street in the direction the girl had been walking, trying to spot the sister. As she does, she listens to her own sister's voice, sighs, rolls her eyes. Saint Polly, self-righteous as always. She bites back her irritation and listens, absently stroking the hair of the girl as if she were a much younger child.

'Yes ... *yes*,' she says eventually. 'I know all that. And I *know* they all need help, but I'm with this one now, and she's ill, and—' And what? Anna. Chicken soup. The little match girl. She can't say any of this. '... And if I leave her, I don't know what will happen to her,' she says instead. It is all she can say. It should be enough.

She holds the girl's hand. *Don't let go.*

She hopes it is enough.

*

'So, Clem. Let's start at the beginning. How long is it since you left London?'

The woman has a kind face, but behind it she's professional, watching me closely as we talk in a cramped office on the second floor, with big windows looking out over an enclosed courtyard. Outside, some of the younger kids are being led out to play. I can't see Billie but she's probably at the back, still putting on her coat and chatting, chatting, as always. Have

13

they given her a scarf to wear, gloves? The wind is bitter today. A memory comes from nowhere, of Billie's gloves with the animals on the fingers. They never got packed. Are they still at home, stuffed into the pockets of her school duffle coat along with a couple of conkers, a pebble, sweet wrappers? Is the coat still hanging on a hook in the hall, in the silence and shadows, dust collecting unseen in its folds?

Some nights when I can't sleep, I imagine walking round our house, filled with all the lost everyday things that got left behind, a museum of us. Through the red-painted front door, tripping over Billie's school shoes abandoned in the hallway ... into the sitting room, where I'm sprawled on the sofa watching TV, to the kitchen where Dad's cooking pasta, a large glass of red wine in hand, Claudia sitting at the breakfast bar with her laptop, telling him about work ... the garden where Billie's on the swing singing made-up nonsense songs about invisible elephants or magical hats. Sometimes I imagine the ghosts of us are still there, living our old lives. Other times I wonder if I'm the ghost and the real me got left behind and I dig my nails into the skin of my arms, to check there's blood inside me, to make sure that I can feel it.

I drag my focus back to the woman talking to me. I don't remember exactly who she is, though I think she must have told me. Someone from the charity, but whether she's some kind of counsellor or just another person filling in more forms I don't know. *Did* she tell me? It's all been a blur since we arrived here. No, that's not right. Things seem very clear as they happen, too clear somehow, too loud and bright. But they don't seem to sink in, so nothing joins together. Like those toys – Billie had one at home, a kind of spinning top with slits in the side and strips of pictures that you put inside. What was it called? When you watched through the little windows the pictures merged and seemed to be moving, clowns juggling and acrobats tumbling. But when you slowed it down to a standstill you could see that really each image was clear and complete on its own. It didn't join on to anything else, it didn't move or make sense.

'Clem?' She looks at me, silent, waiting.

'Sorry?' She must think I'm stupid.

Nah, Mischa says in my head. *She just thinks you're insane. I mean, that must be why they sent you to see her, right?*

'How long is it since you left your home?' the woman says gently.

I count backwards, trying to piece it all together. It seems impossible to measure everything that's happened in days, weeks, months, as if it's something that could be contained in the squares on a calendar. What's happened to us feels outside of time, too big for it. Time is different now. There is now and before, but they don't always go in the order they should, they muddle together, and I forget which one I'm in. Perhaps there will be an after, but I can't imagine it.

'I'm not sure exactly. Months.'

Polly – that was her name, I remember now – is waiting to see if I'll say anything more, still watching me closely. I decide Mischa's right: she's definitely some kind of shrink. I remember them from when I was a kid, after Mum left

15

and everyone was worried about me, leaving gaps to see if I'd fill them. Now I concentrate on smoothing the dog-eared corners of the notebook in my lap. It's hard not to speak when someone's waiting for you to say something, but I guess I got pretty good at it back then. Focus on something else, have an imaginary conversation in your head. It turns out I've still got the knack.

'And you're sixteen years old?'

'Yes.'

She checks a form and some notes. I wonder what's written in them.

'There are no adults here with you?'

'No.'

'At home you lived with your father and stepmother?'

She must know this already. I've told at least three other people this stuff: a form-filler, someone medical, a bored-looking man in a dandruff-flecked suit.

'And Billie.'

'Billie . . .' she prompts gently. 'She's your half-sister?'

Usually when people ask this it's in a tone of disbelief. We couldn't be more different. Me, lanky and skinny, kind of clumsy-looking, mousy hair and skin so pale I'm practically translucent, needing several months of sun before I stop being the colour of skimmed milk; Billie, stocky and fizzing with energy and ideas, a mini-Claudia with the same heart-shaped face, dark-brown skin and determined look. Only her smile is Dad's, wide and mischievous. Mine is my mum's apparently, though I can't remember her smiling much.

'Billie's not half anything,' I tell Polly.

She looks at me, questioning.

'It's what my dad said. When I was younger, I always thought when people called us half-sisters it made it sound like we only belonged to each other half as much as "real" sisters. I always wanted to say, *Don't call her that. She's my sister.* When I said that to Dad he laughed. He said, *Course she is. Billie never does anything by halves.* Because she's so ... Billie. You can't ignore her, you know?' I want to go to the window now, to see what she's doing out in the garden, but it might seem rude. And now I can feel the panicky feeling rising again and Polly is speaking but I can't hear her because there's a roaring sound in my ears and my heart is pounding so hard I can't breathe, I can't breathe—

'Clem?'

Polly's hand on my arm. 'It's okay,' she says. 'Breathe with me. In ... and now out. In ...'

Eventually the fading room comes back into focus.

'That's it,' Polly says. 'You're okay, Clem. You're safe.'

She walks to the water cooler and fills a cup for me and one for herself, putting them down on the table between us. Her nails are painted a glittery dark green, just like Mischa used to wear sometimes, and I want to tell her I like it, that my best friend used to wear nail varnish just the same colour, maybe the same brand even, and that I miss her so much. And I want to explain how I miss wearing nail varnish, which I know seems kind of silly now what with everything else there is to miss, but it was nice to care about what you looked like, right down to whether even your hands looked nice.

'If you can,' Polly says, 'I think it would be really helpful for you to tell me, in your own words, how you came to be here. About why you had to leave home and what happened after you did.'

The air of the room hums with my silence. From outside there are sounds of life, someone whistling in the corridor, a child – not Billie – laughing outside. Inside the room we are in a different world, a muffled place halfway between the living and the dead.

'I know it's not easy, to revisit difficult things, to share them,' Polly says. 'There's no rush. We can take our time.'

I say nothing.

'Do you think you can do that, Clem?'

She waits, her face kind, her blue eyes watching me closely.

Eventually she says, 'I can see you're tired. We can take this as slow as you like.'

She means it as reassurance, but all I hear is that however long it takes, I'll eventually have to tell her everything.

'You're not feeling unwell again?'

I shake my head, picturing myself as she must see me, as I'd seen myself in the mirror of the communal bathroom this morning, a thin, hollow-eyed stranger. A ghost. Billie at my side, trying to talk and brush her teeth at the same time. I tap the table leg very gently with my toe, watching the vibrations shiver the water in my cup.

'I think that's enough for today,' Polly says at last. 'We'll pick this up again next time, shall we?'

Thank God, I can go. I stand, ready to run for the door.

'There's a games night tonight,' she says hopefully. 'Board games, chess, that kind of thing. Come along if you like.'

'Maybe,' I say, knowing I won't.

'What's the book?' Polly asks, apparently casually but you never know with shrinks. Instinctively I hold it close to me as if she might try and grab it.

'It's just a notebook. Billie gave it to me. For my birthday.'

As I say the words, the pure, impossible happiness of that day flashes into my head. It feels like staring into the sun, too bright to look at for long. My grip tightens on the notebook, as if it contains that joy, as if it can take me back there.

'You write in it? A diary?'

'Stories,' I say, feeling myself blush. 'For Billie.'

'Really?' she says. 'What a lovely idea. I'd love to read them sometime, if you'd let me?'

'*No*.' It's out before I can stop it. I can hear the fury in my own voice.

Babe? imaginary Mischa says. *I get it, okay, but ideally you need to not act crazy at the nice shrink lady. Otherwise you'll have to keep coming to see her for ever. Just act normal, if you can remember how. Right?*

Right. I catch my breath.

'Clem?' Polly says. 'Are you okay? I'm sorry, I didn't mean to upset you. Of course, I totally understand that you want to keep what you write private. It's personal to you.'

'Not really. They're just silly stories. Just fairy tales. Not even that really. My grandpa used to tell me all these myths and folk tales when I was a little kid. I loved them.' I know I'm gabbling, trying to distract from that flash of anger, trying to cover it up, but I'm only making things worse. 'I can only remember bits of them now. So I make up my own versions for Billie.'

I force myself to smile at Polly. She nods and smiles back, handing me a tissue, and it's only then that I realize there are tears on my face.

I look out of the window as I leave, to wave at Billie, but it's started to rain and the garden is empty.

*

Once there was a girl who lived at the edge of a great forest with her sister and her mother and father. One day the father sent the sisters off into the woods to pick berries for their supper. 'Stick to the path,' their mother said. 'And keep away from the darkest part of the forest.' Everyone knew that the place where the trees grew thickest and thorniest, and the shadows grew thicker still, was under the spell of a powerful witch.

The berries the sisters picked at the edge of the forest were so delicious that they ate them all, until their fingers and mouths were stained red and the light was beginning to fade. They knew they ought to go home but didn't want to return to their mother and father empty-handed.

'We must pick more berries,' the older sister said. And she led her sister deeper into the trees, deeper into the shadows. But the path grew more overgrown and difficult

to follow, and the only berries to be found in this part of the forest were poisonous nightshade growing among the toadstools and hemlock and all other things that like the dark.

As they rested under a tree, the younger sister saw a flash of colour in the branches above them. It was a dazzling bird with rainbow wings and it sang a song so clear and beautiful that the little girl was enchanted. As the bird took flight, she ran off after it – and her sister followed, forgetting all the warnings she had been given.

But when they reached the tree they'd seen the bird fly towards, it was gone. They could hear its song close by and then spied the flash of its wings as it flew off again, further into the shadowy gloom.

The sisters followed the sound of its song deeper and deeper into the forest and before long they were lost.

*

'Clem!'

I'm deep in shadowy dream, too deep to know the voice or understand it, but not too deep to feel panic: I have to reach it, I have to get to where it is.

'*Clem.*' An insistent whisper.

I open my eyes, staring blindly for a second into the familiar dark of the dormitory, a big, high-ceilinged room divided by makeshift screens and curtains to give some privacy.

Billie comes into focus, clutching Luna, her toy owl, shivering. This happens most nights. Before I'm properly awake I always think we're at home. It's not that I forget where I am exactly, it's more *when* I am that gets confused. I think I've gone back. Time and reality blur at night. It's hard to unpick dreams from memories and shadows.

'Hey,' I whisper, reaching out a hand. 'You okay, B?'

She nods.

'Something disturb you?'

There are lots of us in the dormitory, maybe twenty, maybe more, all women and girls. The building used to be a school, Polly told me. It was going to be turned into flats but the developer went bust or something. Our beds are separated by screens and curtains but they don't keep out the night-time noises: phones, whispers, snoring, people crying out in their sleep, almost-silent crying. The darkness is thick with other people's dreams, with their homesickness.

She shrugs.

'Did you have a bad dream?'

She doesn't answer.

'It's okay,' I say. 'Nothing to be scared of.'

'I'm not scared,' Billie says in a whisper that manages to be scathing. 'I just want to be with you.'

'Come on then.' There's barely enough room for me in the narrow, sagging bed, let alone Billie as well, but we manage. She snuggles in close and I wrap an arm round her, her hair tickly against my nose.

'Better?' I whisper.

I feel her nod.

'Good. Me too.'

Sometimes she wants to talk, or for me to tell her a story. Sometimes just being close is enough.

'I was trying to remember the name of that toy you had at home,' I say. 'The spinning top thing with the pictures.'

'Why?'

'I don't know. I just thought of it.'

'Dad gave it to me,' she said. 'He made pictures to put in it of a bird taking off and flying because that was what I wanted most.'

She's quiet for a minute and I think maybe she's fallen asleep.

'When will we go home?' she says.

I search for an answer in the dark.

'I don't know, B,' I say at last. 'As soon as it's safe.'

Home. Safe. They don't feel real, as much stories as any of the fairy tales I write for her.

'Okay,' she says.

'I love you,' I say.

I close my eyes. After a while I feel her breathing slow as she drifts off. I try to drift too, but I can't. I can't stop thinking.

About the spinning toy.

About Billie's gloves.

About Polly and her questions.

Polly thinks if I answer all her questions, if I tell her everything, then that will make it better.

She's wrong.

I remember the kind concern on her face, her certainty that I will tell her everything if she gives me enough time. *Do you think you can do that, Clem?*

No. I can't do it.

I try to breathe slowly, heavily, try to trick myself into calm, into sleep. But my mind isn't calm, it's racing off into the dark, away from the questions and their answers, getting tangled up in itself, snagged on memories.

Some of the stories Grandpa told me when I was a kid were about the Knights of the Round Table. Swords in stones, wizards, all that. In one story there was this old king who got wounded, and all he could do was go fishing and watch his land fall into ruin and wait for a knight to come and ask him a certain question that would heal him.

'What question?' I asked Grandpa.

'Nobody knows.'

'What do you mean?'

'It depends on who's telling the story.'

'That's stupid,' I said. 'And how could a question heal you anyway?'

'The way I see it,' Grandpa replied, 'everyone's got answers inside them that they don't know till the right question is asked. Or maybe they *do* know the answers, but they aren't brave enough to say them out loud until someone asks them the right question. Either way, the question works like a key.'

'A key to unlock a person?'

Grandpa had nodded then. 'And in this story, only a true knight would be the kind of person to know the right question.'

I think Polly is that sort of person. And she will keep asking me questions until she gets to the one she knows will unlock me and let out everything that's hidden inside.

But I don't want to be unlocked.

I close my eyes but I know I won't sleep now.

From the locker next to my bed I take out socks, a sweater and my rucksack. I tiptoe across to the window, which has a ledge below it just wide enough for me to sit on. It's got one of those blinds with the plastic slats, but stripes of light shine through from a street lamp outside. From a pocket in the rucksack I take out a bird folded from gold paper, a small round mirror with mother-of-pearl roses on the back, a photograph, a blue feather. Finally, I take out the notebook. I lay them all in a row, these precious things from long ago and far away that washed up with me on the shore of this new life. I hold them one by one in the orange glow of the street lamp, like a ritual. I don't wish or pray or anything. I just hold them. Then carefully I put them away. All except the notebook.

You're good at stories, Billie told me that day, my perfect, golden birthday, when she gave me the notebook.

Yes.

I like telling stories.

I turn back through the dog-eared pages of the notebook now, right to the first page. Time bends and twists and collapses in on itself.

Written there in childish writing are the words:

once there was a girl who

Maybe I can do it after all. Maybe I can tell Polly my story. The story of how Billie and I came to be here.

Perhaps I'll even give it a happy ending.

*

'*Happy birthday!*'

I started into semi-consciousness, forcing open an eye, and saw Billie's face millimetres from mine in the grey half-light. Her breath was warm on my cheek.

'Here's your present,' she said.

'Mmmhh . . .'

Something I couldn't see, but which had sharp corners, was pressed hard against my chest and neck so that my head was wedged back against the pillow.

'You're not asleep, are you?' she said, belatedly.

'I mean . . . ?' I squinted at the blur of her. 'I guess not any more.'

'*Yessss,*' she hissed. 'Mum said I had to wait till you were awake to give you my present and now you are.'

'I said I wasn't asleep,' I croaked. 'I didn't say I was awake.'

'Openitopenitopenitop—'

I closed my eyes. 'Just gimme a minute, B.'

She sighed theatrically and removed her elbows from my ribcage. 'One second two second three second four—'

'Okay, okay.' I wriggled myself into a more upright position and blinked till the world began to sharpen.

'I can help you open it if you like,' Billie said, holding out the present, which was wrapped in paper covered with kittens wearing sunglasses. She was breathless with excitement, hopping from foot to foot in her mermaid pyjamas.

'Come on then,' I pulled the duvet back. 'Get in. *Oww!* How are your feet so freezing?'

I tore back the paper at one end and Billie did the same at the other. Inside was an expensive-looking hardback notebook, with a green cover made to look old, and a design of birds flying across it embossed in gold.

'Wow, B! It's beautiful.'

'Do you like it?'

'I love it.' I put my arm round her and kissed the top of her head.

'I saved up my own money for it,' she said.

'No way.'

'I chose it specially because of the birds.'

'Of course.'

'And because you like green. And because it looks really old, like a book from a haunted-house library.'

I smiled. 'It looks exactly like that. Do you think the book might be haunted?' I did a *woooo* spooky ghost noise and waved it at her.

She looked up at me seriously. 'I actually think it might be magic.'

'I think you might be right.' I turned the heavy cream pages of the book. Lined on one side, blank on the other. 'How I am I going to think of anything special enough to write in there though?'

'It doesn't have to be special,' Billie said. 'You can write anything. Anyway, you're good at stories.'

'If it's magic, the stories might come true.'

Billie's eyes went round. 'You better make them have happy endings then.'

'Happy endings are boring.'

'No they're not. Happy stories are the best stories.'

'Okay. Well, you better help me write the first one then, or I'll make all the wrong things happen.'

There was a yawn from the doorway. I looked up and saw Claudia there in her dressing gown.

'Mama!' Billie shouted. 'Say happy birthday to Clem.'

'Happy birthday, Clem. Sorry you didn't get a birthday lie-in.' She walked over and kissed me on the cheek, ever so slightly self-conscious, in the way that affection between Claudia and me always was, even after nine years. It wasn't that we didn't mean it, just that, somehow, we always felt aware of it, like the steps of a dance we were still practising till we could do it without thinking. 'Billie, you do realize it's not even morning yet?'

'After midnight is morning. Because it's the next day.'

Claudia gave her a look.

'She was awake,' Billie added quickly.

'I bet she really appreciated that, B.'

'She *really* did,' I said. 'Thanks, Claudia. You didn't have to get up.'

'I needed to anyway. I've got to go to work. It's a clinic morning.' Claudia was always busy, working as a GP, volunteering, mentoring, being on committees. 'I'll be back for the birthday picnic though. Your dad made me promise on pain of death.'

'What am I being accused of now?' Dad appeared in the doorway in his dressing gown, bleary, hair sticking up. He came over and wrapped me in a bear hug. He'd always made such a big thing of my birthday when I was a little kid, to try and make up for Mum not being there I realized later. He'd never outgrown the habit and I loved him for it.

'Happy birthday, sweetheart,' he said.

'Thanks, Dad.'

'But you need to stop growing up now. No more. Okay?'

I rolled my eyes at him. 'Dad!'

'Fifteen!' he said. 'Where did my little girl go?'

I knew he was joking but I also knew he really was a little bit sad too and I didn't want him to be. I kissed him on the cheek.

'I love you,' I said. 'And I think you should go and make me some coffee.'

He smiled. 'Your wish is my command, birthday girl.'

'I'll do it,' Claudia said, resting her hand briefly on Dad's shoulder as she passed. 'Got to get moving anyway. Come and help me, Billie? Give Clem five minutes' peace on her birthday.'

'Sorry, can't.' Billie climbed back under the duvet and picked up the notebook. 'Me and Clem are writing a story in the magic notebook.'

*

We didn't end up writing our story that day, Billie and I.

On the first page of my notebook, Billie wrote:

once there was a girl who

29

But there were so many possibilities back then that we couldn't decide what came next. And then there were more presents to open and pancakes to eat before Claudia went to work. And then cards arrived and yet more presents, and then Mischa turned up with massive helium balloons in the shape of a 1 and an 8. 'They'd run out of fives,' she told Dad, wide-eyed and innocent, whispering to me later that we might get served in the pub if they thought it was my eighteenth. And then there was the cake to decorate and the sandwiches to make and then and then and then . . .

'Leave a page,' Billie had said. 'Two pages. So we can write the story later.'

But, somehow, we never did.

We can't tell the story now that we could have told then. Those people don't exist any more. They were us, but we are not them.

That story won't be written now.

I must tell a different story instead.

*

'You're looking well today,' Polly says encouragingly as I walk into her office.

In my head, Mischa snorts. *She's just being nice. You look like you have some olden-days disease. Scurvy. Or rickets. Oh, no – wait! Consumption. Actually, maybe all of them.*

Polly smiles and fetches me some water, but I don't drink it because my throat feels so tight I'm not sure I could. I focus on acting normal. My nails dig into my palms.

30

'So,' Polly says. 'Why don't you tell me a bit about your home?'

This wasn't a question I'd been expecting.

'How do you mean?'

She smiles. 'I mean, just about your family ... friends maybe. Whatever you want to share. What life was like, before all this. If you'd like to?'

I wouldn't like to, but it's easier than talking about what came after.

And once I start I find it's hard to stop.

I tell her how we were just pretty normal, me, Dad, Claudia and Billie, even though I know there's no such thing as normal, and some people would probably think we weren't normal at all. But what I mean is that we were just pretty boring.

I tell her about how it had just been Dad and me for a few years, before Dad and Claudia got together. How they had this mutual friend who was a journalist like Dad and who'd been at university with Claudia, and he set them up on a date. And Dad thought Claudia wouldn't be interested in him because she was some high-flying doctor and beautiful and idealistic, and he was, in his words, a 'cynical old political hack with terrible dress sense', but it turned out they had loads in common – they were both only children, had both lost their parents in their twenties, both liked the same (terrible) music, which meant Billie and I later had to listen to it on every car journey, blah blah. They'd tell the story of how they met a lot. It was kind of cute, but kind of nauseating.

And I tell Polly about how Claudia was soon expecting

Billie and they'd worried that I might feel jealous or anxious when Billie came along, so Claudia had got me to talk to Billie even before she was born so that she'd know my voice when she came out, and how I used to tell her stories even then. And I tell Polly how when I visited tiny newborn Billie in hospital and she gripped my finger like she was never going to let go of it, I felt like I remembered her even though it was the first time we'd ever met; like I'd known her all along, all my life, maybe even before that.

Then I tell her about Mischa and how I'd known her since my first day at nursery and how when she argued with her mum she could change from speaking English to Polish in the middle of a sentence, which seemed like a kind of superpower to me. How she bought all her clothes in charity shops and wore crazy eye make-up and always looked amazing. And how she loved horror movies but also cute kitten videos, and was the funniest person I knew.

And I tell her about Danny and how his mum was sick from when we were little kids and he had to look after her, and sometimes he'd get in trouble at school for being late or not doing homework, even though we knew it was because he had to do stuff at home and it wasn't fair. But he never complained about it because he just wasn't a complaining kind of person. And sometimes Mischa and I felt bad because we complained about stupid stuff all the time, but not so bad that we didn't do it.

I tell her how on Sundays Dad always made us pancakes with bacon and maple syrup, and how he's a massive geek and knows all about comics and Dungeons and Dragons, and drinks about five hundred cups of black coffee a day.

And how Claudia is good at everything except cartwheels, which really annoyed her, and how I used to do them all the time because it was the one thing I knew I could do better than her. And how she was always doing things for other people, like taking meals to our housebound neighbour or volunteering at the foodbank.

And how Billie nagged Claudia till she put up a bird table in the garden and Billie used to watch the birds on it and look them up on this app I got on my phone and draw pictures of them that we stuck on the fridge.

And how we were happy.

Until—

'Until . . . ?' Polly prompts.

*

It wasn't until two weeks after my birthday that I found out what had been wrong with Claudia that golden day, that cloud in the blue sky, that pinprick of wrongness.

It was this:

When Claudia had popped home to change before coming to the park she'd found an official-looking letter lying on the doormat with the birthday cards and pizza flyers. She read it sitting at the breakfast bar in the kitchen with the sun slanting in through the glass doors, catching in its glow the smeared line of fingerprints. These had first begun to appear, she remembered, when Billie started walking – yesterday it seemed – and always reappeared no matter how fiercely Claudia resisted them with Windolene and J cloths, their progress climbing higher each year, a rising river. And ghost messages too that Billie and her friend Sakura had written with fingertips in the mist of their breath: smileys and hearts, *Billie!!* and *Sakura!!*, and *HELLO STINKYPANTS*.

I really must clean those windows, Claudia had thought, because it was something she could do, something normal she could cling to when everything else seemed to have shifted around her and come loose. But she didn't move, because in another bit of her mind those messages seemed unimaginably precious suddenly, mystical, ancient marks from a long-distant past like cave paintings or runes carved in stone. *Stupid, I know*, she said when she told me all this, much later. Which it wasn't, but it wasn't a very rational, let's-make-a-list Claudia thing to think either.

The letter, which said that because Claudia's grandparents hadn't been born in this country her citizenship was judged to be discretionary, see Section II ('Immigrants and Inherited Citizenship') of the enclosed booklet, slipped from her hand onto the porcelain floor tiles she'd chosen last year. She didn't move to pick it up. She didn't need to reread it. She remembered every word. How the Office of Homeland Protection had evidence to show she did not meet the requirements, as outlined in Section VI ('Good Character and Upholding British Values') of the enclosed booklet. How she'd be required to attend an interview in due course to determine her eligibility for citizenship. If it was determined she did not meet the criteria for citizenship, she would no longer be entitled to remain in the country. If she remained illegally, she would be arrested and deported. And how she could appeal the decision but should be advised that the chances of a successful appeal were low (see fig. d, Appendix 2, of the enclosed booklet).

She had a sudden urge to set the enclosed booklet on fire using the fancy wok burner on the gleaming range cooker. But she knew that would only set off the smoke alarm. And anyway, she found her legs were shaking and she couldn't move.

So instead she sat and looked out onto our garden, which she'd transformed from the scrubby rectangle of weeds and snails and feral cats into a wildflower haven for bees, with a swing and a wooden playhouse for Billie, and raised beds that had produced never-ending courgettes last summer, which we'd all had to pretend to be pleased about. At the far end was the patio that got the sun all day, where Claudia did yoga at sunrise on summer mornings and she and Dad drank wine with friends on lazy weekend evenings. She'd planned, next year, a small office in the corner so that she could work a day a week from home, pick Billie up from school, take her to the park or for hot chocolate on the way home.

When she looked at the clock, she realized almost an hour had passed.

So that was why she was late to the picnic.

Why she looked at Dad and Billie that way.

It was because she knew. Not what *would* happen, but what could.

She'd understood it long ago, I think, before Toby Knight even became Prime Minister. She understood that he might and what it could mean if he did.

She understood how fragile it all was, and how all of it – the gardens, the family dinners, the plans, the friends, the small, smeary fingerprints on windows and the fingers that made them – all of it can be taken away, can become memories that scarcely seem possible. Can become a handful of possessions – a small mirror, a piece of paper folded into the shape of a bird, a blue feather.

Can become a story.

*

The year I turned eight, Toby Knight was elected to parliament in a shock by-election result. Apparently, before I was born, he'd been an actor in TV shows I'd never heard of, and then, when the acting roles started to dry up, he started a whole new career Saying The Unsayable on social media. He supported the death penalty. He wanted to ban all immigration. He believed that if you didn't love this country you didn't deserve citizenship of it. Some people said he was an extremist. Some said he was a future Prime Minister. Some said he was a joke. I know all this now, but I don't remember any of it. Why would I? What I remember from that year is us moving from the old flat where Dad and I had lived with Mum into our new house where I had a big bedroom and a garden to play in. And Mischa's roller disco birthday party where she wore sequin hot pants and concussed herself. And most of all I remember brand-new baby Billie, with her black curls and her dark eyes that looked at me like she knew all my secrets and found them fascinating.

I do remember how upset Claudia was when he was elected though. Before the election she'd strapped tiny Billie to her front and travelled to support the candidate who stood against him. She didn't belong to a political party herself. She just knew someone like Toby Knight had no place in parliament, she said.

'Why?' I asked.

'I don't want my baby growing up in the world that man wants to create,' Claudia said. 'I want her to grow up in a world where she's safe and valued and so is everyone else.'

This got my attention. I doted on Billie and couldn't bear the thought of anything that might harm her.

'He's going to be a backbench MP,' Dad said. 'He's not going to have any actual power, Claud. They thought he'd get them some good press for once because he's famous and he's well connected in the media, but even half his own party hate him and what he stands for. He'll soon get fed up with it anyway and be off to do something more lucrative. He'll be gone by the next election. Guaranteed.'

The year I was twelve, I remember the skateboard I got for Christmas and the grazes on my knees and elbows from practising flips and tricks Danny tried to teach me. I remember Dad and Claudia and me taking Billie to her first day of pre-school in a little gingham dress that was too big for her and those patent shoes with the buckles and ankle socks, and she honestly looked cuter than anyone's kid sister has ever looked before or since. And every day when we asked her what she did there she'd say, 'I can't remember,' or 'Stuff,' and it would drive Claudia mad. But Dad just laughed and said, 'A girl's gotta have her secrets, Claud. What happens in nursery stays in nursery, right, B?'

That was the year of the stadium bombings. Toby Knight became Prime Minister, elected not by the public but by his own party, after the previous Prime Minister resigned in disgrace and political chaos reigned. *An unprecedented rise to power*, the TV news said. But these were unprecedented times. As Home Secretary he'd shown real leadership in the wake of the stadium bombings, his supporters said. It had proved his point about immigration, he claimed. When was this country going to wake up to the fact that it was allowing its enemies to be welcomed with open arms?

Dad was angry. Claudia was upset. I was confused.

'Why do people even like him?' I asked.

Claudia thought about this. 'I want to tell you it's because they're stupid or evil,' she said. 'And some of them probably are. But it's more complicated than that.'

'Is it though?' Dad said.

'He's very good at convincing people that they've lost something,' Claudia said. 'People want to believe he can take them back to how things were in the past. It feels safer there.'

'Yeah, an imaginary past where everything was perfect,' Dad muttered.

'That doesn't matter,' Claudia said. 'Makes it more powerful if anything.'

It didn't matter that the lost past was imaginary. Things being imaginary doesn't make you care about them less. I understand that now.

'So people think he'll give them back all the lost things?' I said, vaguely imagining them all jumbled up in a heap that smelt of feet like the Lost Property cupboard at school. 'That's why they like him?'

'Some really believe he will,' Claudia said. 'Or hope he will. I think secretly most know he can't, but they don't care.'

'Why not?'

'Because he tells them they're right to be angry about the lost things. And he'll give them someone to blame. Someone to punish.'

'Who?' I said, uneasy.

Claudia shrugged. 'Others. Outsiders. "Them". There's always a Them.'

'But who are they?'

Claudia smiled bleakly. 'Whoever he tells us they are.'

She was right, of course. Toby Knight brought in Community Surveillance, so that people were rewarded for reporting on 'suspicious activity' in their communities. Everyone had to have ID cards. Teachers, doctors, social workers were punished if they didn't report on people they thought might not have the right to be in the country. Anyone whose parents or grandparents had been born in another country could be stripped of their citizenship if they committed a crime. 'That's just the start,' Claudia said.

Finally, the law that banned immigration and began the mass deportations was passed.

Europe imposed sanctions.

Scotland declared independence.

The economy crashed and prices soared.

There were riots.

Toby Knight gave himself new emergency powers to deal with the growing unrest, the 'threat to the decent people of this country'.

And then—

Then it was the summer after my fifteenth birthday, the day Claudia had found the letter waiting for her on the doormat, and everything was about to change.

*

The golden sunshine of my birthday had been the start of a heatwave and the summer weeks had stretched long and hot. Not lazy and golden, though. The summer had been uncomfortably hot, parched and tense. Lawns and parks crisped to hay. Train tracks buckled and tarmac melted. Motorway verges blazed. There were wildfires on the moors that no one could put out.

The curfews were relaxed, then tightened, then relaxed again, as the official Terrorist Threat Level rose, fell, rose again. No one really knew why. There were stories in the media about terror plots, attacks on schools, famous landmarks, football matches that had supposedly been foiled. Dad said it certainly was a coincidence that every single

40

one of these stories all got reported in media owned by Knight's friends.

'So none of it's true?' I asked.

'I'm not saying there aren't terrorist plots,' Dad said. 'There always have been, my whole life. But put it this way: it suits Toby Knight if the public want him to have greater powers to protect them from terror attacks.'

On and on the weeks stretched, hotter and hotter, tighter and tighter until they felt like they would snap.

My room was at the top of the house in what had been the loft. I loved it, but in winter it got cold and in summer it got hot and airless.

We sat in the front garden under the tree in the afternoon because the shade fell on the pavement side. We watched the heat shimmer off the road, and sucked ice cubes we'd made out of lemon squash because ice lollies were so expensive. Everything was so expensive. Toby Knight gave a speech saying are we really not prepared to make a few small sacrifices to stand up for what's right, for the good of our country? Think of the sacrifices previous generations made. We must do the same. They played clips of it on all the news for days.

'I just want a Cornetto,' I said. 'Is it really too much to ask?'

'I just want to be allowed to be a citizen of my own country,' Claudia said. 'Is it really too much to ask?'

She'd had the date through for her interview and couldn't think about much else. She'd spoken to a lawyer friend who told her she should be fine. Yes, she'd gone on protests, she'd argued against government policies, she'd worked with organizations critical of the government. But she didn't have a criminal record, hadn't been involved with any illegal groups. 'Not illegal yet,' Claudia said. 'Give it time.' I'd hear her pacing downstairs late into the night when the rest of us were in bed.

One day while Claudia and Dad were at work I got the sprinkler out for Billie, and we put on our swimsuits and leapt and cartwheeled through its cooling rainbow drops. Only for half an hour because I knew there was a hosepipe ban and we weren't really supposed to – but it was bliss.

Two days later we got a visit from two Community Guardians in their black uniforms, telling us we'd been reported by neighbours for wasting water. Were our parents in? When I told them no, they asked for our ID cards and although I wanted to say I didn't think they could do that, because they weren't actually police or anything, I fetched them anyway. They checked them, nodded. Just a warning this time, but we'd be fined if it happened again. They left a sticker for us to put up in the window. It said THIS COMMUNITY IS GUARDED and it had Toby Knight's signature at the bottom. I remembered seeing one in the window at Danny's but I hadn't known what it was. I put the sticker straight in the bin. I didn't tell Dad or Claudia. Claudia was so on edge and tired that she'd snap at the smallest thing.

I wondered which neighbours had reported us. I didn't like to go in the garden after that. I felt like we were being watched. When I told Mischa she said, 'It's literally your own garden, babe. Maybe I'll come round and sunbathe topless. That'll give the nosy neighbours something to get excited about.'

42

On the last day of the holidays it was the day of Claudia's interview and Mischa and I had promised we'd take Billie to the see the flamingos and toucans at the zoo to distract her, but the roads had all been closed off round Camden and the Tube wasn't running again because of yet another 'counter-terrorism operation'.

So the cemetery seemed the next best option as it was free and we could walk there and Billie could run on ahead and do her bird spotting while we chatted.

'I can't believe it's the last day of the summer holidays and you two are making me spend it in a cemetery,' I said.

'We love the cemetery,' Mischa said. 'Ignore her, Billie. It's got everything. Angels and ghosts for me. Birds and ... nature stuff for B.'

'Me and Dad saw a firecrest once,' Billie told her seriously.

'Cool,' Mischa said. 'That's a dragon, right?'

'Bird,' Billie said, as if a dragon in a graveyard was no less likely. 'And there's rare moths.'

'Exactly.' Mischa put her arm round Billie. 'Rare. Moths.'

'What about for me?' I said. 'What do I get?'

'You get us.' Mischa smiled. 'What more do you want?'

She knew I didn't really mind. The cemetery was a grand old Victorian one, with ivy and statues and paths that disappeared into the trees. Mischa liked to go there so I could take pictures of her looking dramatic next to gravestones. It was surprisingly peaceful once you were in there, like another world, still and timeless. You almost forgot the city existed just beyond the walls.

'Danny's obviously got better things to do than spend time with us,' Mischa said. 'Again.'

'He's with his new friends,' I said, hoping the bitterness in my voice sounded ironic.

It wasn't. The truth was we had lost Danny that summer. We knew it really, but we weren't ready to accept it.

'Summer and Kyle and that lot?' Mischa said.

'Of course.'

We sat in silence for a bit, listening to crickets in the long grass. When Danny had first started hanging out with them we'd assumed he'd realize pretty quickly how awful they were and come back to us. It hadn't worked out like that. He'd joined a Community Guardians youth programme with them. He said they did first aid, boot camps, volunteering, learned about social issues, did online workshops and discussions. 'Indoctrination,' Mischa said. Danny laughed. 'Mischa,' he said, 'seriously? You shouldn't believe all that conspiracy crap. It's more like the scouts than a cult! And they've got us extra help for my mum too.'

He didn't talk to us about it after that. In fact he didn't talk to us about anything much because we never saw him except at school and he didn't hang out with us there any more.

'I just don't get it,' Mischa said. 'I mean, he must actually like them.'

'You know Kyle actually boasts about how many people he's reported on who've then been arrested?'

Mischa shook her head. 'Kyle's a dick. He always has been, ever since primary school. He's a bully, basically. Summer's not like that. She genuinely believes all the Toby Knight stuff.

Her dad works for him or something. You know she took Danny to one of his rallies?'

'A Knight rally? Seriously?'

'Yep. He posted about it.'

'Do you think he likes Summer? I mean ... *likes* her?'

I sighed. 'Maybe. I don't know.'

Mischa looked at me sideways. 'You wouldn't mind, would you? I mean, you wouldn't feel jealous?'

Everyone knew that Danny had had a thing for me for a while. Mischa always joked we'd get married one day and she'd be the maid of honour *and* best man and upstage us all. Danny had always been just a friend to me, but I couldn't deny that the thought of him with someone else was jarring, especially if that someone was Summer. His excuses not to meet up with us stung. I missed him.

'You know what he's like. He's just friends with everyone. He wants to be liked.' I still hoped he'd see sense and things would go back to how they were.

Mischa shook her head. 'Who wants to be liked by *them*?'

'I think he just sees the best in people.'

'There isn't any best to see in Kyle, even with a microscope.'

Billie came running back down the path towards us.

'What are you talking about?' she said.

'Boring school stuff,' I said, because Billie loved Danny.

'Look!' she said. 'I found a feather!'

She held it up like a trophy. It was bright blue and when we looked at it more closely we saw it had rainbow light reflecting in it.

'Wow, B,' I said. 'Where did you find that? It looks like it's come from some magical eagle or something.'

'It's from a magpie,' she said, as though it was obvious.

'Aren't they black and white?'

'Not if you look closely.'

'Look out for more,' Mischa said. 'I could stick some in my hair.'

'Okay.'

She ran off again.

'So when will you find out about Claudia?' Mischa said once Billie was out of earshot.

'The interview's this afternoon.'

'But it'll be okay, right? I mean, it's Claudia. They can't just decide anyone they feel like isn't a citizen any more.'

'Dad says they're just doing it to scare people, so people won't risk speaking out in case they get detained or deported or whatever. He says they won't actually do it, though. It's just Toby Knight trying to silence his opponents because there's an election next year and he knows he's going to lose.'

Claudia thought Dad was being complacent. 'You're part of that world,' I'd heard her say to him a couple of nights ago when they didn't realize I was there. 'You journalists, you're too caught up in the day-to-day drama. It's like a game. You think ultimately everyone plays by the rules. But I'm telling you, Knight's different. He doesn't care about the rules. He doesn't care about the chaos. You can't see the big picture of what's really happening. Maybe you don't even want to.'

There'd been more but I put my earbuds in so I didn't have to hear it, but even so I'd heard doors being slammed.

I'd never known Dad and Claudia to fight like that. Echoes of other arguments I'd forgotten about, half-heard as I'd lain in bed at the old flat, emerged from the dark. Mum yelling. The crash of objects thrown at walls. The sick unhappy feeling felt familiar as it settled in my stomach again.

'So your dad definitely thinks he'll lose the election?' Mischa said.

'He's sure of it.'

'Good,' Mischa said. 'My mum's threatening to go and live on my grandparents' farm in Poland if things carry on like this. And I'm telling you right now, that is not happening.'

'Are you coming?' Billie called. 'I'm hungry.'

'We're coming,' Mischa said.

We followed Billie along the path that wound through the trees and stones and bones.

*

In the dark of the shelter dormitory I carefully take out the blue feather from under my pillow and brush it against my face. In the dark it feels like the touch of a ghost.

*

Claudia had come back from her interview shellshocked.

'They knew all this stuff about me,' she said. '"Evidence", they called it.'

'What stuff?' I said. 'Evidence of what?'

Claudia was the most law-abiding person I knew. She stuck

47

to the speed limit, she didn't park on double yellow lines; she once made Mischa and I go to the police station to hand in a £20 note we found on the pavement.

'I'm black and I'm a woman and I've worked bloody hard to get where I am,' she said when I'd teased her about it once. 'I'm not giving anyone even the tiniest excuse to take it away from me.' I felt stupid then, like it was obvious if only I'd thought about it.

'And they had records of comments I've posted on social media, even stuff from years ago. Protests I've been on, petitions I've signed. They'd gone through my financial records, made notes of when I'd been in debt, or claimed benefits. All my contacts, phone calls I've made, location data ... Really sinister, intrusive stuff.'

'Is that even legal?'

'Yup,' she said. 'Emergency Surveillance Powers. Supposedly to stop terrorists or people who are a threat to the state. But in reality to stop anyone you don't like. The worst thing was they'd got testimonies from colleagues. People I thought liked me. I'd said in a meeting last year I believed it was our duty to treat a patient in need even if they didn't have the right paperwork. All that got reported back. Like it was a crime.'

Claudia had appealed the decision, but in the meantime she wasn't allowed to work until she heard whether her appeal was successful. So now she was waiting, stuck at home, going slightly crazy. She'd cooked and frozen batches of soup and chilli, pies and patties, Yorkshire puddings and curries, until the freezer was full. She'd alphabetized everything in the house: books, Dad's old CDs, records. Dad, trying to lighten the mood, joked that he expected to come home and find the food in the cupboard lined up by sell-by date. He was worried all the tension in the house would affect Billie. But Claudia hadn't laughed.

'Glad you think all this is funny,' she snapped.

'I don't, Claud,' Dad said. 'You know I don't.'

I knew he was worried now, but he still thought it would be okay, that the appeal would be successful.

'How come all this stuff isn't in the papers?' I said. 'Why aren't you writing about it?'

But Dad had his own problems. His paper was about to be taken over by a businessman who just happened to be an old schoolfriend of Toby Knight.

After the cooking and the cleaning and organizing, Claudia started writing lists. I didn't know what they were lists of. She filed them in ring-binders.

She talked to Billie about her own mum, who had died before Billie was born, and about her grandparents, who'd come to London from Jamaica way back when. She showed her pictures of them and spent evenings poring over family albums.

Some of Claudia's friends came round to see how she was. Some didn't.

'You certainly find out a lot about people at times like this,' she said.

I mainly tried to keep out of her way. I felt bad, but it was too easy to say the wrong thing.

One day when I got home from school I found Claudia in the kitchen, restlessly folding ironing while muttering at the radio. I made myself some toast as quickly as I could and tried to escape.

'Can you tidy up after yourself for once please?' she snapped as I went to leave. 'I've just cleaned this kitchen. Is it really too much to ask?'

'Okay, okay,' I said. 'I was going to do it after.'

I wiped the crumbs off the side, put the butter back in the fridge. Claudia snapped off the radio. 'There,' I said, glaring at her, then noticing how tired she looked. 'I was going to make tea,' I lied. 'Do you want some?'

Claudia looked at me and half-smiled apologetically. 'Thanks,' she said. 'I know I'm not exactly great company right now. It's just the waiting. I'm not really sleeping. I can't stop thinking about the appeal and that bloody interview.'

'I'm sure it'll be fine,' I said.

'And you're a legal expert, are you?' Claudia said, then put her hands over her face for a second. 'Sorry. Sorry. Ignore me.'

'It's okay,' I said. 'It's not surprising you're stressed.'

'I shouldn't take it out on you though, Clem.' She tried to smile. 'Tell me about normal things. How are you? How's Mischa? How's Danny?'

'Oh, they're fine.'

'Yeah? Danny hasn't been round here in a while. You haven't fallen out or anything?'

'He's busy,' I said. 'You know. He has to do a lot for his mum.'

Claudia put the pile of folded ironing into the basket and looked at me.

'It can be hard when friends move on,' she said, because annoyingly she always seemed to know what I wasn't telling her. 'But it usually means you didn't have as much in common as you thought.'

'Who said he's moved on?' I snapped. 'Anyway, I don't really want to talk about it.'

She held her hands up. 'Okay,' she said. 'Sorry. It's not my business. I just want you to know, I know I'm preoccupied at the moment and not in the best mood ... but I'm here if you want to talk, okay?'

'I do know,' I said, but somehow it came out wrong, like *Why would you think I want to talk to you?* I didn't mean it to but somehow it always did. I wished that Claudia didn't always try so hard to be a Great Parent™ and that I didn't always end up pushing her away. I knew that I loved her and that she loved me, but in the way that you know a place if you've read about it in a book instead of seeing it for yourself. It was a careful, learned sort of love. It was a coat that had to be put on, that sometimes felt so big it swamped me and other times just a bit too tight so that I couldn't quite move in it properly. It took concentration, from both of us. Sometimes I wondered what would happen if we stopped concentrating.

Billie assumed we loved each other as totally and as effortlessly as she loved both of us. It was Billie who bound us together, from the day she was born. Billie made everything simpler with Claudia and me. We each knew the other would do anything for her.

'Do you want me to go and get Billie from Sakura's for you?' I said, an awkward peace offering.

'No,' she said. 'It's fine. I could do with a walk.'

'Shall I walk with you?' I said, trying to convince either Claudia or myself that I wasn't a total bitch.

Claudia smiled. 'I'd like that.'

She paused. 'Clem?'

I looked round at her.

'If anything happens ... I mean if the appeal doesn't work out—'

'It will.'

'Okay. But if it doesn't, and I'm not here ... If things get dangerous—'

'Dangerous?'

'I'm not saying they will,' she said. 'But if they do, I want you and Billie to get out of London. I thought maybe you could go and stay with your grandpa.'

'With Grandpa?' I was surprised. Claudia and Grandpa had only met a couple times and not for ages.

'I was just thinking you'd be safe there.' The words came out in a tumble, the manic edge of the cooking and list-making returning. 'It's just an idea. But we're a bit lacking in relatives, me and your dad. And it's such a sleepy little village, isn't it? And you and he were always so close when you were little. I know he'd take good care of you and he's a good man. He'd take you both in. He might even appreciate the company now he's on his own. And Billie would love it, wouldn't she? You know how she always goes on about wanting to live in the countryside.'

Claudia's intensity was unnerving.

'Have you talked to Dad about this?'

She half-smiled again. 'You know what he's like. Relentlessly optimistic about everything. He thinks I'm overreacting.'

She paused.

'You do too,' she said. 'I know. Maybe I am. Maybe you could mention it to your grandpa if you speak to him.'

'Okay,' I said, but only to make the conversation stop. Claudia was freaking me out. 'I'll call him. But I can never get through to him these days and he never gets in touch with me. I haven't spoken to him for ages.'

Claudia took my hand and squeezed it. 'Thanks, Clem. I just need to know you'll both be safe. It means a lot to me to know Billie would have you around. I always wished I had a sister. I'm so happy she has you. She couldn't have a better sister.'

'Oh,' I said.

I turned away, feeling myself go red. I hadn't expected her to say that. I always felt like deep down Claudia thought I was a bit flaky. She was so organized and determined and good at everything. I was so different from her.

'Thanks,' I said at last. 'But don't worry. Everything's going to be okay.'

'She's got too much time to think,' Dad said when I mentioned what Claudia had said about going to Grandpa's.

'You don't need to worry about it, Clem. Claudia's anxious, understandably, and she's got too much time to think at the moment. And she loves you and Billie, and she's worried about the effect all of this is having on you. But you're not going to have to go anywhere. This is your home.'

Still, I did call Grandpa anyway. It had been ages since we'd spoken and I missed him. Since Granny died, he never called, never texted me with jokes or random weird facts like he used to, or sent me pictures of Merlin, his dachshund. For a while I'd tried calling him, but he never wanted to talk, not like before. He'd sound vague, make excuses and say he'd call back, but he didn't. I'd tried not to mind but we'd always been so close when I was a kid, especially after Mum. Now I found I felt almost nervous as the phone rang and rang until eventually the answerphone clicked on. I felt a shock of disorientation; it was Granny's voice, warm and jokey. Grandpa still hadn't changed it two years on. I imagined Granny's voice echoing into the hallway in their empty house like a ghost. How much he must miss her. I found I couldn't leave a message. I'd call him again soon.

*

Polly is watering her plants when I step into her office, a row of shrivelled-looking cacti lined up along the windowsill. I'd had a cactus on my desk at home that Mischa gave me. She chose it specially because it looked particularly obscene. Polly's cacti do not. They look as though, if they could speak, they would plead in their tiny cactus voices for the sweet release of death.

'Whatever the opposite of green fingers is, that's what I've got,' Polly says. 'My girlfriend calls me a herbicidal maniac. I thought it would be different with a cactus but . . .' She gestures hopelessly at the stunted evidence of her failings.

'I kill plants too,' I say and she smiles. 'You need Claudia. She's like some kind of plant whisperer.'

'Claudia? Ah yes, your stepmother.'

I almost smile. 'She hated me calling her that.' I don't add: *So I did, just because I knew it bothered her.*

Polly looks confused.

'Because, you know, fairy tales,' I explain. 'I'd introduce her as my wicked stepmother.'

'Right,' she says, smiling. 'It was a joke.'

Almost, I think, but nothing ever managed to be completely a joke between Claudia and me. There was always an undertow of effort that somehow flattened any attempt at humour into earnestness (her) or snark (me). But I couldn't explain it to this woman. I couldn't even explain it to myself.

'They say it actually does help if you talk to plants,' Polly says. 'Is that what she does?'

'She used to sing to hers,' I said. 'It was kind of annoying to be honest. She said you just had to love them. Anything you do with love you do well, she said.'

'She sounds like a very wise person.'

'Oh yes, she was.'

I couldn't tell her that it had bothered me. It seems so stupid now. It did even back then. I didn't know why it did. But I've had time to think about it and now I do. It was because Mum *hadn't* been full of wisdom. I didn't know much about her but I did know that. I wish I could explain it to Claudia, now I understand it. But maybe, knowing Claudia, she already knew.

'Can you tell me what happened to Claudia, Clem?'

*

Here it is. The point where everything changes. The door between before and after. It shimmers in the air, a cherry-red-painted door with a brass number five on it. I must push it open and walk up the stairs to my room. The final seconds of our old life. There I am, not knowing it, just thinking it's another day.

There I am, peering into my bedroom mirror, horrified, trying to blank out the morning noise of the house, Billie's whining ('But I don't like tights, they're itchy'), Claudia's snapping ('Just come and eat this cereal now otherwise it'll be soggy and you'll still have to eat it') ... It was still dark outside, cold even with the heating on, and I'd left it till the last possible moment to force myself out of bed. My head felt as grey and foggy as the outside world. I took a close-up picture of my nose and sent it to Mischa.

See what I mean? Literally a boil.

I dabbed at the spot some more with concealer but it only made it look worse. I waited for Mischa to reply with some sarcastic comment but she didn't. I was probably going to miss the bus and be late for school again, but I couldn't quite bring myself to hurry. I was wondering whether I could convince Claudia to call in sick for me (not a chance) and, mouth wide open, was trying to peer at my tonsils for tell-tale signs of illness that definitely required a day of TV-watching and ice cream, when there was a crash from downstairs so loud that I jumped and got mascara smeared across my forehead.

'What the . . . ?'

I leapt up, taking my earbuds out.

'B? Claudia? You okay?'

There was shouting from downstairs, men shouting.

I froze. Dad wasn't here. He'd left early today. So who was that shouting?

And then Claudia yelled, 'No, stop! You can't do this. Get your fucking hands *off* me—'

– Claudia doesn't swear like that –

and then Billie, screaming –

'Mama! No!'

Shit.

By the time I got to the stairs there was a crowd of men and a woman, all with black uniforms and blank faces, crowded in the hall. Loads of them, it seemed, with all their noise and bulk and force, though afterwards I realized it could only have been four or five. Two of them had hold of Claudia. Her hands were handcuffed behind her back. The woman was in the sitting-room doorway holding on to Billie – one leg in her tights, one still bare – as she tried to get to Claudia. My slow, morning brain tried to take all this in: Claudia, the handcuffs, the uniforms and whatever weapons were concealed in them, like a movie or something off the TV – and all of it in our hall, the family portrait Claudia had insisted on having done by a professional photographer, all of us fake-grinning down on everything from the wall, Billie's packed lunch on the hall table.

'You've got no right!' Claudia was shouting.

It's a mistake. They must see this is ridiculous.

'You can't do this. There's an appeal . . . I'll get my passport if you just let me *go*—'

'Don't worry,' one of the men said. He was tall and broad, red-faced. 'We'll take what we need.' He nodded two of the men towards the stairs. They pushed past me as though I wasn't there, heading up towards our bedrooms.

'Hey!' I tried to shout, but it came out quiet and high, not like my voice at all, like a little kid's voice.

I thought of the knickers lying on my bedroom floor, my posters and photos, my *stuff*—

'*Hey!*' I tried to sound angry, not scared. 'You can't go in there!'

But obviously they could. I heard them opening drawers and knocking things over and I wanted to go up to stop them but Billie was screaming and Claudia was almost out the door and as Billie struggled I thought, *Have they got weapons? Have they got* guns? *I mean, they couldn't use them, could they?*

'Please,' Claudia said, her voice different now, not shouting. I could hear she was fighting to sound calm. 'Okay. I'll come.'

'No!' I said. 'Claudia, this isn't right! Tell them. It's a mistake.'

'Clem,' she said, sharp. 'Leave it.'

'But—'

'See?' she said to the men holding her. 'I'm not resisting. Just let me say goodbye to my little girl – you can see how upset she is.'

They didn't let go of her.

'Have you got kids, any of you?' Claudia said, desperate beneath the forced calm. *'Please.'*

Red Face said, 'Wait.' He nodded towards the woman who was still holding on to Billie.

She walked forwards till she was close enough that Claudia could have reached out to them if her hands weren't cuffed behind her back. The woman kept a grip on Billie's arms.

'Let go of her, can't you?' I said, unable to stop myself, breathless with fear and adrenalin and fury. 'She's just a kid. What do you think she's going to do?'

No one seemed to hear.

'Say what you've got to say,' Red Face said to Claudia.

She took a breath. 'Billie, it's okay,' Claudia said. 'Don't cry. Look at me, B. I'm all right. See?' She even smiled. I knew it was superhuman, the strength it took for her to do that.

'Mama . . .' Billie's voice was small and scared.

'It's all right. I'm going to go with these people now and I'm going to get this sorted out, yeah? You hear me. It's wrong. I'm going to put it right, okay? And you mustn't worry about me. Promise?'

Billie said nothing.

'It'll be okay, B. You'll be okay. Dad will be here. And you've got Clem. She'll take care of you.'

She looked up at me, her face taut, trying to hide her fear. In a low, urgent voice, she said, 'Call your dad. Tell him what's happened. And, Clem . . .'

She stopped. I realized there were tears on her face, but her voice stayed steady.

'Claudia—'

'Look after B for me. Remember what I said to you, before. You made me a promise, yeah?'

I stared at her. I did remember.

'Keep it,' she said.

'Enough,' said Red Face. 'Now move.'

'I love you, B,' Claudia called over her shoulder as they pushed her out of the door, but Billie couldn't see her as she said it, there were too many people in the way.

'Mama!' Her scream echoed the panic I felt pounding in my chest. *This is really happening.*

The woman who'd been holding Billie back let go of her arms and I ran down to her, holding my little sister tight as she flung herself at me.

There were heavy footsteps on the stairs behind us. The door slammed.

And it was just us, just Billie and me, her sobbing, inconsolable, though I tried, pulling her to me, rubbing her back, holding her head against me, stroking her hair.

'It's all right,' I could hear myself saying, over and over. 'It's all right.'

I called Dad, still holding Billie to me, hardly able to find words to describe what had happened, unsure even what *had* happened, everything so unreal except for Billie, her shuddering breath, my arms around her.

And then—

The strangest stillness. The radio still chattering in the kitchen. *Traffic moving very slowly on the M25 anticlockwise between junctions 19 for Watford and 15 for Heathrow . . .* It's faraway, maybe not even real, an echo of something from very long ago. We can hear it but we're somewhere else now, in a place caught outside of time, everything stopped.

No. As I pulled Billie tighter to me, I could feel my heart thud against her. As long as she was close to me, I knew that I was still here, still breathing, that time was moving. We were moving with it, carried by it to an unfamiliar place. We clung to each other, adrift in the strange, new world we found ourselves in, the wreckage of our old life floating around us: plastic lunchboxes, PE kits, Claudia's half-drunk cup of mint tea, Billie's upturned cereal bowl, the milk and Weetabix mush soaking into the carpet.

I carried Billie through to the sitting room awkwardly, remembering how easily I used to swing her up onto my hip when she was a toddler, showing her off everywhere like a pet. She was too big to be carried now, but she clung to me tight and wouldn't let go. The TV was still on, cartoons that Billie pretended to be too grown-up for but still watched every morning while she got ready for school.

Then Billie and I just sat there, staring blankly at adverts for nappies and yoghurts, waiting for Dad.

'When will Mama come back?' Billie said at last.

'Soon,' I said.

I was wrong.

'Clem?'

I surfaced from deep blankness and saw Billie standing by my bed holding her rabbit nightlight and Luna. She looked very small.

'Billie. You okay?'

She shook her head.

'Can't sleep?'

She shook her head. Dad and I had tried to persuade her to sleep in with one of us, but she'd insisted on staying in her own room. 'Maybe she just wants things to feel normal,' Dad had said.

'Want to come and sleep in my bed?' I said.

I could see she wanted to say yes but she hesitated.

'If Mama comes back late from work, she always comes in to give me a kiss. If she gets home tonight and I'm not in my bed she'll be worried.'

She was waiting for her mum. I remembered what that felt like.

'She won't be back tonight, B,' I said, gently.

Billie frowned. 'How do you know?'

'It's late now, isn't it?'

'Will she be back tomorrow?'

I wanted to reassure her but I couldn't lie. After Mum left, no one exactly lied to me, but I remember the blurring of the possible and impossible, the maybes and the let's see tomorrows. The hope just made things worse.

'Dad might know more in the morning, okay? But, for now, we need to sleep.'

'Where will Mama sleep tonight?'

Where *would* she sleep? I couldn't imagine, or didn't want to.

'I don't know, B.'

'She didn't take her pyjamas. Will they give her some?'

Claudia's neatly folded pyjamas would be under her pillow, where she'd put them this morning, in that other life.

'I think so. Come on. Why don't you get in.'

Billie climbed in but she didn't lie down. 'Why did they have to take her when she hasn't done anything wrong?'

'I don't know, B.'

'What if they come back and arrest me? Or you or Dad?'

'They won't!' I hugged her. 'I promise.'

But even as I said it the thought slid into my head: did I even know that? I'd believed Claudia was safe, even after she got the letter, because things like that just didn't happen, not here, not to us ... Now though, what was impossible and what wasn't, who was safe and who wasn't, seemed less clear.

'Dad won't let them. And I won't let them,' I told her firmly. But now I *was* lying. Billie knew it too, of course. She'd seen me watching helpless as they took her mum away. She knew we couldn't stop them.

I remembered my promise to Claudia.

'If we need to, we'll go and stay at my grandpa's,' I said, knowing Billie would love the idea. She fantasized about living in the country, so much so that Claudia used to find houses in the middle of nowhere on property websites and say, 'Look! We could live in a bloody palace compared to here. This one's got five bedrooms and a paddock!'

And Dad would roll his eyes and say, 'Apart from the eight-hour commute, sounds great. And I'm sure the paddock will come in really handy for that horse we haven't got.'

So now I told Billie how Grandpa lived in a house like that, just not as big. And I told her the village was just like how you'd draw a picture of a village, with thatched cottages and a duckpond, and how the woods started at the back of Grandpa's house. I saw her relax at last as she imagined it.

'You mean, the garden just turns into a forest?'

'Yeah, pretty much.'

'Is it enchanted?'

'It's like ancient woodland or something so it's bound to be enchanted.' I was sure it was when I was a kid. 'I used to play out there all day. Just me and the dogs. And the witches and wolves, obviously.'

'Can I play there?'

'Of course.'

'What's your grandpa like?'

'He's the best,' I said. 'He's funny and he knows about all sorts of weird, interesting stuff that no one else does.'

'What weird, interesting stuff?'

'He used to be a teacher in a university. He knows all about language and words. He's got these huge dictionaries – they're so big that they have their own little magnifying glasses – and they tell you all about the history of the words and when they were first used and all that. And he's Welsh. He grew up in a mining village so he knows all sorts of things about that. And he knows about stars and space.'

'Does he know anything about birds?'

'Probably. But not as much as you.'

She looked pleased.

'And he loves telling stories,' I said. 'When my mum went away, Grandpa used to tell me stories to make me feel better.'

Billie looked at me curiously. I never talked about my mum to her, or to anyone really.

'What stories did he tell you?' Billie said.

'Old stories. Welsh myths. Greek myths. Fairy tales. But he made them his stories.'

'Is that why you're good at telling stories? Because he was?'

'Maybe.'

'Will you tell me one now?'

'Sure,' I said.

'About a magic forest?'

'You lie down and close your eyes.'

I switched off the light and held Billie close, and in the dark the forest grew up around us.

*

Now in my narrow dormitory bed I pull the blankets tight around us. I pull the twine necklace from under my pyjama top and close my hand around the ring with its green stone.

It is warm from lying against my skin. I close my eyes and, instead of the coughs and low voices and buzzing of phones of the dormitory beyond the screens, I tell myself I can hear the whisper of the trees in Grandpa's forest all around us, lulling us to sleep, keeping us safe.

*

The sisters realized they were in the deepest, densest part of the forest where no sunlight broke through the leaves, and they were scared.

'I know!' the older sister said. She took out some bread from her pocket and tore pieces off to make a trail they could follow. Before long, night had fallen and it was so dark in the forest that they could hardly see their way. The rainbow bird had disappeared and they could no longer hear its song.

In the darkness the sisters had the strangest feeling. They felt there were eyes watching them.

At last, they came to a wall of thorns. The spikes scratched at their hands as they tried to push the branches aside. There was no way through it.

'It must be the witch's castle!' the younger girl cried.

'We need to get away from here,' the older sister said.

They held hands and began to run, but the witch's enchantment meant that whichever path they took they always ended up back at the same place.

'Keep hold of my hand,' the older sister said. 'We'll find our way home together.'

But the trail of crumbs she'd left had been eaten by hungry birds and there was nothing to show them the way.

*

Rain pelts against the window. Polly tells me horizontal rain is an Edinburgh speciality. The cacti look like they're dreaming of the Mexican desert.

'You were telling me last time about Claudia's arrest,' Polly says. 'Was it after that happened that you left your home?'

'No,' I say.

I couldn't explain now that, as terrible as it was, we still thought everything would be okay. That Claudia would come back. That Knight would lose the election. That everything would return to how it was.

A business ally of Toby Knight took over at Dad's newspaper.

Dad lost his job. He said he couldn't have worked for that man anyway.

Somehow we still thought it would be okay.

Somehow, despite the shock of Claudia's arrest, and how much we missed her, and the feeling that everything was falling apart around us, we just carried on.

What else could we do?

*

'Can they even do that though?' Mischa said. We were supposed to be in maths, but instead were huddled together trying to shelter from the rain behind the hedge at the back of the sixth-form block.

'They can do whatever they like,' I said. 'It wasn't just my dad. The new boss fired all of them.'

'So what's he going to do now, your dad?'

'He's working with this resistance network. Other journalists, lawyers, IT people . . . I dunno, trying to publicize what's happening and organize against Knight ahead of the election next year. He's kind of obsessive about it.'

'Isn't that dangerous?' Mischa said.

'I don't know. Maybe. He's worried about surveillance. Spyware or whatever. He has to keep changing his phone. He said I might have to too. They target people's families.'

'Aren't they only supposed to use that on people they think are terrorists? Your dad doesn't exactly seem the terrorist type, babe. I mean, he posts pictures of parkrun and weird bread he's baked.'

I shrugged. 'Claudia never even returned a library book late. Didn't stop them arresting her, did it?'

'You still haven't heard anything from her?'

I shook my head. Claudia had phoned every week for the first month after her arrest. She couldn't say much because there was always someone with her when she called, but she told us she was being held at a detention centre somewhere in Kent. She hadn't even known whether they were going to charge her or try and deport her to Jamaica, even though she'd never lived there and only visited once when she was a little kid. Then they told her she was being moved and after that we hadn't heard from her.

'It's so horrible, not knowing. Especially for Billie. She can't understand why her mum's not phoning. It's hard for everyone but her most of all.'

'I'll come over and cheer her up,' Mischa said.

'It's all right for you. You get to be Fun Aunty Mischa. And then you get to leave.'

'Talking of fun,' she said, 'Halloween party at Belle's. We have to go.'

'Do we though? I'm not really in a party place, Misch. Anyway, I might have to babysit Billie. Dad's out.'

'Can't she go to a friend's?' Mischa said. 'We're not missing this. It's Halloween. They've dropped the curfew for once. And Adi's going, he told me.'

'Oh, so Adi's why you want to go.'

'Not the only reason. I just think we all deserve a night out and a good time. My mum's driving me crazy at the moment. One minute she's fine, the next she's freaking out saying the world's gone mad and that we'd be better off going to Poland before we get kicked out.'

'Seriously?'

'She doesn't mean it. Anyway, I told her she can go but I'm staying here, thanks.'

'My dad said one of his journalist friends is moving to France. He told my dad he should get out of the country too if he can.'

'He's not going to though?'

'No way. He needs to find Claudia. Anyway, he thinks everything's going to get back to normal soon. After the election anyway.'

The rain was getting harder.

'Why are we out here?' I said. 'We should have just gone to maths.'

'No, we definitely shouldn't.'

The bell rang.

'Okay,' Mischa said, 'we'd better go.'

She held her bag over her head and started running, swearing as she trod in a puddle. I ran after her laughing.

'Okay,' I said. 'You're right. Let's do it. We deserve a party.'

Mischa turned and hugged me in the middle of the playground.

'Too right, babe. We *shall* go to the ball.'

*

I can't sleep again. Billie woke me earlier but she's sleeping now, her soft breathing next to me in the bed. I pick up my notebook, open it and take out the gold paper crane that's folded into its pages.

I wonder how many we've made since. I lost count long ago. I see in my mind a trail of birds marking the path of our journey here, folded into books, hidden under pillows, fallen down the side of seats, drifting out to sea, made out of newspaper and flyers and anything that came to hand.

But this was the first one we ever made.

*

Billie hopscotched her way along the cracked pavements, splashing me with puddle-water as she went.

'Billie, can you not?' I snapped. 'My tights are soaked.'

I had to take Billie to breakfast club every day and I was sick of it. In the old days, I'd walk to Mischa's and we'd get the bus together. Now I had to get up an hour earlier, and with the extra ID checks on the bus and the army checkpoint that had been set up on the main road which took for ever to get through I was always getting detentions for being late for school. Today everything possible had gone wrong and now we were both going to be late for school.

Billie looked at me, eyes wide with reproach. 'Mama never minded.'

According to Billie, Mama never minded anything. From Billie watching TV till midnight to Billie's packed lunch consisting entirely of chocolate or being allowed the day off school because her favourite socks were in the wash, Claudia had apparently just smiled and let her get on with it.

It has to be said, that's not exactly how I remembered it ('I don't care if Freya goes to bed at eleven. You go now' ... 'No, orange flavour sweets are not a fruit, Billie') but I knew that wasn't the point. Billie missed Claudia. Everything was right when she was here and now it was wrong. That much we could all agree on. In the weeks since she'd been gone, I'd realized just how much Claudia did to keep everything running smoothly, keeping everyone happy, seeing arguments brewing and defusing them before the rest of us had really noticed them, spotting difficulties on the horizon and dealing with them in advance so that by the time we got to them they weren't problems any more. And all the while making sure Billie's favourite socks had been washed, packing a healthy lunch that Billie would actually eat instead of leaving it mouldering in her bag all week, getting her PE kit to school on the right day, making dentist's appointments, not forgetting to fill in the forms for after-school clubs, remembering when Billie's friends' birthdays were and buying them presents, staying calm and reasonable, doing yoga every day and being a doctor. I'd always quietly mocked Claudia's uber-organized control-freakery, but now, too late, I was in awe of it.

'Sorry, B,' I said. 'Hopscotch all you like. Just try not to splash me. And try to do it at Olympic hopscotching speed because we're so late it's not even funny.'

As I said it, a car drove past spraying me with water from the roadside and I couldn't help swearing.

'I wish Mama was here,' Billie said to the pavement, standing on one leg.

'I know, B,' I said. 'I was just thinking the same thing.'

'Why can't we go and see her?'

'You know why.'

We still hadn't found out where she'd been moved to.

'But why doesn't Mama even phone?' Billie asked, taking hold of my hand.

'You know she would if she could. She's just not allowed.'

'Why is nothing allowed? It's not fair.'

I sighed, trying and failing to think of something positive to say. 'I know, B.'

'Sakura told me something,' Billie said as we turned into the road where her school was.

'She did?'

72

'She told me about it because I like birds.'

'Like' was an understatement. Borderline obsession might be closer. She knew all sorts of random facts about them and her room was full of bird toys and pictures and ornaments and books. I think it started with Luna, her toy owl, or maybe I just think that because Luna was my present to Billie when she was born.

'Oh yeah? How did she know that when you only mention birds ten times in every conversation?'

Billie didn't even notice my teasing. She was too focused on what Sakura had told her.

'She said in Japan, if you fold a thousand birds out of paper – what's it called again, the paper-folding thing?'

'Origami.'

'If you make a thousand birds out of origami, you get a wish and the wish definitely comes true.'

'It does?' I didn't need to ask her what her wish would be.

'Sakura gave me one she'd made to get started,' Billie said. 'Look.' She reached into her school bag and rummaged around till she found it, pulling out a complicated-looking bird folded from red paper.

'Wow, impressive,' I said. 'It's a crane, I think.'

Billie nodded. 'They're lucky in Japan. Kind of like horseshoes and four-leaf clover, but even more special.'

I took it from her and examined it as we walked the last few steps to the school gate, trying to protect it from the rain. 'And you're planning to make a thousand of these? Not gonna lie, B, that could take a while.'

'That's why I need you to help. Sakura showed me how

to make one but I can't remember. She says you can look on YouTube though.'

'*Okaaay*,' I said. 'And exactly how many years of my life is this going to take?'

Her eyes filled with tears. 'It's for a wish, Clem. It's really important. *Really*. It's not a joke.'

'I know, B,' I said quickly, putting an arm round her. 'I know. I get it. We'll google it when we get home, okay? Anyway, you'd better run.' It was so late that everyone had already gone in.

She kissed me and I watched her hopscotch across the empty playground, her head full of the magical birds that would bring her mum home. I looked at the folded bird in my hand and found I had tears in my eyes. I remembered how it felt when Mum left. It felt like the safe, solid ground I'd been walking on had turned into a tightrope and at every moment I thought it might snap. I'd do anything to stop Billie feeling that.

Less than an hour before, as she'd stood in her pyjamas yelling at me because I'd put milk in her cereal bowl, I'd felt like yelling right back at her, that she was a brat, that I didn't want to have to look after her, that it was boring and exhausting and I hated it. I'd had to lock myself in the bathroom so I didn't, and so I could cry without her seeing. Now I hated myself for even thinking those things.

I took out the stupid old phone Dad had given me and texted Mischa.

Soooo late. Can you say I've got a hospital appointment or something.

If anyone really was spying on my messages, they were going to be very bored.

Mischa replied straight away:

> U okay?

I replied:

> I am NEVER having kids. If I ever get broody kill me.

Mischa sent something that I assumed was emojis, but the phone was so old it just did a row of question marks instead.

I walked towards the bus stop, thinking. About how angry I'd felt with Billie this morning, how overwhelmed and desperate and lonely. What if you really didn't know you didn't want kids until after you had them? Could that happen? Was that what had happened to Mum? I tried not to think about her, or to try and make sense of why she'd gone. It had got easier over the years but sometimes I couldn't help it.

I saw the bus just pulling up to the bus stop. I knew I should run but I didn't. I was already going to miss half my first lesson and it was maths, and I'd get a detention either way so why bother? I decided to walk even though the rain was starting to fall again, Billie's red paper crane still in my hand.

It turned out I was right: origami cranes are very difficult to make, even with the help of a step-by-step tutorial on YouTube.

Our first attempt was a complete failure because the paper was too thick and wouldn't fold properly.

The second time round, I got so annoyed with the calm and patient tone of the YouTube tutor that I didn't listen properly and rushed ahead, which caused a massive argument between Billie and me. The mangled piece of paper that should have been a crane ended up in the bin.

The third one, which we didn't try till two days later because we weren't talking to each other, seemed to take us hours to make but we were very, very careful. I had found a sheet of gold paper in Billie's craft box, left over from some Christmassy creative project Claudia had done with her last year. We were going to do this properly. We folded precisely, corner to corner, edge to edge, and we were gentle with the tricky petal folds when it would have been easy to tear the paper. And, at the end of it, we had an actual recognizable paper crane. We'd somehow managed to create this delicate creature out of a piece of paper, with no mistakes or rips or lopsided wings, no drama or slamming doors, against all the odds, and we were so ecstatic about it that we danced around the kitchen and Billie had to call Sakura to show her.

'Just nine hundred and ninety-nine to go,' Billie said.

*

I could make them in my sleep now, those birds, I've made so many of them. I almost don't notice I'm doing it. Sometimes I find my fingers moving along imagined folds even when I

don't have any paper. If we followed them, the trail of magic
birds we've left behind would lead us home.

*

*The sisters sank down under a tree and hugged each other
close to keep warm. The dark was all around them and, as
they shivered and wondered how they would ever get home,
they had the feeling they were being watched.*

*Just then there was a great sound of rustling and
flapping in the branches about them and a huge vulture
swooped down and flew around them, once, then twice.
Its eyes glowed orange in the dark, its beak was cruel
and tearing, and its talons were sharper than knives. The
sisters knew immediately that this was the terrible witch
in disguise. They knew that if they let her fly around
them a third time they would be rooted to the spot,
unable to move.*

*'Run!' the older girl said, grabbing hold of her sister's
hand and holding it tight in hers.*

*But as they ran they heard the great swoosh of wings
behind them. The girl felt her sister's hand slip from hers
and found that all she held was a single blue feather. When
she turned, she saw that her sister had been transformed
into a bird with wings the colour of a summer's sky.*

*Then the vulture shape-shifted into the witch. She
snatched up the colourful bird and ran back with it towards
the castle, her long blonde hair streaming out behind her.
The girl tried to follow but the red roses grew up thick*

around her and their thorns ripped her skin and tore her clothes and she couldn't find the castle.

*

Mischa is turning and walking away from me.

She says something I can't hear.

She turns and looks over her shoulder—

But when she turns to me she has no eyes, just blank emptiness where eyes should be.

She can't see me—

Mischa! I try to call out but I can't . . .

And I realize it's not her at all, it's not her—

So where is she?

I look around desperately, trying to find her, but there are too many people – people everywhere crowding in, pushing so I can't breathe – but I have to find her, I need her—

Mischa! I try to shout again . . .

But nothing comes out—

I wake, jolted out of sleep by terror, heart pounding, sweating, trying to scream—

I try to breathe slowly, wait for my heart to slow itself.

'Mischa?' I whisper into the dark.

But all I can hear is muffled Peppa Pig music coming from a phone someone's given their kid on the other side of the dividing curtain.

The relief of waking from my nightmare fades.

I reach for my notebook and take out the photo of Mischa and me that's tucked inside.

Mischa. I need her.

But she isn't here.

And I'm falling.

*

Mischa turned up at the bus stop where we'd agreed to meet, exactly twenty-five minutes late.

'Hiya, babe,' she said, hugging me. She smelt of cherry blossom body spray and chewing gum. 'How do I look?' She turned around so I could admire her from all angles. She looked amazing, as always, all beehive and eyeliner and curves.

'Why do you always have to be so late? And you've got lipstick on your teeth,' I said, even though she hadn't.

I wasn't in the mood for a party. Billie had been clingy all week, especially at bedtime. She threw a proper tantrum when I said I was going out, like she used to when she was a toddler, lying on the floor, screaming. As I'd tried to get out of the door, I had a memory of Claudia surrounded by parenting books about the terrible twos, trying to work out what she was doing wrong with Billie.

'But they all say different things,' she'd said, slamming one shut and looking around despairingly at the others. 'And how am I supposed to ignore her when she's lying on the pavement in front of someone's mobility scooter, swearing?'

'Ignore the books,' Dad had said. 'There's a whole industry based on making people feel they're failing because they haven't found the magic way of stopping their kids behaving like kids.'

'You're not helping,' Claudia had replied. 'And the swearing is your fault by the way.'

I couldn't see then why Claudia had to get so angsty about everything. But back then I could be the fun one. Now I had to take more responsibility for Billie and it was different. Eventually Dad had arrived home and prised Billie off me. I'd grabbed a pair of cat ears from Billie's dressing-up box as a token gesture towards a costume and escaped to meet Mischa, only to find she wasn't there.

She rubbed at her front teeth with a finger.

'Sorry, Clemzi. I did try to call you but I couldn't get through. They've got all this extra security round the flats now, since they arrested those guys last week. They took ages checking my ID and I'm sure it was just because the guy wanted to look at my cleavage a while longer. Better?' She bared her teeth at me.

I relented. 'You look amazing. Got your ID card for the bus?'

'Of course.'

When we were sitting side by side on the bus Mischa said, 'What the hell is that?'

'It's why I didn't get your messages.' We looked at my ancient phone, one of Dad's old ones from years ago. I held it up to show her. 'It's like something out of a museum.'

'Oh my God, is it even a phone?' She took it from me to examine. 'It's so big and heavy. Where are you supposed to keep it?'

'Right? I told him he might as well have given me one of those old contraptions with the dial and the curly wire to carry round with me.'

Mischa laughed. 'Why though? I mean, why's he given it to you?'

'He's paranoid about surveillance. You can't go online with it or anything. No apps, no messaging, nothing except SMS. He said I should only use it in emergencies and always assume people are listening into my calls or reading my messages.'

'I mean, no offence, babe, but do you really think they want to listen to you and me moaning about science homework or our menstrual cycles or whatever?'

'That's what I told him but you know what he's like.'

'Here's our stop. Do you think Danny's going to be there tonight?'

'I don't know, Misch,' I said. 'Do you really want to do this? I'm so not in the mood for a party.'

'You'll enjoy it once you get there,' Mischa said.

'That's what my dad always used to tell me when I was a kid,' I said, nearly falling down the stairs as the bus lurched to a stop. 'And he was always wrong.'

The party was too loud. There were loads of sixth-formers there and people who weren't from our school and most of them already seemed really drunk when we got there. Mischa had brought a couple of cans of beer that she'd found in her fridge and gave me one, even though I didn't want it.

'Let's go and dance,' she pleaded, tugging on my arm. But dancing was the last thing I felt like doing.

'You go on,' I shouted above the noise. 'I'll wait here.'

'Fine, be miserable then,' she said and stuck her tongue out at me.

'Thanks, I will,' I said and went and sat on the stairs, which got annoying because people kept treading on me on their way up and down, but there was nowhere else to sit that wasn't either really loud or in the kitchen, where Danny and Summer were wrapped around each other.

This nice, earnest sixth-former came and sat with me for a bit and talked in a slurred, sincere way about how bad it was that they'd changed the curriculum so that it censored history, and how he really admired the teachers who'd resigned over it. I agreed with him, but the music was giving me a headache and it was really hard work to hear what he was saying. He poured me a paper cup of neat vodka before he went. I took a sip but it was like drinking petrol. My head was throbbing, worse than ever.

Time passed. Maybe an hour, maybe two. I moved from the stairs to a landing and ended up sitting with two people I didn't know who were talking about elephants and made no sense. I decided I'd go and find Mischa and see if I could persuade her to leave. But when I saw her, she was blatantly flirting with Adi and I knew I wouldn't be able to get her to come away yet. I needed air. I gestured to Mischa to say I was going outside.

I found the back door and slipped outside into what wasn't so much a garden as a small yard with a skip taking up one side. There was a single wooden chair with several slats missing that I perched on, and a bike leaned against a wall. The cold and quiet were a relief. I realized I'd drunk more than I thought, though not enough to do anything embarrassing. I just felt sad.

'Clem!'

I turned to see Danny.

'I saw you come out,' he said. 'You okay?'

I nodded. 'Just got a headache. I think I'm going to go.'

'Not on your own?'

I shrugged. 'Where's Summer?'

'Dancing,' he said. He sat down on the ground next to me. 'You don't like her, do you?'

'No.' I'd drunk enough vodka to be honest then. 'Or Kyle. I don't know why you do.'

'They're a laugh when you get to know them.'

'They're not a laugh. Mischa and me are a laugh. They're . . .'

'What?'

'I dunno, Danny. The Community Guardians thing. The whole grassing-up your neighbours thing. Call it what you like, it doesn't seem like much of a laugh to me.'

'Don't be a kid, Clem. Grassing people up? It's not the playground. Don't you think if someone's a criminal, maybe dangerous, you've got a duty to keep people safe?'

'Yes, I do.'

'And, actually, you're judging me and my friends right now, deciding you're better than us. You don't know them properly, but you've decided you know what they're like. Isn't that being prejudiced too? You think everyone who doesn't agree with you is racist or bad or something. They're not like that.'

'If you say so.'

'How could Summer be? Her dad's whole family's from India.'

83

I shrugged. 'She and Kyle literally boast about getting people arrested and deported.'

'They only deport people who shouldn't be here. And if people are detained, they've obviously done something wrong, haven't they?'

'Like my stepmum?'

He looked uncomfortable. 'You know I didn't mean it like that. Maybe. I don't know. Like I said. If she hasn't, they'll let her go.'

'*If* she hasn't? Danny, this is Claudia we're talking about. You know her. She's not dangerous. She's not a criminal. She's done nothing wrong.'

'Well then, she's got nothing to worry about, has she?'

I shook my head. When Danny had come outside, I'd thought – hoped – that he was trying to get away from Summer, that he knew he was wrong and wanted to come back to Mischa and me and for things to go back to how they used to be. Now I realized he'd only come out to try and convince me that he was right.

'Danny, I came out here to get some peace. Why don't you go back in and find Summer?'

'Look, I don't want to argue. I just think you've got the wrong idea about them, about Toby Knight and all of that. I don't want us to fall out over it. There's going to be an election, right? People can decide for themselves. I just want to get on with my life, don't you?'

'Not everyone can just get on with their life though. Look at Claudia.'

'I'm sorry about Claudia,' he said. 'I know it must be tough for you. Come on, Clem, we've been friends since for ever. This can't change that. We're still us, aren't we? Let's just agree to disagree.'

I looked at Danny. Pale skin, shaded with stubble now, curly brown hair. He was nearly a man, I realized, seeing him for a split second through the eyes of someone who didn't know him. But really, he didn't look so different from the skinny little kid sitting in the front row of our reception class photo. His hazel eyes watched me, concerned, wanting to make things okay for me, like he always had. I remembered how we used to talk when he was worried that his mum would die. I'd told him stuff about what it was like after my mum left that I hadn't told anyone else. He'd always been kind and straightforward and thoughtful. He still was all those things. But he was other things too.

If it wasn't for all of this, I'd probably never have known. I'd just have known the kind, straightforward Danny who sometimes tried a bit too hard to be liked. We'd have been friends for ever. Maybe more than friends, who knows. Does the kind of person you are depend on luck? On living at the right time, in the right place, with the right people around you? I never thought about it like that before.

'I don't know. Are we still us?' I said, slowly.

He laughs. 'What do you mean? Course we are.'

I stood up. I didn't feel drunk now. I felt clear-headed.

'Clem? Where are you going?'

'Away.'

'Clem!' he called after me. 'Come on. Don't go!'

I didn't look back.

*

I take out the photo of Mischa and me again. The right side of the photo has been cut at a slight angle. On Mischa's shoulder there's a hand. The hand is Danny's. This photo used to be of the three of us, my favourite photo of us. Danny printed it for me. I look at the space where he should have been. I can remember exactly what he looked like in the photo, grey T-shirt, looking not at the camera but at Mischa and me, laughing. We'd been on a school trip to the Globe Theatre. There'd been a pencil case in the gift shop I wanted to buy for Billie but I couldn't afford it, so I got her a badge instead. When we were on the train home Danny got the pencil case out of his school bag. He'd bought it so I could give it to Billie.

Where is Danny now?

Do I hate Danny? Yes.

Do I hope he's okay? Yes.

Do I still care about Danny?

I don't know.

Nothing makes sense.

*

When I knock on the door of Polly's office there's no reply but, after hesitating for a moment, I go in anyway.

I sit down on the plastic school chair and wait.

The room feels different without Polly in it, darker, colder.

After a while, I stand up again, because the chair is uncomfortable and the room is too still and quiet. There's a pile of boxes stacked against a wall which turn out to contain swimming nappies and tins of beans and sardines and assorted cleaning products. I squeeze between them and the desk to the window to check on the health of the cacti. The jug next to them has a dribble of water in it. I pour it onto the parched soil of the one closest to me and hum Jingle Bells for the benefit of the others.

Then I look at the postcards and notes on the pinboard behind Polly's desk. There are a couple of photos of her with people I assume are her girlfriend and her family. I look more closely at the family one and realize I recognize the woman in it. I close my eyes. I can smell her expensive perfume, see her concerned face looking into mine. *Stay awake, little match girl.* The woman at Grandpa's café. Polly's sister.

As I'm looking at the photo, Polly bursts in through the door.

'Oh!' she says, breathless. 'Clem. You're here already.'

'I just came in to wait,' I say, feeling my face flush. 'Sorry. That photo,' I say, pointing at the pinboard, 'it's your sister, isn't it?'

'That's right.'

'I'd forgotten. I can't really remember it.'

'You were very ill. Delirious.'

'She was kind.'

Polly looks at me with an expression I can't read. 'That's not the word most people would use to describe Nina,' she says. She walks over to the pinboard, takes down the photo and looks at it. 'But you're right. She is kind.'

'And sad,' I say. I don't know why.

Polly looks at me, curious. 'You reminded her of someone,' she says. 'Her daughter actually.'

I nod. *Anna*, I think, but don't say. I'm surprised at the memory, which seems to come from nowhere: the woman, Nina, talking about her, stroking my hair as I lay on the cold ground.

'I'll be seeing Nina over Christmas, as it happens. It's the first time in a while we've spent it together. I'll be off for ten days so we won't have any sessions during that time.'

I find, to my surprise, that I'm disappointed by this. I try not to show it.

'I know it's hard,' she says. 'Being away from family. Even harder than it always is, I mean.'

I remember last Christmas, without Claudia.

*

'She asleep?' I said to Dad as he collapsed onto the sofa and helped himself to a handful of Quality Street.

'Yeah,' he said. 'At last. As she should be, given she woke up at five a.m.'

There was nothing new about Billie waking up painfully early on Christmas Day, but everything felt different this year. She was excited, but Christmas Day just made the gap where Claudia should have been more empty. Billie's excitement was fragile and felt like it might shatter at any moment.

Somehow, though, Claudia was still organizing us anyway. Dad had found a bag of stocking presents for Billie and me at the back of the wardrobe that she'd bought and wrapped throughout the year. She'd baked the Christmas cake with Billie's help back in early autumn when the leaves were just turning orange outside the kitchen window and the weather was still surprisingly warm. It had sat in its tin in the cupboard under the stairs, wrapped in layers of greaseproof paper and foil, steeped in brandy, undisturbed by the upheaval of our lives around it. Billie remembered it at the last minute, because icing it and adding the decorations was a Christmas Eve ritual, and then Dad had panicked about whether you could even get hold of marzipan and icing sugar any more with all the food shortages. There'd been mass brawls in supermarkets over turkeys and Christmas puddings and they'd had to bring in extra security and ticketing systems that led to people queuing all round the car parks for hours, all of which just caused more fights.

'Season of goodwill, eh?' Dad said. 'Nobody even liked Christmas pudding until they thought they couldn't get it.'

But it turned out Claudia had thought of that too. I understood now why she'd seemed so frantic and distant in those weeks she'd been at home: she'd foreseen all this. She'd prepared herself for what was coming and then she'd tried to prepare us for life without her. There was marzipan and icing sugar stored away with the Christmas cake tin, and the star and angel cookie cutters and photocopied recipes in a folder. She'd also bought the Quality Street we were now eating; tubs like ours were now selling on eBay for more than cars and diamonds, according to Mischa, who may have been exaggerating. And there were the sprouts and potatoes Claudia had planted in the garden and the Christmas wrapping paper and leftover crackers saved from last year.

It was just as well because, without Claudia's income, money had already been tight, and since Dad lost his job I knew we were really struggling. Dad told me not to worry, he had savings, we weren't going to starve. I knew he skipped meals though and didn't switch the heating on while we were at school even when it was bitterly cold.

Billie had insisted on buying Claudia a present with money from her piggy bank, wrapping it and putting it under the tree. Mischa and I had taken her out and bought it with her: a tube of Claudia's favourite fancy hand cream, which luckily no one was stockpiling but was unbelievably expensive anyway. I had to give her the money I'd been saving for Mischa's present, but Mischa didn't mind.

'You know your mum won't be back to open it, B?' I said, just to be sure, handing her the fancy little black and white bag tied up with a ribbon.

'I *know*!' she yelled at me, in the middle of the boutique. 'I'm not *fucking STUPID*!'

Several people gave us disapproving looks and Mischa said, 'If you think this is a performance you can pay for your tickets,' and the disapprovers all looked embarrassed and pretended they were actually really busy looking at something else. Mischa marched out and we trailed behind her.

But I knew really that Billie still hoped Claudia would be there to open it, magically, somehow. I knew because I'd had that hope myself once, as Christmases without Mum ticked by.

Between us, then, Dad and I had kept Billie busy all morning with presents and games and TV and food, and she'd enjoyed it, but none of us ever forgot for a second that Claudia wasn't there and we didn't know where she was. I didn't want to imagine what her Christmas was like, how much she'd be missing Billie.

By the afternoon Billie was exhausted, sitting glassy-eyed in front of a movie on the sofa with Dad.

By bedtime she was tearful.

Claudia's present still sat under the tree.

'Bit of peace and quiet at last,' Dad said once Billie was finally asleep and it was just the two of us sitting in front of some Christmas Special neither of us wanted to watch.

'Yeah.'

We smiled and then our smiles faded and we looked away from the lonely parcel and tried to seem busy, Dad concentrating very hard on the TV schedule, me checking my phone to see if Mischa had messaged.

I looked at Dad, not knowing what to say. I'd felt a weird kind of distance between us over the weeks since Claudia had been arrested. It wasn't just that he was so busy and preoccupied, although that was part of it. His work with the resistance network, the campaigning, the fight to find out what happened to Claudia, took up all his energy. It was obsessive. He was often out early and back late, and when he was working at home he barely looked up from his laptop. We hardly ever saw each other and when we did, he was exhausted and stressed. And he wouldn't tell me much about his work, and as that was the only thing on his mind, there wasn't much to talk about.

But it was more than that. Claudia wasn't mine in the way that she was Dad's and Billie's. I felt like I missed her because they did, and because it made my life more difficult now she wasn't there. I did feel a pang of loss, of wishing when I went down bleary-eyed in the morning that she'd be there in the kitchen with her post-sun-salutation cup of green tea, or I'd just see her pottering about in the garden on a Sunday, making things grow. I even sometimes missed her asking me stuff I didn't want to talk to her about or offering me advice I didn't need. And I worried about her, of course. But it just wasn't the same for me as it was for them. I didn't feel that physical pain in the chest, that homesick longing, that I knew they must have. It made me feel disloyal. I wanted to say something now that would connect us, Dad and me, that would show him that I did care about Billie, that I understood how much he was hurting. But what could I say?

'It's all so weird, isn't it?' I blurted out at last. I could hear how childish my words sounded. 'Everything. It's just *wrong.*'

It wasn't what I meant to say at all. It was ridiculous and obvious and, even worse, as I said it I found I had tears springing to my eyes.

Dad looked at me and half-smiled. 'Hey,' he said. 'Clem. Come on. Things will get better.'

'Sorry,' I said.

'Don't be. It's been a long day. Christmas reduces people to tears at the best of times. Which this definitely isn't.'

I tried to smile back but I felt worse than ever. I'd wanted to comfort him, and now he was having to comfort me.

He came and sat next to me and put his arm round me. I leaned my head against him. We hadn't sat like that for so long. For that moment I felt like everything was fine, and everything would carry on being fine, as long as we were together.

'Do you remember the first Christmas we had without Mum?' he said.

I looked at him, surprised. We didn't talk about Mum. Not in a Never Mention Her Name In My Presence way. We just didn't. I thought back, sifting through my Mum and post-Mum memories.

'I'm not sure.'

All the Christmases when I'd hoped for her return blurred in my memory, but I do remember those months after she left, her presence so tangible I sometimes talked to her still, the silent space where she should have been always there with us. The rawness of her absence bound me with Dad so tightly I found even his being in another room made me chew my nails and count silently until he was back where I could see him, holding his hand.

'It was hard,' he said. 'Really hard. For a while I thought we'd never be happy again. But we were.'

'Yes,' I said. 'We were.'

'And we have to believe we will be again.'

'I know,' I said. But it was hard.

'Things are changing, Clem. We've just got to get through this next couple of months. Knight's going to lose this election.

93

He gambled that whipping up all this fear and uncertainty would strengthen him, that he could convince people he was the only one that could keep them safe and lead them forward. But it's done the opposite. His support is fading and he knows it. That's why he's letting the protest go ahead. He wants to appear reasonable. But it's too late.'

There was a huge protest planned for January that Dad was helping to publicize. The rules controlling mass gatherings were being relaxed for this and the organizers wanted to get as many people there as possible.

'I know it's been tough,' he said. 'But we will get through it. Things will get better.'

'I know,' I said, even though I didn't.

'I love you,' Dad said.

'Same.' I reached over for the Quality Street. 'Hey, you've eaten all the purple ones.'

He laughed.

'Of course. I don't love you *that* much.'

When I went in to see Billie that night, she was fast asleep. I sat down on her bed watching her breathe, in and out. When I bent down to kiss her, I realized she smelt of Claudia. It was the expensive hand cream. She'd sneaked down at some point and taken it from under the tree, smeared some on her hands and put the tube under her pillow. After that she put it on whenever she was really missing Claudia, which was most of the time, and sometimes I'd catch the scent of it unexpectedly and I'd turn round thinking Claudia was there. I realized in those moments, before I had time to think, just how much I wished she was.

I went and lay in my own bed but I couldn't sleep. I messaged Mischa but got no reply. I switched my lamp on, opened my bedside drawer and took out the small round mirror that Claudia had left for me as a Christmas present. It had belonged to her mum and had an old-fashioned design of mother-of-pearl roses on the back. I'd always liked it. It felt precious, that Claudia had given this to me. I knew it was her way of telling me that we were each other's family. I wanted to tell her that I understood this and that I was grateful, although if I'd tried it would probably have come out wrong, as always, so maybe I'd just have hugged her without saying anything.

I wished I'd worked out how to sound genuine whenever I tried to say something nice to Claudia. I wished I could have told her that I didn't mean to be sarcastic or awkward on purpose, not most of the time anyway.

And I wished I could tell her that I was proud that she wished she'd had a sister like me, and that I'd kept my promise, that it hadn't been easy but I'd made sure Billie was okay and I always would, until Claudia was home.

*

'Clem,' Polly says as I walk into her office. 'Happy new year! Can I interest you in an only-very-recently expired vegan and gluten-free mince pie? I've got about five hundred of them.'

'Tempting,' I said. 'But no. Thanks.'

'Good call. They have an aftertaste which is ...' – she

muses – 'not festive. Anyway, I've made you a coffee. Milk, one sugar, right?'

'Thanks.'

I take the mug she hands me and sit. 'How was Christmas? How was your secretly kind sister?'

'It was good,' she says. 'Really good actually. And Nina managed not to offend anyone for almost an entire hour. How was yours?'

'Fine,' I say, even though it wasn't, which she knows. But everyone was kind and wanted us to be happy, and they gave the kids toys and books that people had donated, and Billie loved the games and making paper chains and singing.

There's a small spider plant in one of those knotted hanger things, perched precariously on top of a tin of festive shortbread on her desk. She sees me notice it and smiles apologetically.

'It was a Christmas present, can you believe?' she says, holding it up for me to admire.

'From someone who doesn't know about you and plants?'

She laughs. 'From someone who's trying to improve me.'

I watch as she hangs it carefully from a hook so it dangles above the windowsill where her other victims are lined up.

You've missed coming to see her, Mischa says.

I have not. I only come because I have to.

You don't actually though, do you? Mischa continues. *I mean, what are they going to do if you don't?*

I don't know, Misch, but it's just easier to go along with it, okay?

She sighs. *Don't you think maybe there's just a little bit of you that wants to tell her what happened?*

I feel sick.

No. I don't. I can't tell her.

'So,' Polly says, sitting, leaning forward. 'Clem. Shall we talk about what happened next? About when you had to leave home?'

I think about my story with the happy ending. That story is my protection, from Polly's questions and where they will take me.

I sip the coffee. It's hotter than I expected and burns my mouth but I swallow painfully down.

'Clem? Was it too dangerous to stay in London?'

Yes.

Yes.

I can't. I'm not strong enough to tell her.

I close my eyes.

You're good at stories.

Yes. This is my story. I can tell it.

*

As we walked up the steps from the shadowy Underground station, past the line of armed guards at the entrance and out into the sharp, spring light, the world felt new. There was the hum and chatter and shout of the crowd, the smell of frying onions and cigarette smoke and something else in the air too. Even on the Tube on the way there we could feel it. Something different. Something crackling in the air and for once it wasn't anger or fear, although those hadn't gone away.

Dad had left early that morning and was up at the front of the march helping to set up the stage. There were speakers coming from all the political parties, and from families of people who'd been detained and deported, and even some celebrities, although he wouldn't tell us who. 'Couldn't he have got us in to meet them?' Mischa said, but Dad had made it very clear that wasn't going to happen so we'd arranged to meet him afterwards.

People were nervous, you could feel it. There had been rumours of a counter-protest, but Dad said the police would keep the two groups apart. They didn't want trouble any more than we did.

'I didn't realize there'd be so many people,' Mischa said.

'There's going to be thousands, my dad says. Like, tens of thousands.'

'Do you think they'll try and arrest us?' she said, looking at the ranks of police and army lining the route. 'My mum didn't want me to come. She's convinced I'm going to do something crazy and get myself into trouble.'

I smiled. 'I mean, why would she think that, Misch?'

'You don't think there will be trouble, do you?'

I shrug. 'I think it's fine. Dad says it's all been agreed with the police and the army and everyone. I mean, he wouldn't have let us come otherwise.'

'I suppose. But if I get arrested or something, my mum will actually kill me.'

'We've got Billie with us. They're not going to arrest a little kid, are they?'

'Hey,' Billie said. 'I'm not a little kid. I'm the tallest in my class. Nearly.'

'Yeah, Clem,' Mischa said, 'stop bullying Billie.'

'Yeah, *Clem*.' Misch and Billie always ganged up on me.

We moved slowly along from the Tube station exit but there were so many people we didn't get very far. I held Billie's hand tight. 'Don't let go,' I said to her every few minutes. 'Make sure you don't let go of my hand.'

'I *know*, Clem. You told me a billion times already. You don't have to hold so tight, you know.'

We walked slowly in the pale sunshine, along Oxford Street, people packed in across the whole of the road that was usually full of buses and taxis. There were people as far as I could see in all directions and after a few minutes everything slowed down, so that eventually we were at a standstill.

'My feet are killing me,' Mischa said.

'Told you heels were a stupid idea.'

'Yeah, but I do look amazing.'

I shook my head, laughing at her. 'Course you do.'

'Seriously though, how much longer till we can move? I'm starving. Do you reckon we could quickly go to McDonald's?'

'I don't even know if it's open. Anyway, they're keeping everyone together on the road. They won't let you through.' I nodded at the police and army and cadets lined up along the pavement.

Mischa gave me a *duh* look. 'I can be very persuasive you know. I'm going to try.'

'Can I go?' Billie said. 'I'm starving too. I want fries. And I need a wee.'

'No, B,' I said. 'You need to stay with me.'

'Why?' Billie whined.

'Because that was the deal. I'm looking after you. You've got to stay with me and hold my hand.'

'You hold too tight. Your nails dig in.'

'I don't want you to get lost, that's all. We'll find toilets somewhere further along.'

'See you in a minute,' Mischa said, calling over her shoulder as she turned and walked away. 'I'll bring you some fries, B. If I can't find you, I'll call.'

'Don't get your hopes up,' I told Billie. 'They won't let her through.'

'They will,' Billie giggled. 'She's Mischa.'

But as time went on and nothing happened and Mischa didn't reappear, Billie started to whinge. Suddenly the crowd started to move.

'Let's wait for Mischa,' Billie said. But we couldn't. The crowd was too tightly packed and we had to move with it. I remembered with a lurch how much I hated being in big groups of people.

'I'll message her,' I said, but when I tried the signal kept cutting out. 'Too many people all on their phones,' I told Billie. 'I'll try again in a minute.'

Losing Mischa and the lack of phone signal just added to the feeling of being not quite in control. I tried to squash down the anxiety. The drone of helicopters overhead buzzed in my ears.

We moved on towards Oxford Circus and turned down Regent Street. For a while we moved along quite freely, Billie looking longingly at the boarded-up windows of Hamleys as we went past. As the road curved down towards Piccadilly Circus we slowed. The people in front of us couldn't go fast enough, there must be a bottleneck or maybe they were being blocked by the police. People were still moving up from behind, so we were being squashed closer and closer together.

'What's happening?' Billie said.

I stood on tiptoes, trying to see what was going on, and glimpsed a line of police on horses in high-vis jackets blocking the road ahead.

'Ooh, horses,' Billie said when I told her. 'Can we stroke them?'

Surely they'd move and let us through in a minute? The panic that I get in small spaces bubbled up inside me, pressed in among all these bodies, not tall enough to see over people's heads to know what was going on, but I tried to breathe slowly and tell myself there was plenty of air for everyone, it wasn't for long, we'd be moving soon. I looked up at the big sky and focused on all that space instead of the crush of people around us.

My phone started ringing in my pocket. I assumed it was Mischa, but when I looked I saw it was Dad.

'We're nowhere near Trafalgar Square yet,' I said, having to shout to make myself heard. 'We're not even at Piccadilly Circus. They're not letting us move. And I've lost Mischa.'

'Clem, listen to me.'

Even in all the noise I could hear there was something weird in his voice. I let go of Billie's hand and put my finger in my other ear to try and block out the voices around me.

'What is it, Dad? Are you okay?'

'Can you get away from where you are? Can you get to the station?' His voice sounded tense, like he was trying not to sound panicked even though he was shouting.

'I don't think so. There's so many people . . . I can try.'

'Okay—' His voice cut out. ' . . . as quick as you can.'

'What?'

'Just do it, Clem!'

'Do what?'

'You need to get away from the march.'

'What? Why?'

'Get to the station and get on a train. Or, if you can't do that, walk, *run*—'

I rolled my eyes. 'Dad, we can't even move.'

His voice cut out again.

'Dad,' I said. 'Can you hear me? Dad?'

I looked at Billie who blew a bubble of gum at me until it popped with a crack. I pulled a face back.

' . . . and Billie—' His words became garbled.

'Dad?'

Silence.

'I'll call you back in a minute, Dad,' I said. 'When the signal's better.'

But the line had already gone dead.

'Can I speak to him?' Billie said.

'He's gone.'

I called Mischa's number but it went straight to voicemail.

'Misch, call me back will you—'

As I was speaking, something changed. There were shouts and screams and then like a wave crashing towards us there were people running, pushing, crushing. People started to fall over as the crowd tried to push through the barriers at the sides of the road. I saw police on horseback, truncheons raised—

'Billie!' I shouted. She stumbled and almost got trampled. I grabbed her and tried to lift her up as best I could but I was being jostled from all sides, trapped among people taller than me so I couldn't see ahead, carried along by the surge of the crowd, my feet barely touching the ground.

'Are you okay?' I gasped. 'Can you breathe okay?'

She nodded at me with wide eyes as we came to a standstill again. I knew I couldn't keep carrying her like that for long. My arms were burning and I had to put her down.

'What is it?' I asked a woman in a purple puffa jacket next to me. 'What's happening?'

'Run,' she said. And she was gone, swept away by the crowd, and we were being pushed, squashed together.

If we could just get to a shop doorway out of the tide of people—

'Come on, Billie, we have to—'

I looked down and somehow—

'Billie!'

Jesus.

'Billie?'

Somehow she was gone.

'BILLIE!' I yelled. I looked all around, between the running people, but I couldn't see her. I stood, frozen. I wanted to run, but in which direction? I could be running away from her.

'BILLIE!' I screamed, blind and paralysed with panic. Oh, God. Please. 'Billie!'

She couldn't have gone far. She couldn't have. She'd been there a second ago. I'd been holding her hand . . .

'Billie!' I couldn't breathe.

And then—

And then . . .

Then I saw her. Standing, crying as she looked around her blindly, calling out, 'Clem! Clem!'

'Billie, I'm here,' I called as I ran towards her, but it came out as a gasp and she didn't hear me in the noise of the crowd.

'Billie!'

And then she turned and she saw me. I reached her and grabbed hold of her and she wrapped herself round me like a limpet.

'I thought you'd gone, Clemmie,' she sobbed. 'I thought—'

'Hey,' I said. 'I wouldn't leave you, would I? Now come on. We need to get away from here. It'll be okay, B, but we've got to get somewhere safe as quick as we can, yeah? Can you do that? Can you run?'

She nodded.

'Okay,' I said. 'That's it. Hold my hand. Don't let go.'

*

Polly's watching me.

'A lot of people died at that protest,' she says quietly.

She waits for me to say more. I say nothing.

There is a blank hole of unguessable time after that day.

'Clem?' Polly says. 'Are you okay?'

Flashes of memories surface and then disappear into the dark.

Blood on a pavement above me, the sky below—

The beep of a heart monitor—

The hospital smell, detergent and fear—

'You were in hospital?' Polly says. 'You were hurt at the protest?'

But the beep of the heart monitor drowns her out.

Someone is crying.

Through a window, clouds heavy with snow—

'And so, you left London,' Polly says. I nod.

*

Things had changed in that blank, empty time. I remember being in the car with Dad, driving home through grey streets, past the army patrols and the slushy remains of thawing snow.

He was talking, far away.

'There were riots after the protest march,' Dad said. 'Knight blamed all the violence on the protesters – "Extremists who didn't care who got injured or died in their cause". He's declared a State of Emergency. This is what he planned. It's why he let the protest go ahead.'

I wanted Dad to stop talking but I couldn't say so. I couldn't say anything.

Opposition politicians had been arrested, he told me. Others were in hiding, trying to form a cross-party emergency government. But the army was with Knight, so far. Judges, journalists, anyone who spoke out, all being rounded up.

I leaned the side of my head against the window and looked out and watched the small cloud of my breath grow and fade, grow and fade on the glass.

'They've cancelled the election "until security concerns can be addressed". He planned the whole thing! The violence . . . it was all for this. An excuse to bring in martial law. To deny people the chance to vote him out.'

Dad's face was tight with anger. His voice shook.

'Democracy had to be protected, Knight said. Can you believe he actually said that?'

I could believe everything and nothing. None of it made sense. None of it mattered.

'People who can leave are getting out. Out of the city, out of the country . . . You need to leave too, Clem. Like we agreed. You need to go. Clem? Are you listening to what I'm saying?'

I just needed him to stop talking.

'Drop me off by Mischa's flat,' I told him.

He refused, so I tried to get out of the moving car.

Dad yelled at me. He held my hand. He cried.

None of it made sense. None of it mattered.

He stopped outside the block of flats.

'Ten minutes,' he said.

I climbed the stairs to Mischa's, stopping at every floor to catch my breath. I hadn't been able to call her. My phone had gone in the panic and crush. And you couldn't go on social media now. They said terrorists and dissidents were using it to plan attacks. Most people couldn't even go on the internet half the time.

See you in a minute. I'll bring you some fries.

That was the last thing she'd said to me.

I stood out in the corridor, still breathless from the stairs, shivering, imagining Mischa's mum answering and saying—

Her mum telling me with gestures and tears, breaking into rapid-fire Polish—

But there was no reply. I sat down with my back against her front door and closed my eyes.

'You're not here for Mischa, are you, my love?'

I opened my eyes. How long had I been sitting there? Wendy, Mischa's elderly neighbour, was looking down at me, cigarette in hand. Mischa had always liked Wendy, with her dyed black hair and jingling bangles and her many, many cats. She did tarot readings for Mischa sometimes, and Wendy had given her a crushed-velvet tunic with medieval sleeves she'd worn in the sixties. She'd once told Mischa she'd 'had it off' with one of the Rolling Stones when she was very young. Mischa hadn't known whether to be impressed or horrified. 'Not in this top though, right?' Wendy had just laughed.

'I'm so sorry, love,' Wendy said now, taking my hand and giving it a squeeze. 'She's gone. Didn't you know?'

The world faded to grey as I stood up and I sagged dizzily against the door until the faintness passed.

'Gone?' My voice sounded like someone else's.

'Gone,' she said dabbing under her eyes where tears and black eyeliner were mingling. 'God bless her.'

'Gone where?'

Wendy shook her head.

'Do you mean ... Wendy, do you mean she's gone away to, like, family in Poland, or ... ?'

'I don't know, sweetheart,' Wendy said. 'I just don't know. There's so many gone and everyone's heard something different. You don't know who to believe. I was at my sister's for a couple of nights – no one to feed the cats of course, I was worried sick about them but I had to go because she gets herself in a right state, my sister. And when I got back, next door was empty and someone told me ... oh, my lovely Mischa.'

'Told you what?'

'They told me they'd heard something ... something bad had happened. She was on that march, you see. And her mum, Renata, bless her, she was so distraught she's gone away, to family, back home.' She took hold of my arm as I felt my legs sag under me. 'Now, now, lovey – don't lose heart. There've been all sorts of stories going round – none of them true. They told me Nathan from number thirty had died – said he'd been trampled by a horse – then I saw him this morning with my own eyes. Miserable as ever, like he always is. Wild rumours, you see, love. Or wishful thinking in Nathan's case.' She gave a short cackle of laughter. 'But not Mischa. I'd *know* if she was gone,' she said fiercely, stabbing at the air with her cigarette. 'I'd know.'

And then there was a yowl from inside Wendy's flat.

'That's my Benjy. They'll all be wanting their tea. Stay strong, my darling. She's still with us. Believe it. I can feel her vibrations.'

And Wendy disappeared into her flat, the door clicking shut behind her. I was left standing in the corridor, just a waft of smoke where she'd been.

I didn't want to leave. I wrote: *Please be okay, Misch. Call me as soon as you can. Love you, Clem* on a page in my notebook, because you don't write notes to people who aren't coming back, so if I wrote her a note she couldn't be gone. I was about to rip it out and post it through the letter box when I realized she couldn't call me: I had no phone. So I crossed it out and wrote instead *I'll be at my grandpa's. This might or might not be his number.* I wrote out a row of digits that seemed like Grandpa's number but might not be. It was the best I could do. I sat and folded the note into a paper crane and posted it.

I thought I'd be able to find out what had happened to Mischa in the end, because of course I would. How could I not? For all my life till then, almost nothing was unknowable. It could all be googled, all possible information was everywhere. You had to work really hard – as hard as Mum had done – to leave no trace. It had been almost impossible for people *not* to know where you were all the time, and what you were doing and who with, even when you didn't want them to. Now, with no phone, no internet, I didn't know how to find out anything. Secrets and rumours and vanishing acts were possible again. People disappeared. You could lose them in the moment between one heartbeat and the next.

Mischa is one of the things I lost in the darkness.

She smiles over her shoulder at me from the other side of it. *See you in a minute.*

*

'You didn't see her again?' Polly says. 'After that day, the march? You didn't hear from her?'

I shake my head.

'I'm sorry. It must be hard not knowing what happened to her.'

I nod.

'And you must miss her.'

Miss her? I don't just miss her. I can't be me without Misch. There's a whole part of me that only exists with her. If she is gone for ever then so am I.

I remember lying on my bed at home. Dad sitting on the edge of it.

'We've run out of time,' he'd said. 'You need to leave. First thing tomorrow.'

Most of the people he worked with had been arrested already. Someone had reported on them. They didn't know who. Maybe someone inside the group betrayed them. It would only be a matter of time till they got to Dad. I begged him to come but he said it would put us in too much danger,

110

and anyway he had to carry on the work he was doing, it was more important now than ever. He couldn't tell me where he'd be, I wouldn't be able to contact him. But once it was safe, he'd come.

He gave instructions. Train tickets, maps, cash – not much. It was all he had. In the inside pocket of the rucksack, false ID.

'But won't they know if they check?'

'No,' Dad said. 'These are good. The best. I promise you, Clem. It's safer than you being linked to me or Claudia. But keep your head down. Try not to get stopped.'

Then he'd had to go out. I hadn't wanted him to.

'I'll be back before you go,' he'd said. 'And if I'm not, go anyway.'

He kissed me. He was crying.

I'd half-woken in the night to find Billie curled up next to me in bed, her eyes fluttering open.

'Try to sleep, B,' I murmured.

'Tell me again about the magic forest,' she said, only half-awake.

'It's waiting for us,' I told her.

'Clem?'

Dad's voice didn't belong in my hazy dream.

'Clem! Wake up!' I forced open heavy eyelids. The room was still shadow-grey, the sun not yet risen. I blurrily thought of summer holidays, Dad hauling me out of bed in the dark in order to get on early-morning planes or ferries, cases packed the night before, promises of bacon sandwiches at the airport and swimming in the sea before teatime.

'You need to go. Now. The back way. Quickly, Clem.'

Pulling on clothes, grabbing my purse, my notebook, a photo, Claudia's mirror.

'We mustn't forget Luna,' Billie said and I grabbed the owl toy.

Running downstairs.

Dad waiting with the rucksack he'd packed for us, lifting it onto my back. Saying goodbye. Dad's face.

Polly watches me remember.

'And so that's what happened?' she prompts. Her voice is gentle. 'Your father got away? You and Billie made it to safety?'

Running over the lawn, heart racing, past Claudia's vegetable patch, across the patio to the back fence. Shouts from the front of the house. Dad. He must have gone out there so that we could get away out back.

My face, wet with tears.

The grip of Billie's fingers, tight around mine.

Scrambling over the fence, swearing, falling into the rose bush on the other side, splinters and thorns embedding themselves in my hands, barely felt till later. The gap at the bottom of the fence, where Billie used to crawl through to play on the trampoline in the back neighbours' garden.

'That's it. Stay with me, B.'

Panting through the garden towards the back of their house, a mirror image of ours. Through the looking glass. Round the trampoline, dodging patio furniture. No risk they'll see us, the family left weeks before. The neighbour's dog yapping as I squeezed through the narrow passage between the houses, trying not to get entangled in the rusting bikes abandoned there. Holding my breath, waiting for a voice. If there was a voice, would it help us or report us? Impossible to know. Best not to find out.

Silence.

Deep breath. Then through a side gate with its broken lock, thank God. Quickly through the square of front garden, hidden from the road by an overgrown hedge, and out onto the pavement, walking as fast as possible without actually running so as not to attract attention.

And then thinking of Dad, panicking. I need to go back. I can't leave him. I can't go back.

Dad—

'Clem?' Polly says again.

I open my mouth to speak but words don't come. I close my eyes and I feel like I'm falling.

I can't breathe.

I see – . . .

I see a bird, flying in a blue sky far above us, far, far away. Make a wish.

Don't let go.

'Yes,' I say to Polly. 'That's what happened.'

FLIGHT

The action of flying or moving through the air with or as with wings. The action of fleeing or running away from danger. An extravagant or far-fetched idea, an exuberant display of imagination.

The girl tried in vain to claw her way through the wall of thorns but the spikes tore at her skin and she could not fight her way through.

She wandered the forest in despair, the blue feather in her hand. She had lost her sister and even if she could find her, she had no idea how to break the witch's enchantment.

At last, bleeding and exhausted, she lay down under a tree.

'I wish I could see you again, my sister,' the girl said, tears falling onto the ground where the tree's roots spread deep. She curled up among the roots, in a space that was just the right size and shape, as if it had been made just for her. With tears still flowing from her closed eyes, she fell asleep.

The girl did not know it, but the tree she lay under was an ancient and powerful one. It was said that if you made a wish beneath that tree and left it an offering, your wish would come true.

The girl had wished and she had given the tree the gift of her tears.

As she slept, she dreamt of a blood-red flower that only grew on a faraway island. The flower bloomed once a year and could only be picked at midnight on midwinter's night. Its petals were able to break even the most powerful of enchantments.

The girl woke knowing she must find the flower.

It was the only way to save her sister.

*

All around were people, pushing, pressing, crowding round the train departure screens, running for the platforms, hauling luggage and children after them, shoving people out of the way. The tension made the air thick, harder to breathe. Harder to think. Queues snaked around the concourse and back on themselves.

'Keep hold of my hand, Billie. Don't let go.'

I was dizzy. Everything was too bright, too loud.

I started to push through the crowd, back towards the entrance to the station, needing to get back outside to the air, the rain. It was impossible to breathe now and the noise all around was almost drowned out by the roar in my head. But I couldn't fight through and the bulk of the rucksack on my back slowed me down and kept knocking into people around me. A woman carrying a baby in a sling swore at me and I might have apologized or yelled at her but my throat felt too tight to do either. Eventually I reached a wall by a sandwich shop, its shelves picked clean, and leaned my head against the cool of the stone.

'Clem?' Billie's voice was far away. I tried to speak but I couldn't.

I couldn't do this.

I couldn't be here.

I couldn't leave Dad.

We had to get out of the station.

But then what? There was nowhere else to go.

The crowd noise pulsated, loud, quiet, close then far away, like a tide. I breathed and counted like one of the post-Mum shrinks had taught me to. In for six, out for eight. In for six—

'You all right?'

A tall woman with beaded braids was peering at me through thick glasses.

I nodded, still unable to speak.

'Here.' She held out a bottle of water. I tried to nod or smile or something. She watched me fail to open the bottle and gently took it back, returning it open. I managed to gulp the water, felt the cold of it inside me. I was real. I was here. I breathed in and out. Took another gulp. Wiped my mouth.

'Better?' she said.

I nodded.

'Here,' she said. 'Take this.'

She handed me a plastic pot of pallid fruit salad and a cellophane-wrapped square of cake.

'No,' I managed to say. 'I'm fine. Really.'

She pressed it into my hand. 'The sugar will help,' she said and smiled at me before turning and disappearing into the crowd.

'Thank you,' I tried to call after her, but she was gone.

The hours before we could get on a train blurred, till they were only the ache in my hips and back from standing for so long, the throb inside my head of the endless loop of threatening tannoy announcements, the readiness always for the surge and crush of people when the barriers opened. The constant effort of keeping the panic inside me. Every so often people would be searched, hauled away. I found myself looking away in case their bad luck was catching and because I couldn't help wondering who they were, if they'd actually done anything wrong, if people they loved would be waiting for them somewhere and worrying when they didn't show up. I hated myself for looking away. I felt sick and shaky as we got near the barrier, but in the end no one asked for ID and we were through and time sped up.

Trying now to run down the platform past carriage after carriage packed full of people, slowed by the weight on my back, Billie's hand holding mine, as the whistle blew . . .

Desperately cramming into the damp heat of the last, packed carriage just before the doors locked shut and at last the train moved slowly out of the station, the people who hadn't got on sliding backwards, away from us, out of sight . . .

Breathing. Breathing.

I was so relieved to be on the train that it wasn't until long after we'd left the station and trundled out through the graffiti-covered bridges, past the empty, glass-walled offices, the tower blocks of the city, and then the lawns and trampolines and washing lines of the suburbs, not until there was nothing but fields and sky, that I realized our home was gone. I'd missed it as we'd trundled onwards. I'd let it slip away without noticing, without saying goodbye. That was the first time I wondered whether I'd ever see it again.

Then there were more hours spent at a grey, non-descript station on the edge of a grey, non-descript town, busy but not as bad as London, before finally, in the early evening, getting on another slow, meandering train that would eventually get us to Grandpa's.

This train was almost empty and we sat at a table. Billie stretched out on the seats opposite, her head on my rolled-up coat, and slept. I wished I could call Dad or message him to tell him we'd made it; we were on the train.

I wished I knew whether he was safe too.

Wherever he was, our train was creaking and jolting through the night taking us far away from him. The darkness all around felt overwhelmingly huge, stretching out for ever in all directions, and we were lost in it. I had a flash of an out-of-place memory of visiting the Science Museum with Mum and Dad when I was a little kid. I could only have been five at most, but I don't have many memories of the three of us on days out together so I suppose that's why it stuck. Dad couldn't wait to show me all the old rockets and space modules. Some of them really did look like something you'd make at primary school, a lemonade bottle wrapped in tin foil, just bigger, a tin can, with bits bolted onto it like Meccano. Then Mum and Dad had a row, which had started on the Tube on the way there, continued in the café, and came to a head in Space.

Dad went outside to smoke because he was angry and I sat with Mum among the weird-looking rockets. She became more interested in them once Dad had gone.

'Imagine it,' Mum said. 'Going to space. In that. Not knowing if you'd make it there, let alone back again.'

I did imagine it. It made me feel a bit sick.

'I'd do it in a heartbeat, wouldn't you?' Mum said.

My heart beat. It beat again. I wasn't like Mum. I wanted to be, but the thought of the astronauts, with all of space and time around them and no gravity to hold them down, made me feel like I needed to hold on to something.

'What if you just floated off, into nothing?' I said to her.

'I know.' Mum's eyes went all faraway, as though the idea was just that tiny bit tempting.

That's how I feel now: small, cut loose, lost in something too big.

Stop with the melodrama, I told myself. *You're on a train going to Grandpa's. Just like you used to.*

But I hadn't spoken to Grandpa in months. I remembered the times he'd waited for me on the platform, waving, smiling, in bright scarf, woolly hat and garish jacket in winter, Hawaiian shorts and sandals with stripy socks in summer. This time Grandpa didn't even know I was coming. This time he wouldn't be waiting. This time Granny wouldn't be there. I tried to imagine Grandpa without her and failed.

The last time I'd been to the village was for Granny's funeral, two years ago. It seemed like in another life. Dad had driven us. I'd felt sick all the way there, at the loss of Granny. But more than that, secretly, I was wondering if Mum would be at the funeral. I'd tried not to be distracted by the thought. But I was shaking as I walked into the crematorium, at the thought of seeing her again. I needn't have worried. She was just as not there as ever. I cried silently all through the service. Grandpa didn't cry. He just looked confused, as though he'd walked into a room and then couldn't remember why. I'd held his hand, which was shaking. That had made me sadder even than Granny.

Someone in the village had organized a wake at the pub afterwards but we couldn't stay because Dad needed to get back. 'Will he be okay?' I eventually managed to ask Dad when we stopped at a service station for coffee. Dad sighed. 'Maybe not for a while. But he's lucky being in the village. He's got people around to look out for him. Friends and neighbours. They'll see he's all right. And you can go and visit him soon.'

But I hadn't gone. Grandpa had made excuses when I suggested it. 'Give him time,' Dad said. But he never wanted to chat when I called. And then he stopped replying to my messages and my calls.

Grandpa had always been my rescuer, always picked up the pieces, made sense of things. He'd done that a lot after Mum had left. Could he do it now? It didn't seem possible.

I shivered. The carriage was empty now except for an older

woman who was reading and had a cat in a carrier. Would she think we looked suspicious? I was so exhausted I felt danger could be anywhere, everywhere. But the woman didn't even look at us, just made soothing noises to her cat and read her book. I tried to stay awake, to stay on guard, but I felt my eyelids drooping, snapping awake as my head nodded forward. I drifted into darkness and patchy dreams. I was in space, alone, floating. I looked for stars but there weren't any. Just darkness and me, floating . . . No! Not floating. Falling. I tried to grab hold of something but there was nothing to save me, just nothing and more nothing—

And now there were shapes in the darkness. A different fear settled on my skin, on my blind eyes. This dark place wasn't somewhere vast and full of nothing. It was somewhere small and full of shadows, the air warm and damp like breath. Not in space at all. Underground. Trapped. And what else was here with me in the dark—

'Clem,' Billie said. 'Clem!'

'Billie,' I tried to say, foggy with sleep, forcing my eyes open.

She was sitting up in her seat. 'You were asleep,' she said accusingly over the table in between us. 'You shouldn't sleep.'

'Right.'

But it wasn't right. I looked out of the window and I didn't know where we were. It was still dark. Not night dark. Tunnel dark. It was closed in around us, noisy and black.

'Hold my hand,' I said to Billie, my voice slow and slurring, but the noise of the train in the tunnel drowned me out. I reached out to her but instead of hands there were feathers. She had wings and I was falling again, with a feather in my hand, holding it as tight as I could—

'Oh,' I thought in my dream. 'It's still a dream.'

I forced my eyes open again. I saw Billie stretched out, asleep on the seats opposite, her head on my folded coat. I breathed, in and out, gripping the cold edges of the table, till my heartbeat slowed to the rhythm of the trundling train.

'It was just a dream,' I said.

The woman with the cat looked up at me for a moment but then went back to her book.

Billie didn't stir.

I told myself it was the wind making my eyes sting as we stood in the midnight stillness outside the station. It was colder here than in London and so quiet that the silence seemed loud. Back home, I was so used to the constant background hum of traffic and police sirens and planes that I didn't notice it. Now its absence made my skin prickle. There was no one around. No one at the ticket office. No one stumbling out of the pub or driving home from whatever it is that people do in the evening in places like this. Had it always been like this or were there curfews here too? I realized I'd been expecting nothing to have changed here, away from the city, but now I wondered.

Dad had said, 'Don't draw attention to yourself, you know what villages are like, all those nosy parkers twitching their net curtains. They could teach Toby Knight a thing or two about Community Surveillance – they invented it.'

Mischa had asked me once what it was like in Granny and Grandpa's village.

'Imagine if Narnia and the place where hobbits live had a baby. That's what it's like,' I told her. 'You know how Americans imagine any bit of England that isn't London? It's exactly that.'

Mischa nodded. 'So, cute cottages and pointless feuds and general bigotry?'

'No!' I was shocked. 'It's not like that. It's just pretty. The people are nice. It's quiet.'

'It *is* like that,' Mischa said. 'Believe me. Those places exist everywhere. My grandparents' village is like that too.'

Was that where Mischa was now? Please let her be there. Let her be moaning about the lack of WiFi and coffee shops. Let her be alive.

I shivered.

'Come on,' I said to Billie, trying to sound brisk and like a proper grown-up. But my voice just sounded small, swallowed up by the night. 'We'll warm up once we're walking.' I was anxious to get moving. There might be curfew patrols, even here. The quicker we got to Grandpa's the better.

I looked at the map Dad had put in a pocket of the rucksack. Grandpa's village was the next one over, forest and farmland between. A single road joined them, the road Grandpa usually drove us along in his ancient Mini, always with the roof down because it was the only time I got to ride in a convertible, always playing jazz really loud because the CD had got stuck in the player sometime in the last millennium and (Grandpa

126

claimed) the volume control was broken. When Grandpa drove it it had seemed no distance at all. But now, walking, I realized I had no real idea of how far it was. I knew it would be much quicker if we cut through the forest. I'd done that walk with Grandpa before, in the daytime, in summer, with a picnic. The thought of the forest at this time of night was very different. We'd stick to the road.

I wrestled the weight of the rucksack to sit more comfortably on my back, my breath puffing out in front of me.

'Come on,' I said to Billie. 'The sooner we get going, the sooner we'll be there.'

We walked down the High Street, still eerily quiet, but we tried to keep to the shadows anyway. We followed the road to where the new houses straggled on the edge of the village and then on to where the road got darker. It was hard to see anything once the street lights ended. I stopped and felt around in the rucksack, praying Dad had packed a torch. He had. We started walking again.

The moon was hidden behind thick cloud. Billie lagged behind. Her feet hurt. Her hands were cold. It was too far.

'Are we nearly there?'

'No, of course not,' I said, trying not to sound impatient.

'But I'm *tiiiired.*'

'I know,' I snapped. 'You know how I know? Because I'm tired too. Also, because you keep whining on about it.' I felt bad about snapping then. I didn't look at Billie. My heels had blistered and the pain had become agonizing as the skin peeled off. Each step made it worse.

'I felt a raindrop,' Billie said.

'No you didn't.'

'I did. And another one.'

Fat, undeniable raindrops started to fall, multiplying till the air was filled with them.

Seriously? We were wearing jackets but they weren't waterproof and the rain was so heavy that in a few seconds we'd be soaked. There were raincoats in the rucksack but if I tried to get them out here they'd be wet before we even got them on.

As I was thinking this I heard a car engine coming towards us fast. The glare of its headlights turned the streaks of rain silver for a second and we had to jump sideways into the thorny hedge to get out of the way.

I was breathing hard as the car disappeared.

'Okay,' I said. 'Let's get off the road. We'll go through the forest.'

Billie looked at me through the rain.

'Won't it be dark?'

'I mean, yes. But it'll be dry. Drier than here.'

'But there might be wolves.'

'There are no wolves in this country,' I said.

'There might be witches.'

'Billie,' I said, 'there won't be witches.'

'How do you know?'

I sighed. 'There might be owls.'

She said nothing.

'Come on. It'll be an adventure,' I said, trying to sound

128

like someone who likes adventures. I did my best to push thoughts of axe murderers and evil forest spirits and witches out of my mind.

*

Polly watches me closely as I tell her about our journey.

She isn't sure about my story now. I can see it in her eyes, although her face still shows the same kind, attentive expression it always does when she's listening to me. Her eyes say: *What aren't you telling me? What are you telling me that I shouldn't believe?*

Does she know? Can she guess?

I don't know.

But I'm good at stories.

Stories build cities and grow forests and make people appear from empty air.

They're a good place to hide.

But Polly knows this. *Coming, ready or not.*

'Carry on, Clem,' she says. 'We have time. Tell me more.'

*

We scrambled up over the stile into the field, the forest looming ahead of us, the small fan of torchlight ahead of us, darkness and shadow all around.

'Quick. Let's get to the trees.'

Rain was running into my eyes and down inside my collar; my hair stuck to my face. Billie ran ahead and disappeared among the trees, but sprinting after her with a rucksack was impossible. I lumbered forward and tried to force my heavy legs to hurry. As I reached the edge of the trees my ankle caught on a root and twisted and I lost my balance, falling heavily, the weight of the rucksack dragging me down. As I hit the ground the air was knocked out of me and my head flashed with light and shock at the blow.

I lay on the wet ground, not knowing where I was for a few seconds. Gradually my breath came back and I began to reorientate myself. But I had no energy to lift myself up. I lay on the wet ground, the rain pelting down on me.

'*Fuck*. Fuck fuck FUCK.'

Tears of pain and self-pity stung my eyes, mingled with the icy rain. It was too much. I couldn't go on. It was just all too much.

I swear you're so dramatic when you're hungry, I heard Mischa say.

I'm not being dramatic, I answered back. *I'm in pain. I think I've broken something.*

You're fine, she said. *Come on, Clem. Get up now.*

I clambered painfully to my feet, wincing as I put weight on my ankle, looking around for Billie. 'B, wait for me.'

I pointed the torch after her and saw the flash of her red coat as she disappeared into the trees.

'Billie! Wait!'

I started to limp after her as quickly as I could, which was not quickly at all, gasping with pain at every step. When I reached her I had to pause and lean against the enormous tree we were under so I didn't lose my balance again.

'I thought I lost you,' Billie said and started crying. 'I looked round and you weren't there.'

'Sorry, B,' I said. 'I fell.'

She sank down between the roots of the tree. 'I want to go home,' she said, her voice small. She leaned back against the tree and closed her eyes.

'Mustn't fall asleep, B,' I said, trying to stop my teeth chattering. 'Not yet. In stories, if you fall asleep under an ancient tree in the middle of a forest, do you know what happens?'

Billie ignored me.

'You get taken off to the Otherworld. And when you're there it's like one big party, but then you get tired and you want to get home. And when you do it turns out hundreds of years have passed.'

She looked at me.

'I don't care,' she said. 'I just want Mum. And Dad.'

But she let me pull her up.

'Come on,' I said. 'Hold my hand. It's not much further.'

The noise of the wind and rain all around us was loud, like the sea, and I felt as though the forest was tilting and tipping around us like the waves of the ocean. I rested my hand against a tree to steady myself. I blinked hard, trying to focus my vision.

Billie was watching me. 'Are you okay?'

'Yeah, I'm fine.'

But I couldn't shake the feeling of being watched, that anyone or anything could be hiding behind every tree. A sick shakiness rose inside me. I wanted to run.

We carried on, and all the time I was looking out for something – anything – lights, something familiar, a thinning out of the trees, that would tell me where we were. But there was nothing. I had no idea whether we were even heading in the right direction. It was so dark, and everywhere looked the same in the small patch of torchlight. I couldn't go on much longer. I was just wondering what would happen if we decided to sleep in the woods when we came to a dip, almost falling down into it. I stopped. Something about it was familiar.

'Wait!' I said. 'I know this place. I know it. Just down here . . .'

I scrambled down the slope, holding on to tree roots as I went to steady myself.

There it was.

A small wooden shelter, almost hidden unless you knew it was there. A kind of hut, made of wood and branches. Grandpa had found it when Mum was little, all falling down and rotten. He'd replaced some of the boards, made it waterproof and patched up the holes. Mum had played there as a kid and then 'got up to no good' there when she was older. It was her place to escape to, Granny said, when she wanted to get away from everything. Relief flooded through me.

I pushed open the door cautiously and flashed the torch inside. It was empty.

'Let's just go in out of the rain for a minute,' I said.

I opened the rucksack with clumsy, cold-numbed fingers. Rain dripped from the end of my nose and my hair as I felt inside, trying to identify what things were. I found us dry jumpers and the fold-away raincoats. As I rolled the wet clothes up in a plastic bag and stuffed them in the rucksack, I remembered the food the woman at the station had given me and fished it out of the side pocket. We stabbed at cubes of unidentifiable fruit with a plastic spork. It tasted like the most delicious food we'd ever eaten. I found Dad had stuffed some cereal bars into the rucksack too. It was like a feast. I felt euphoric, in a light-headed, unreal way. Everything hurt a bit less. I wasn't as cold.

I wrestled Billie into her raincoat and did up the zip.

'Better?' I said.

She said nothing.

'Come on,' I said. 'It's not far now, I promise. And it's all going to seem better once we get there.'

I shut the door of the hut carefully behind us. The rain had eased off and I wasn't scared now. It was as if the forest had shown me the hut, that it had known that was what I needed. And I felt a connection to Mum – that for once, somehow, Mum had been there for me when I needed her. It was her hut after all.

As we set off again I told Billie how pleased Grandpa would be to see us. I told her he'd fry us up some bacon and we'd find hot-water bottles, and there'd be a big crackling fire to get warm by and Grandpa would toast bread on a toasting fork and maybe he'd let Billie do it too but she'd have to be careful not to set it on fire. All the things I remembered about trips there when I was a kid. I told her about how Grandpa used to teach me card tricks and how we used to play duets on the piano and he'd get it all wrong on purpose. How he was accompanied at all times by Merlin, his dachshund, and, in the evening, a tumbler of whisky which smelt like smoke and tasted like fire.

Then I told Billie about the stories of the forest Grandpa used to tell me when we'd come walking here together, about thieves and knights and kings and wizards, and magical stags. About children lost in the forest, or princesses hiding there, and trees that turned out to be people put under a spell and owls that turned out to be witches in disguise.

Her eyes were glassy with exhaustion and she was silent.

And then, at last, the trees began to thin and we weren't in a proper fairytale wood any more. There was a bike path, a dog poo bin, a playground where everything was made of logs and rope that looked smaller than I remembered it. And at last—

'Look! Can you see it?'

Through the tree trunks, a light.

I opened the wooden gate at the end of the garden. In the dark it looked strange, wild, unfamiliar. It wasn't the dark, I realized, as I made my way slowly through the long grass. The garden didn't look how it should. What had been the lawn was a meadow up to my knees. Grandpa's vegetable patches, usually neat with rows of canes for runner beans and sweet peas to grow up, were thick with thistles and weeds.

The light turned out not to be from Grandpa's house but one of the houses further along the track. Grandpa's house stood in darkness, all shadows and blank windows.

I felt a flash of anxiety. What if Grandpa wasn't here?

I clenched my teeth to stop them from chattering and

limped round the side of the house and up to the front door before I could really start to panic. I pressed the old-fashioned bell and expected to hear it jangling inside but perhaps it was broken. I knocked, gently, so as not to wake any neighbours.

Billie sank down and sat at my feet, her head against the rucksack.

I listened carefully for footsteps inside but heard nothing. The only option was to knock louder. The taps rang out, sharp, into the stillness of the garden, echoing down the track. I saw a light go on upstairs in the house next door and a crack open in the curtains. Minutes passed. Could he really not have heard?

Then I remembered Granny used to keep a spare key under a little ornament shaped like a frog, round the side of the house. I felt my way round through the shadows, stepping carefully in the dark, to where I thought the frog should be. As I got closer I could see its pale shape in the dark, and when I lifted it up there was a rusty key underneath on the damp soil. I was so relieved I felt dizzy.

I hurried back, wincing with the pain of my twisted ankle, put the key in the lock and turned it.

I pushed the door slowly, braced for an alarm or at least a barking dachshund—

Silence. I stepped inside and felt around for the light switch, then blinked at the too-bright hallway: the tiled floor, the chest of drawers with Granny and Grandpa's wedding photo in a silver frame, the painting Granny did of Mum when she was a kid, curled into an armchair, sleeping. All so familiar and safe it felt like a dream.

No point in waking him now, I decided. I'd leave a note on the kitchen table and explain everything in the morning. I crept to the downstairs shower room to find a towel, dried us off as much as I could, dug pyjamas out of the rucksack, lay Billie down on the sofa.

'I'll make us some tea,' I said, but she was asleep before I'd finished speaking, Luna tucked under her arm. I tiptoed into the kitchen to put the kettle on, still shivering. The kitchen was a mess, dirty plates in the sink and a clutter of food packets and old milk cartons on the food-crusted counter. Granny would always say, 'A tidy house, a misspent life.' But Grandpa had always kept everything spotless. I was too tired to wonder too much about it and certainly too tired to clear it up, but it did make me uneasy. I made tea, and even though I had to have it without milk because the milk had gone off, the warm bitterness of it was comforting. I was just about to settle myself on the sofa that Billie wasn't on when I heard footsteps overhead.

'Who's there?' It was Grandpa.

'Grandpa, it's me,' I called back. 'It's okay! It's me, Clem.'

I went out into the hallway and waited for Grandpa to come downstairs.

I tried not to let my smile falter as I saw him. He looked so much older than when I last saw him, so much thinner and frailer.

'Grandpa, I'm so sorry to wake you up,' I said. 'I was going to explain everything in the morning . . .'

He was staring blankly at me.

'What are you doing in my house? Who are you?'

I felt like I'd been punched.

'Grandpa, look!' I said. 'It's me.'

My mind was whirling, trying to make sense of it all. *It's the middle of the night. He's still half-asleep.* I knew, though – I knew something wasn't right.

'I'm so sorry to turn up like this in the middle of the night, Grandpa,' I tried again. 'Why don't you go back to bed now and I'll explain it all in the morning?'

I heard myself talking to him like he was a kid, like he was Billie.

He peered down at me. Was it his eyes? Maybe he was losing his sight? I moved closer so that he could see me better and he took a step back. He cowered away. Sick panic rose inside me. He could see me, but he didn't know me.

As he stared at me, for a mad moment I thought maybe it wasn't Grandpa at all, because there was something about his face that wasn't like him, a kind of emptiness. He just stared at me, his eyes wide with fear, no hint of recognition. I felt like I couldn't breathe.

'What do you want?' He sounded like a little kid. He looked scared.

'Grandpa' I said again, desperate. 'It's me. It's Clem. Your granddaughter.'

Grandpa looked at me curiously now, as if there was a flicker of something, some connection he couldn't place.

'Clem . . .' He said it like it was a word in a foreign language he'd heard once a long time ago and he was trying to remember what it meant.

'That's right,' I said. 'That's me. Clem. Remember, Grandpa?' The blankness in his face cleared.

'I didn't know you were coming,' he said, his voice worried but somehow calmer. 'I didn't know . . .'

I climbed up the stairs to him and held his hand. It felt fragile as a bird's bones in mine.

'It's okay, Grandpa,' I said. 'Don't worry, it's fine. It's a surprise.'

'A surprise?' he said.

'That's right. Lucky you, eh?'

'Lucky me!' he said and smiled back at me. I gave him a kiss on his thin cheek.

'Come on,' I said, leading him up the stairs. 'You go back to sleep and I'll explain it all in the morning.'

When we'd said goodnight, I sat on the top stair looking down at the hall, the tiles, the painting, the wedding photo on the chest of drawers.

I cried, silently. I thought I would never be able to stop.

I slept late the next morning. I had no idea what time it was when I woke. The alarm clock on the bedside table had stopped at ten past three who knows how long ago. The light coming in through the curtains of the spare room was filtered to a pale apricot-pink glow like the inside of a shell. This room used to be Mum's. I tried to imagine her here, the ghost of her when she was my age. I pushed the thought away. I didn't want to think about her. I closed my eyes. I felt safe in this room. I didn't want to step through the door into the real world. I remembered the empty look on Grandpa's face and felt the hollow fear of the night before. I wanted to stay here, perfectly quiet, perfectly still, in my safe, enchanted shell where it would always be ten past three a long time ago.

I knew I couldn't though. I sat up slowly, wincing with the pain in my shoulders and neck from carrying the rucksack and the stinging of my heels where the raw bleeding skin had scabbed over. As I got up, stiffly, every muscle ached. This must be what it felt like to be old. I carefully tried putting weight on my twisted ankle. Sore but not unbearable. I limped to the window and opened the curtains. I remembered pinning the hems of those curtains for Granny when she made them years ago. It was easier for my small fingers, she'd said, than hers with their swollen knuckles. And I remembered Grandpa telling me bedtime stories in this room, sitting by the bed, his eyes bright, filling my head with monsters and magic. Now it seemed he couldn't even remember who I was. I didn't think I could bear it.

Out in the wilderness of the garden, Billie was already exploring, still in her pyjamas with a sweater pulled over the top. I waved but she was too busy making a track through the overgrown grass with a stick to see me.

I turned away and took clothes from the rucksack. Before I put them on, I breathed them in. They smelt like home.

'Dad,' I said, as if he might hear me. 'I need you.'

Hot tears spilled down my cheeks. I didn't know where he was. I didn't know when I'd see him again. All I could let myself think about yesterday was getting here. But now, here alone, the thought that I didn't know when I'd see him again was unbearable.

'I can't do this,' I said.

In Grandpa's stories people often seemed to find themselves in the Otherworld. Babies left gurgling in their cradles near open windows were taken there and changelings left in their place. Or some innocent person fell asleep under the wrong apple tree in the midday sun and was stolen away to where time stands still, waking up years later to find that everyone they knew died long ago. Princesses were taken there as a payment because some stupid human didn't follow a fairy's instructions. Even goddesses could end up there, snatched away while picking flowers or else bitten by a snake while dancing, and then someone had to make a great journey to try and bring them back.

For a while after Mum left, I wondered whether maybe this could be where she'd gone. If so, who would go to get her back? Not me, surely? I knew from Grandpa that these journeys to the Otherworld tended not to go well.

'Where is it though?' I'd asked him, just in case. 'The Otherworld.'

'Well,' he'd said. 'Depends who you ask. It can be under the ground, or hidden inside the green hills, or faraway over the seas of the west, beyond the great Ninth Wave. Or it might be under a lake in the crater of a great volcano. Or it can be right here, lurking in the shadows or on the other side of the mirror.'

Later, I wondered whether maybe it wasn't Mum who had

140

gone to the Otherworld but me, without realizing, and I was living the wrong, Other life while someone else, a changeling, had taken my rightful place. I'd stare at the girl on the other side of the mirror. Was she me? Or was she someone living my life instead of me, with my real mum who hadn't left, and my happy dad who was always laughing and was never worried or sad? I'd try to catch her out, the girl in the mirror, by sticking my tongue out suddenly. I'd scan her features, looking for the smallest sign that she wasn't really me, earlobes, eyelashes, irises studied closely for discrepancies.

Billie changed all that. When Billie was born, I belonged in my life again. I knew it was my life, my real life, once Billie was in it. We were a family. Dad was happy. I was happy.

But now I had that feeling again, that I had lost my real life, become separated from it. I took from my rucksack the photo I'd grabbed from my bedroom of Mischa and me, the blue feather, the gold paper bird Billie and I had folded together, and put them on the windowsill next to my notebook.

Last I took out the small mirror, the present from Claudia. It had a crack running across the middle it. I hated myself for not having looked after it better. *Seven years bad luck, babe*, Mischa said. But luck didn't exist any more, good or bad. There was just this. Just broken things.

I searched the face in the glass, as I used to do. In the house in the mirror, Grandpa might be downstairs making bacon sandwiches, Dad might be there too, chatting with Grandpa about the football or the garden, Granny might be about to knock on the bedroom door with a cup of tea and a story about something funny Merlin had done. The girl in the mirror watched me, fractured. I hated her.

'I'm sorry,' I whispered to Claudia.

I made my way slowly downstairs, my ankle stiff and sore. My smaller self ran ahead down these stairs two at a time, calling to Merlin, singing.

I tried to prepare myself for Grandpa's empty stare when he looked at me.

Focus on the plan, I told myself. This was what Claudia always said. When you're scared or overwhelmed, make a plan. Put a couple of achievable things at the top so you can tick them off. Action will make you feel calmer and energized, success even more so. And then you'll be less scared and overwhelmed and you can tackle the bigger things. This was her answer for everything from revision (me) to parenting a small baby while having a very important job (her) to hangovers (whoever needed to hear it). Obviously, I had always made a point of ignoring her in the past. Now things had changed. I had to be the Claudia of the situation. So my plan was, first, to get some fresh milk, and second, to tidy the kitchen, and then . . . and then, well, it was just to do everything else. I'd make the 'everything else' list later, when coffee and the energizing sense of achievement had kicked in.

I opened the door to the kitchen with a smile plastered on my face that even I could tell would look unconvincing. There was no one there. Through the sliding glass doors to the garden I could see Billie, crouched down, looking intently at something she'd found in a weed-filled flowerbed and singing to it. A snail probably, or a flower fairy, or a special stone. She looked up at me and waved but I could see she was far too busy to come inside.

The kitchen was even worse in the daylight than it had looked the night before so I hurried out again before the second item on my list began to feel impossible. I found Grandpa on the sofa in the sitting room, Merlin's head on his lap. It all looked so normal and right that relief flooded through me. Maybe he really had just been half-asleep and confused last night. Maybe.

'Morning, Grandpa,' I said, trying to sound like a bright, cheery, morning person, not someone who had just been crying inconsolably and had a sprained ankle and didn't even like mornings on normal days.

He looked up from the paper and smiled at me. Merlin didn't stir. He was deaf now, I realized, grey-muzzled. That was why he hadn't barked when I'd arrived the night before.

'Oh, hello there!' Grandpa said, and if I hadn't known him all my life, and known how his face always lit up with joy and love and mischief when he saw me, I'd have been fooled. But I knew. It wasn't like last night – he wasn't afraid, he didn't think I was stranger. He just couldn't quite place me. I tried not to let myself feel the hurt of it.

'I'm Clem,' I said breezily as if it was completely normal to have to introduce myself. 'Your long-lost granddaughter. Sorry to scare you last night, turning up out of the blue. You were half-asleep I think.'

143

He stared at me. Then 'Clem!' he said, his voice different. And there it was, the look that was just for me. 'I hardly knew you for a moment there. What a lovely surprise.'

He stood up painfully and shuffled over to me. He was shorter than me now, I realized, stooped over.

'It's so good to see you, Grandpa,' I said hugging him, my voice a bit hoarse.

'You too, *cariad*, you too. Let me look at you now.' He held me off from him. 'How did you get so tall? My little Clem. It must be a while now since I saw you, I think?'

I didn't want him to start thinking about when we'd last seen each other in case he remembered it was at Granny's funeral.

'Yes,' I said. 'Too long. I've missed you.'

'Well, I'm glad you're here,' he said. 'Now, where's Granny got to? Have you seen her?'

I stared at him.

'Nancy!' he called. 'Nance! Come and see who's here!'

I felt myself grow hot with panic.

'Grandpa . . .'

What should I say? What *could* I say? He watched me, expectant. It felt wrong to lie to him but I certainly couldn't tell him the truth.

'Granny's not here,' I said at last.

He looked anxious for a moment, then smiled.

'Out at the shops I expect,' he said. 'You'll see her later. You're staying a while?'

'A while, yes. I don't know how long.'

'Well,' he said, taking my hand, 'you know you're

always welcome here. We'll look after you. Stay as long as you like.'

'Thank you, Grandpa,' I said. 'I thought I'd just pop down to the shops and get a few bits. We're out of milk. And I'll get us some breakfast things. I'd love a walk.'

This was a lie. My ankle was still sore and my whole body felt stiff and heavy. But I found I did want to see the village, after all this time. As a kid I'd always loved the contrast between village life and what I thought of as my own faster, louder, harder-edged life in London. I'd felt superior and worldly-wise, but I'd also envied the chocolate-box prettiness of this rural place and the way everyone seemed to know everyone else and looked out for each other. Now the thought of everything carrying on here as it always had was reassuring after the tension and fear back in London. And Grandpa was so frail and slow when he moved I wasn't even sure he could make it as far as the village. How had he been managing all this time? Neighbours helping out probably. I'd go and see them later. Now it was morning, Dad's warning about village gossips and keeping out of sight seemed silly. Paranoia didn't belong in this sleepy place.

Billie was definitely not up for walking anywhere ever again after yesterday and anyway she said she had important tricks to teach Merlin, so I set off down the track on my own. Every time I thought of Dad I still wanted to cry. But I told myself he would want me to be doing this, to be trying to make things okay. He always said, if you're scared, act like you're not and eventually you might even kid yourself that you're not. And if you don't, at least you'll kid other people. 'Fake it till you make it, Clem.' So I tried.

It was a perfect spring day, the sky clear blue, the sun pale. Last night's rain had left a fresh smell of things growing in the earth. I breathed it in. Even my aching ankle felt a bit less stiff as I walked, careful not to put too much weight on it. I remembered as I went how ridiculously idyllic the village was, the track surrounded by woodland, the duck pond, the church with its pointy-arched gateway and sloping graveyard full of wonky gravestones, the village hall.

I'd expected to find kids playing at the swings on the green, people walking their dogs and stopping for a chat, but despite the sunshine there was hardly anyone about. Still, the peace was a relief after the tension of London, the checkpoints, the cadets, the patrols, the feeling that things could tip over into something angry or violent or dangerous at any moment. Now I was here it was hard to imagine any of that really existed.

I walked on, past the dog groomers, the café, the closed chippy and the pub, till I reached the village store where Grandpa used to buy me sweets out of big jars behind the counter. Inside, a lot of the shelves were empty, like at home. I found a loaf of wholemeal bread that was past its use-by date – better than nothing – and a pack of butter. There was no fresh milk but I picked up a carton of UHT and took it to the counter.

The woman behind the counter – Jade, according to her badge – looked up and smiled, then stopped smiling and looked at me harder, her coral-glossed lips pursed. I smiled awkwardly. She didn't smile back.

'Got your village card?' she said as she scanned my shopping.

'No,' I said. 'I'm just visiting.' I assumed it was like a loyalty card and if you got ten stamps you got a free coffee at the café or something.

'Thought I didn't recognize you.' I looked at her, surprised at the hostile edge to her voice. 'Well, sorry. You'll have to put all that back. Can't sell to outsiders.'

'Oh,' I said, 'no, I'm not an outsider. I'm visiting family here.'

'Right,' she said, pointedly looking me up and down. 'Well, maybe you are and maybe you aren't but I can't sell to anyone without a card.'

'Seriously?'

'Do I look like I'm joking?'

I couldn't imagine Jade ever looking like she was joking.

'But why?' I said. 'What's the big deal with the card?'

She shook her head, like she couldn't believe how stupid I was. 'Take a look at the shelves! There isn't enough even for us in the village. There's families without enough to feed themselves. No bread for days. No formula milk for weeks now. When it does come in there'll be fights over it. We can't have people from all around buying everything up. People coming in from the cities, the second-home-owner lot.'

'But that's not me. Like I said, I'm staying with family.'

She put her hands on her hips. 'Well, if you're staying with family, *they'll* have to come and do the shopping. But unless you're a registered visitor they can't get extra rations for you.

147

Who is it you're staying with anyway? I'm bound to know them.' She said it like a challenge to catch me out.

I wanted to tell her it was none of her business but bit it back.

'My grandpa. Huw Morris.'

The woman's face changed instantly.

'Aww, Huw,' she said, smiling. 'You should have said. Poor Huw. How is he?'

'He's fine,' I said, like you do.

'Hasn't been the same since Nancy left us, bless him. Dear Huw. And you're his granddaughter, are you? Seren's daughter?'

I felt myself flinch at the unexpected sound of my mum's name in this stranger's mouth. It felt far too personal, an invasion into the part of my life I kept hidden. But of course, everyone knew everyone here.

'Yes.' I tried to sound casual. 'That's right.'

'Hmmm.' She looked at me differently now, interested, trying to compare me with her memory of Mum perhaps.

'So,' I said quickly, before she could ask me something about her that I'd have to admit I didn't know the answer to, 'as this is Huw's shopping ...'

'Shaun usually does Huw's shopping for him. But he goes to the supermarket.' She sniffed disapprovingly, either at the supermarket or Shaun, whoever he was.

'You know Shaun, I expect?' There was something too bland in the way she said it.

'No?'

'Oh,' she said it in a loaded way. 'Well.'

'Is he a friend of Grandpa's?'

'Depends who you ask.'

I waited for her to go on but she didn't. She was enjoying this, wanting me to ask more. But I didn't want to play whatever game she was playing. I just wanted to get out of there with the shopping and get back to Grandpa.

'So . . . I need to put all this back?'

She looked disappointed. 'Well, I shouldn't really, but seeing as it's for Huw . . .' She looked around but there was no one else in the shop. 'I'm not giving you extra, mind. Bring his card in next time and I'll take it off your ration for the week. Don't tell anyone, or there'll be trouble.'

'I won't,' I said, putting the things in my bag, wondering what kind of trouble and whether for me or her. 'Thanks. That's really kind of you.'

'He's a lovely man, Huw. I do feel for him since Nancy passed away.' She handed me the receipt. 'How long are you staying by the way?' She said it casually, like she was just making polite conversation, but she didn't look at me as she spoke.

'Oh, just a few days,' I said, not knowing why I was lying. 'Just wanted to see my Grandpa and make sure he was okay.'

She looked relieved.

'That's good,' she said. 'I mean, it's a shame for Huw not to have you around longer. But it means you won't have to get approval to stay. And it's just you, is it?'

'That's right. Just me.'

She nodded, satisfied.

Well, give Huw my love, won't you?'

'I will.'

'And if anyone's funny with you in the village, just make sure they know you're not staying long. Some people are a bit . . . Well, it's understandable, isn't it?'

'Bye,' I said, smiling, trying not to show how relieved I was to be getting away from her. 'Thanks again.'

'And keep an eye on Shaun,' she called after me. 'He's always been trouble, that one.'

I wanted to get back as quickly as I could but my ankle had begun throbbing from the walk and I felt lightheaded and weak with hunger. The quiet seemed wrong now, sinister even. I wanted to cry. I wanted to call Dad and tell him about Grandpa not knowing who I was and talking to Granny like she was in the next room, and about the weirdness of the village. I wanted to ask him what I should do. But I knew that was impossible. I was on my own.

I sat on a bench on the green to catch my breath, then pulled a slice of the bread out of its plastic wrapping and stuffed it into my mouth. It was dry and stuck to the roof of my mouth. I chewed it slowly, looking around at the play park, the duck pond, the cottages that overlooked the green. When I'd been a kid it had all seemed perfect. But how would it feel to grow up here, with everyone knowing everything about you? Who your family were, where you lived, everything you ever did and who with, everything you bought at the village store, what medication and personal stuff you got from the pharmacy . . .

I couldn't imagine it. Maybe you'd feel cared for, certain that everyone was looking out for you. Or maybe you . . . maybe you wouldn't. Maybe it depended on the kind of person you were.

Or on the kind of person everyone else decided you were.

What had it been like for Mum?

This was the question I was really asking. Mum with her silky dress, hiding behind her film-star sunglasses that meant you could never really see her expression, Mum who never stayed in one place, who never left a trace. What had it been like for her here in the village? I thought of Jade's expression when she'd mentioned her, greedy for gossip. Maybe it was no wonder Mum had wanted to escape into the forest. And then to keep on escaping.

As I sat there a dog like a miniature wolf ran up to sniff me and then sat, waiting to be petted. She looked at me with her ice-blue eyes. I leaned down and stroked her head as the owners walked over, a woman, a teenage boy and a younger girl, all very blonde and beautiful-looking, in a glossy, healthy sort of way like they'd just stepped out of one of those catalogues that used to arrive in the post for Claudia, catalogues that she moved straight from doormat to recycling bin without opening. I imagined they were the sort of family that got up early to play tennis together at the weekends and I tried not to dislike them.

I felt very conscious of my own rumpled clothes, pulled out of the rucksack that morning, and the fact that I now hadn't had a shower for two days, my hair stale and greasy, scraped back in an elastic band.

'Your dog's beautiful,' I said, smiling at the woman in her expensive jacket, hoping to focus attention on the dog rather than me.

'Skadi!' she called sharply, as if I hadn't spoken, and the dog trotted obediently back to her.

'Well trained too,' I said.

'Put her on the lead,' the woman said to the girl behind her, who I guessed was about twelve and was a smaller version of her mother.

The woman walked towards me. 'You're not from around here, are you?'

Ah, the traditional friendly village greeting. At least I was prepared for it this time.

'Oh, no. I'm just here visiting family. Not for long,' I added quickly.

'Could you tell me exactly who you're visiting and when you're leaving?' the woman said, in a voice that suggested she was used to being obeyed by people as well as dogs.

I looked at her, taking in her perfectly bobbed hair and her surprisingly unlined face for someone with a son older than me.

Botox, imaginary Mischa whispered. *Either that or she's done a deal with the devil. She looks the type.*

The three of them stared back at me.

Is it me, Mischa whispered, *or are they all a bit Village of the Damned?*

'Well?' the woman said, not disguising her impatience.

'Why do you want to know?' I said, feeling myself flush as I spoke. 'Are you going to check up on me?'

'Yes,' she said, as if it was a stupid question.

'Don't you believe me?'

'If you've got nothing to hide, you won't mind telling me.'

'But it's none of your business.'

Her perfect complexion turned a mottled pink. She was about to speak when her phone rang. She took it out of her bag and sighed.

'I haven't got time for this,' she snapped. 'Jonas, take her details. Saskia, you bring the dog.' She turned away to take her call and marched off across the green.

I looked at the son and daughter, half-hoping for a conspiratorial smile or eye roll now their mum had gone, but was confronted by matching cold, blue-eyed stares. The son, Jonas, took out a notebook and pen from his jacket pocket and held them out to me while his sister stood behind him, looking me up and down with undisguised contempt.

'Just write down the name and address of the person you're staying with,' he said.

I looked at him. 'Actually,' I said, 'no. I don't know you and it's kind of a weird thing to ask, don't you think? I've told you I'm staying with family, even though it's none of your business by the way, and if you don't believe me that's not my problem.'

I held the notebook out for him to take. His face was blank. The girl, Saskia, looked shocked. For another second I thought she was going to yell at me.

'It could be your problem,' Jonas said.

'I'll take my chances,' I replied.

'Show us your ID card then,' Saskia snapped.

I looked at her. 'You aren't the police, are you?'

'We're junior Community Guards.'

Compared with the Community Guards at home, they didn't exactly seem threatening.

'That sounds fun,' I said. 'But I haven't got my ID with me. Sorry.'

The sister looked angry and took a step towards me but before she could say anything her brother stepped in.

'Have it your way,' he said.

'Jonas!' his sister said.

'We'll find out who she is and where she's staying soon enough anyway.' He turned to me. 'If you're staying longer than a week, you'll be in trouble. And so will whoever you're staying with.'

'Is that supposed to be a threat?'

'I'm just warning you,' he said.

'Nothing happens in this village that we don't know about,' Saskia said, staring at me again as if she was memorizing my face, before they stalked off giving me a last scornful look as they went.

Once they'd gone, I stood up and walked in the opposite direction, back towards Grandpa's.

Wow, imaginary Mischa said. *They seemed nice.*

I tried to smile, thinking about what my friend would have said to them, but it just made me miss her more. I found I was shaking.

Focus on the plan.

I hid inside the hood of my coat and limped on back to Grandpa's.

It was only as I opened the door to Grandpa's that I realized I should have bought cleaning stuff and cloths. I felt stupid, like a kid playing at being a grown-up.

'I'm back,' I called. There was no reply. I walked through to the kitchen to put the kettle on and stifled a scream, dropping the carton of milk on the floor where it burst open.

Standing at the sink was a huge man with his back to me and headphones on singing along to Britney Spears. He spun round, surprisingly quick for someone so big.

'Who the bloody hell are you?' he said.

He really was massive, the same size and shape as Kris, the bouncer Mischa's mum dated for a while (*Like a wall made out of human flesh*, Mischa told me after she met him, unimpressed). The intruder was in his late twenties, I'd guess, with a buzz cut, fair eyelashes and pale blue eyes. His pinkish skin was covered in tattoos. His nose looked like it had been broken many times. I'd probably have been more scared if he hadn't been wearing Granny's pink washing-up gloves and the apron she'd won in a raffle years ago at the village fete that said I RUN ON LOVE, LAUGHTER AND PROSECCO!

'Who the bloody hell am I? Who the bloody hell are you?' He put his rubber-gloved hands on his hips. 'I'm the carer of the gentleman who lives here, thanks very much.' He had a strong accent, Liverpool maybe. Definitely not from the village anyway. 'Now, your turn.'

155

'You don't exactly look like a carer.'

'Is that right? And what exactly does a carer look like, in your opinion, eh?'

He watched me, unblinking, his muscly, tattooed arms folded. I realized this was a fair question. I also realized it was highly unlikely an intruder would have broken into Grandpa's house to do the washing-up.

'I didn't even know he had a carer,' I faltered.

'Well, now you do. But you still haven't told me who you are.'

'I'm his granddaughter,' I said. 'Clem. I've come to stay for a bit.'

The suspicion disappeared from the man's face.

'Clem! You've grown so much I didn't recognize you.'

I looked at him in surprise.

'I saw you at Nancy's funeral but never got a chance to speak to you. You look so much older.'

I remembered the painful blur of Granny's funeral. Then I remembered Grandpa asking where she was this morning and the sick panicky feeling returned.

'I'm Shaun by the way,' he said.

'Oh! Of course. Someone in the village mentioned you.'

'I bet they did.' He said it in a way that made me think he guessed it hadn't exactly been complimentary. 'But what are you doing here? I had no idea you were coming.'

I explained. His expression changed.

'Oh, Clem, love,' he said. 'I'm so sorry.' And he came over and hugged me. Normally I'm pretty strict about who I'm prepared to be hugged by (Mischa says it's my worst trait and blames it on the fact that there's a lot of Gemini in my star chart) and the list of acceptable huggers definitely doesn't include strangers, but I found I didn't mind too much apart from the stray soap suds.

'Well, you're here safe now. We'll look after you. I'm just sorry I wasn't here when you arrived. I've been away for a couple of days, hence the chaos in here. Normally I'm in every day. I'll make us a cuppa, but I'd better clean up that milk first. By the way,' he said, in a way that was supposed to sound casual, 'who did you speak to in the village?'

I told him about Jade and then about the Village of the Damned family. I tried to make it sound funny but he didn't smile.

'Did you tell the woman much?'

'No. She wasn't very happy about it. You know her?'

Shaun nodded. 'Imogen Glass. Nasty piece of work. She's on the council.'

'They said it would cause trouble if I stayed longer than I'm supposed to. Not just for me, for Grandpa too.'

'Look,' Shaun said, 'don't you worry about it. You're here now. You're safe. You stay as long as you need to. It's just ... it might be better to keep your heads down. Stay out of the way. Just for now.'

I was so tired I told Shaun I was going to go and lie down. I went to check on Grandpa first, who was dozing on the sofa. I hadn't felt brave enough to ask Shaun about Grandpa's memory yet. That could wait.

I picked up Grandpa's glasses from where they had fallen

on the floor. 'Please remember me when you wake up,' I whispered and kissed him on the cheek.

Billie was fast asleep in the spare room with a little pile of paper cranes next to her. Luna had fallen on the floor, so I picked her up and tucked her under Billie's arm. Then I curled up next to her.

'It's okay,' I said softly. 'We're here now. We're safe. We can stay as long as we like.'

I closed my eyes and listened to the silence of the stopped clock as I drifted into sleep.

*

'You look tired,' Polly says. 'How are you sleeping?'

What she means is, you look like the sad ghost that haunts a Victorian asylum, babe, Mischa says. *And not in a good way. I'm saying this with love, you know that. But maybe brush your hair once in a while? And could you not blag some concealer from somewhere? Your eyebags literally look like Danny's when he got hit in the face by that cricket ball that time.*

'I'm sleeping fine,' I lie.

Polly and I have met outside today at her suggestion, maybe because she thinks fresh air will do me good or maybe she can't stand being in her tiny, messy, damp-smelling office with those windows that only open half a millimetre.

She sits down on a bench and gestures to me to join her.

'It's good to be outside, eh?'

It's cold, but just being in the sunlight, among green,

158

growing plants rather than quietly desiccating ones is an improvement, I have to admit.

We sit quietly for a while, as if we're just people rather than interrogator and victim.

But it can't last. Eventually she will ask, and I must answer.

*

After that first day in the village, I slept. For days, maybe even weeks, I wasn't sure. I slept most of the time. It was like I had to just not *be* for a while, like I'd used up my lifetime supply of being and now it was time to stop. I didn't want to go out even into the garden. I'd watch Billie playing outside from the bedroom window, and I'd look out to the forest beyond, and then I'd close the curtains and lie down and sleep again.

I dreamt sometimes, though I could only remember glimpses of my dreams afterwards. The weird blonde family on the green singing a song I was supposed to know the words to; Danny wearing a surgical mask, trying to say something I couldn't hear; the flat Dad and I had lived in with Mum when I was little, hiding the pieces of something precious I'd broken— When I woke, I couldn't remember what it was but I could still feel the panic and shame of it. *What had I broken?* I was damp with sweat.

As I lay in Mum's old room, Billie would appear at the bedside, to sing me a song she'd just made up or tell me about a fox she'd seen in the garden or to ask me whether I thought it would be more fun to be a ginger cat or a magpie. We folded more cranes. We wished.

Shaun would bring me tea and bowls of porridge, or stewed fruit, or rice and beans. I'd promise to get up and help more tomorrow.

'You've been through a lot,' he said. 'You need to recover. Let yourself heal.'

Mischa said, *You're like a wrinkly old tortoise all tucked in its cardboard box for winter.*

I ignored her.

Okay, fine, she said. *Not a tortoise then. A seed. You're like a seed in the ground. You've got a load of life inside you but no one can tell. Not even you.*

Better, I said.

Just don't forget to come out when it's spring, babe, yeah? No one wants to live in the dark for ever.

As the days grew longer my energy began to return and I stretched my tortoise neck out of the cardboard box. I got up. I got dressed. I started, slowly, to be again.

Only inside the house though. Shaun told me he'd had a visit from Imogen Glass two weeks after my arrival to see if I was still there.

'What did you say?'

'I said, what a shame, you've just missed her, she's gone to stay with cousins in Great Yarmouth.'

'Why Great Yarmouth? Where even is Great Yarmouth?'

'I dunno,' Shaun said. 'First place that popped into my head. She looked at me like I was lying, but then she always does. So nothing new there.'

'Do you think she'll be back?'

'Knowing her, I'm sure she'll make trouble if she can,' Shaun said. 'But you let me handle her. Nothing for you to worry about, love. But, like I said, you're going to have to stay in the house.'

My new, strange life navigating Grandpa's unexpected shifts in time and place, never venturing beyond the garden, soon became normal and took on its own rhythm. In the mornings, Grandpa usually had more energy and could remember more and I'd sit with him and chat. He often thought I was Mum. The first time he called me Seren I froze, unable to speak. The strangeness, the wrongness of it. Over time I minded less. Perhaps I almost liked it, a connection between Mum and me that I'd never had before. I grew curious about her, about her life here when she was my age. I'd never thought about it before. There were so many things I wanted to ask Grandpa. Was I like her? What was her favourite movie? Who were her friends? A million other things. All of them part of the one big question, I suppose: why had she left? Perhaps by understanding her better I could understand that. Why had I never asked him before? It was too late now.

In the evenings, I'd help Shaun to invent edible meals with the ever more limited ingredients he brought back from the supermarket, and he'd tell me colourful stories of his past, the village tearaway who'd arrived from Liverpool to live with a dad he didn't even know and who had never fitted in, and then later his life as boxer.

'What do you say to Grandpa when he thinks Granny's still alive?' I asked him. 'Do you lie to him? Do you pretend she's still here?'

He thought about it. 'It's not really pretending,' he said. 'In that moment, she is still here, for him. So it's not really a lie. Is it?'

Later we'd watch old movies from Grandpa's DVD collection. Sometimes there were power cuts in the evenings and we'd play Scrabble or card games by candlelight.

I missed Dad so much those evenings. He'd have loved them. I told Shaun that Dad was even more competitive than him.

'I'm sorry, love,' Shaun said. 'You must miss him so much.'

I had to pretend then that I'd left something in the kitchen because I didn't want Shaun to see me cry.

I didn't ask Shaun why we were getting power cuts. I didn't ask about what was happening in London, about what Dad had said, about the army and Knight and the opposition. I never watched or listened to the news. Words escaped sometimes from the kitchen or the sitting room – *economic sanctions martial law attempted coup dissident groups another night of rioting clampdown* – and they were like gunshots going off in my head. My ears rang, my chest constricted, I had to get away from them.

I didn't even ask Shaun about what was happening in the village. I pretended the world ended at the garden gate.

Time stood still.

At last, I grew restless. Through the window I saw blossom in the trees and hedges and flowers blooming all over Grandpa's wild garden.

'Can we go into the forest?' Billie asked.

It was what I wanted too.

I wanted to go to Mum's hut.

Shaun wasn't keen but I begged him. 'Okay,' he said at last. 'Most of the forest is off limits for the villagers now. The powers that be want to keep people where they can see them. So you should be okay. Just stay right away from the path and the kids' playground. That's the only bit of the forest villagers are allowed into. You don't want anyone to report you. But there's bound to be some that don't stick to the rules so be careful.'

Billie helped me pack a bundle of fruit and some cheese that Shaun had bartered from a farmer he knew, and together we set off into the forest. We went straight to the hut. Later we brought cushions and a blanket and jars to collect things; we picked bluebells and primroses, collected pine cones and feathers. We pressed flowers in the pages of my notebook. Billie scooped up all the spiders in the hut and gave them names. We decorated the hut with paper birds and listened to the real birds singing outside. I told stories.

*

'Billie was right,' Polly says. 'You're good at stories.'

I say nothing.

'It sounds idyllic.'

'It was,' I say.

And it's true, almost.

*

One summery evening I was sitting in the garden with Shaun. We'd cooked rice with wild garlic and foraged mushrooms (which Shaun assured us he knew for sure weren't poisonous or hallucinogenic) and we'd all agreed it was the nicest meal we'd ever cooked. Billie was in bed and Grandpa was dozing in the sitting room. Shaun was drinking home-brewed mead which he'd made with honey a beekeeper friend of his had given him. Brewing mead was a new skill Shaun had learned because the landlord of the village pub, who apparently was good friends with Imogen Glass, had barred Shaun along with anyone else he didn't consider true members of the community.

'Monks used to brew it in medieval times,' Shaun said.

He poured me some but I only had a few mouthfuls as it was incredibly strong.

'I guess medieval monks needed something to liven things up,' I said.

He laughed. 'You'd be surprised.'

'Shaun,' I said, made brave perhaps by the mead, 'do you know if Grandpa's been in touch with Seren recently? My mum, I mean?' I'd been wanting to ask him for ages but always found an excuse not to. I didn't want him to know how much I'd been thinking about Mum since I'd been here. I'd searched the hut, hoping I'd find some sign of her, something left behind, but there was nothing. I'd shown Billie the witch marks carved into trees centuries ago, told her, just as Grandpa had told me, how they were supposed to give protection against the evil spirits, witches and demons who lived in the woods. But really

I'd been hoping I'd find Mum's initials carved into the bark, just a sign that she'd been there.

Shaun looked at me carefully.

'No,' he said. 'I don't think so.'

'Does he know where she's living?'

Shaun sighed. 'I know he had an address for her when your granny died because he wrote to her. Whether she wrote back I don't know, but she didn't come to the funeral and he never got in touch with her again. He was very upset that she never showed up, you know.'

'So you know her address?'

He shook his head. 'Huw would never talk to me about Seren. He found it too hard. Sorry, love.' I knew he really was sorry. Shaun had told me one evening while we were cooking potato surprise (the surprise being mainly cabbage, unfortunately) that his own mum had left when he was a baby and his nan had brought him up. 'Families are complicated. Even the ones that don't look it from the outside,' he'd said.

'Sometimes Grandpa thinks I'm her,' I said.

'I know,' Shaun said.

'I don't tell him I'm not.' I wasn't sure whether I was asking for sympathy or forgiveness.

'He still knows *you*, you know,' Shaun said.

I nodded. I did know it.

'Now I think of it, your granny had a box of things that were Seren's. I found it when I was sorting out her stuff to take to the charity shop. Nothing much, like. Just a shoebox. I don't

165

know what's in it. But you should have it, if you want it. Hang on, I'll go and find it.'

As I waited for Shaun, I tried to suppress the thrill of excitement I felt at the thought of the box and what might be in it.

He reappeared sooner than I'd expected.

'Huw hasn't come out here, has he?'

'No. He's asleep in the living room, isn't he?'

'Not any more he's not.'

'Is he upstairs?'

'I'll check.'

Shaun came back a couple of minutes later.

'He's gone.'

I looked at him, trying not to panic. 'Wouldn't we have heard the front door slam if he'd gone out?'

Shaun looked at me. 'The front door's open,' he said.

'What?' I said, jumping up. '*Shit*. When did you last see him? He was there when I went in to get my jumper. What time was that?

'An hour ago?'

'Did you see him after that?'

Shaun shook his head.

'So he could have been gone a whole hour! Jesus, Shaun.'

'He can't have gone far . . .'

'You don't know that!' My mind was racing. 'He could have gone anywhere. How are we going to find him? I mean, he could have gone into the forest or he might have fallen—'

'Clem,' Shaun said, 'stop. We've got to stay calm. We've got to think.'

'You should call the police.'

'No,' he said flatly. 'We can't do that.'

'Because of me?'

'Because we don't need to. I'll find him.'

'Fine. I'll come and help.' I moved to go into the house but Shaun put his hand on my arm to stop me.

'Clem, you can't.'

'But I—'

'Look,' he said sharply, 'if you get seen and someone makes a fuss, it won't just be you who's in trouble, will it? It'll be Huw as well. So you won't be helping him. You could be putting him in more danger.'

'Than I already am, you mean?'

Shaun didn't meet my eye. 'I know the places he's likely to go. I'll find him. Seriously, Clem, don't worry. I'll be back before you know it.'

He wasn't. I sat for a while in the garden thinking of all the terrible things that could have happened to Grandpa or could be about to happen to him and how they were all my fault and now I couldn't even do anything about it.

The wind was picking up. I took the glasses inside. Shaun had been gone more than half an hour. I couldn't bear it. I went upstairs to get a hoodie and the torch.

'I'm just going to find Grandpa,' I whispered to Billie but she didn't hear me.

I'd just go up and down the track to check. I wouldn't be long and I'd keep my hood up so no one would see me. Anything was better than just sitting there waiting.

And then, as I sat on the bottom step to put my trainers on, there was a knock on the door.

I jumped up.

But then I stopped. What if it wasn't Grandpa? I stood for a second, paralysed, not knowing what to do.

The doorbell rang and still I stood frozen. Then I realized there was one of those peephole things so you can see who's outside. Shaun must have fitted it.

I peered through it.

Grandpa! Relief flooded through me. But he was with someone. They stood further away, with their hood up and back to me. They looked like they were on the phone.

What should I do? I'd just have to get rid of them quickly and hope they didn't ask any questions. I couldn't leave Grandpa outside in the cold. He looked frailer than ever, confused in a way that was so childlike it made my heart hurt.

I took a breath and opened the door. The relief on his face when he saw me . . .

'Grandpa!' I hugged him. 'Come in. You're cold.'

Then the person he was with turned round and my heart flipped. It was the guy I'd last seen on the green, Jonas, that first morning in the village. The son of Imogen Glass. I half-expected him to do some kind of citizen's arrest on the spot, but instead he just looked concerned about Grandpa.

'Oh,' he said, 'hi. I found Huw down the track.'

Didn't he recognize me? I'd assumed he would, and although I was relieved, I couldn't help feeling a tiny bit annoyed as well. Was I really that forgettable?

'He'd got a bit confused,' Jonas went on, 'and couldn't work out where he was. Easily done – it's so dark down there with no street lights. So we decided to walk back together, didn't we, Huw? I was just trying to call Shaun in case he was out looking for him but I can't get a signal.' His voice was kind and reassuring. I didn't understand how he could be so different.

Grandpa looked blank. 'Where's Nancy?' he said. 'Jonas? Where's Nance? I don't know where she could have got to.'

'It's okay, Huw,' Jonas said gently. 'Don't worry about Nancy. She's fine.'

I looked at him, surprised, then away again. 'Let's get you inside, Grandpa,' I said quickly, anxious to get him indoors where he'd feel safe and also keen to get rid of Jonas as quickly as possible.

'Is he okay?' Jonas said. 'Can I do anything? I could wait with you till Shaun gets back?'

'Thanks for bringing him back,' I said. 'We'll be fine.' I took Grandpa's other arm and helped him in.

'Okay,' Jonas said in the end. 'If you're sure.' He turned to go, then remembered something, reached into his pocket and took out Grandpa's reading glasses. 'He dropped these. I didn't want them to get lost or broken.'

I took them without saying thank you. Why was he acting like this, like he was just a nice, normal guy? I started to close the door.

'Wait,' he said. 'That day I met you on the green—'

I slammed the door and then stood still for a second, trying to process it.

He did remember. The nice-guy act was just a trick.

And now he'd be heading straight back home to tell his mum.

'Come on, Grandpa,' I said. 'Lean on me. Let's get you sat down.'

I needed to get my head straight, to work out what to do. But first I needed to make sure Grandpa was okay. As we made our slow progress to the sitting room, I heard something being put through the letter box. I tensed. What was it? A warning of some kind? A threat?

Once Grandpa was settled next to the fire, reassured, with Merlin by his side, I went back to see what had come through the door. Lying on the mat was a piece of lined paper that looked like it had been torn from the notebook I'd refused to write in on the green.

It had just one word written on it.

Sorry.

By the time Shaun got back I'd warmed Grandpa up with blankets and tea and as far as I could tell he'd forgotten about getting lost.

'Oh, thank God!' Shaun said, and I realized he'd been a lot more worried than he'd let on. He hurried over to Grandpa, crouched down in front of him, and held

Grandpa's hand in both his. 'You had us worried there for a minute, Huw.'

'Did I?' Grandpa looked pleased. 'Well, you know, I like to keep you on your toes.'

'I had noticed,' Shaun said. 'Still, all's well that ends well, I suppose.'

'Maybe not,' I said. 'He didn't come back on his own. Someone found him and brought him back.'

Shaun looked at me sharply. 'Who?'

'Imogen Glass's son,' I said heavily, knowing it was the worst possible answer.

But Shaun looked almost relieved. 'Oh, okay. Jonas.'

'Why aren't you freaking out?'

'It's okay,' Shaun said. 'He won't tell anyone.'

'Are you crazy? He's probably telling his mum right now.'

'He won't be.'

'He's already apologized for it!' I waved the piece of paper at him.

'That's not what he means.'

'Seriously? I think it's pretty obvious that's what he means.'

'Clem, I trust him, okay?'

I stared at him.

'What are you talking about? Have you forgotten about that first day I was here? How he threatened me? And Grandpa? Why are you acting like it's no big deal?'

Shaun wouldn't meet my eye and busied himself tidying up the dinner plates. 'I've got my reasons.'

'But you don't want to share them?'

Shaun sighed. 'We'll talk about it tomorrow. For now, all that matters is that Huw's safe.'

I went to bed, but I couldn't sleep. I was listening, waiting for a knock on the door, a shout. That day when they'd come for Claudia played out in my head. I hadn't been ready that time. None of us had. What could I do this time if they came for us?

Nothing, that was the truth of it.

I was furious. With Jonas. And with Shaun for being so complacent. Why wasn't he worried? If he'd had a proper reason to trust Jonas, he'd have told me. It didn't make sense.

The more I didn't sleep, the more feverish my thoughts became. Could I trust Shaun? I remembered the warning Jade in the shop had given me on that first day.

I thought of how Shaun got here before it even got light in the morning so he'd be here when Grandpa woke. How he'd change Grandpa's sheets and bathe him and deal with all the gross personal stuff that I never could. How he never lost patience with him, even when Grandpa was having a bad day. How he was stretching the food to make sure we all had enough, how he never pushed me to talk about what had happened back home, or about Mum or Grandpa, but he understood anyway. I hated myself for doubting him.

'Clem?' Billie said sleepily in the dark.

'Hey.'

'The cat said the ball was his.'

I smiled. 'You're dreaming, B. Go back to sleep.'

She rolled over and I lay staring into the dark, listening to her breathing.

Even if he was right and Jonas wasn't going to report us, for whatever mysterious reason, it didn't change the fact that the danger wouldn't go away.

The danger was real.

No. It was worse than that.

The danger was me.

*

Billie hasn't woken me tonight, yet I just can't sleep.

I go through the notebook until I reach pages with no writing. Instead, there are flowers pressed in between, bluebells and dandelions, and oak leaves – beech and hazel too, a fern with its tendrils tiny and delicate. I even labelled some of them for Billie, looked up the Latin names in Grandpa's pocket book of trees and wildflowers. I lean towards the page, close my eyes and inhale, as if I'll be able to smell them, to breathe in the forest.

Perhaps I'll show them to Polly next time. I know she's interested in my notebook. I won't let her read my stories but this would be okay. She likes dead plants after all.

*

Shaun hadn't given me a proper explanation of why I should trust Jonas and I still wanted to know.

'Don't judge him by who his parents are,' he said when I'd pushed him on it.

'I'm not,' I said. 'I'm judging him on his actions.'

I could see Shaun trying to be patient. 'Just trust me, will you? I've met all sorts of liars in my time, from psychopathic gangsters to two-timing boyfriends to estate agents. One was all three at the same time. I know a wrong 'un when I meet one, and Jonas isn't one. Believe me when I tell you that you don't need to worry.'

But as time went by I began to realize that there were other things Shaun wasn't telling me. He'd take phone calls and go into other rooms to talk in a low voice so I couldn't hear him. Once he had to go away overnight and was very evasive about where and why. Eventually he told me some story about a sick cousin that I didn't believe for a second.

I knew Shaun just wanted to keep me safe, but what secrets did he have, I wondered, that were too dangerous for me to know?

It had been raining heavily for days so we hadn't gone off into the forest all week. Billie never minded the rain and happily put on her red raincoat and splashed in puddles in the garden, made a tent from the clothes airer and an old plastic sheet she'd found in the shed, collected rainwater in jam jars and sprinkled petals in to make perfume that she was going to sell for a million pounds a bottle. I sat and watched her through the raindrops that trickled down the patio doors.

After a week indoors, I was edgy and irritable. I just needed to get away from everyone, from the house, from myself. I felt trapped, closed in. I needed the peace and secrecy of the forest. It was my only escape.

Billie decided to stay and play with Merlin, who was far too old and arthritic for walks in the woods these days, so I made my way towards the hut alone, going the long way and staying off the path. The smell of wet leaves and damp soil, the sound of the rain on the trees, made me feel alive. I sensed the tension begin to lift. I felt almost euphoric after the stale, constricting days in the house. It was just me and the trees.

Inside the hut, I sat down with my back against the wall. The forest quiet pressed in around me. I'd wanted to be on my own but, now that I was, there was nothing to distract me from the noise inside my head. It was just that pretending everything was okay when it so obviously wasn't felt like such a struggle some days; I thought I'd crack with the effort of it. Pretending I wasn't worrying about Dad and Claudia. Worrying about whether we'd be found out. Worrying about the danger I was putting Grandpa in. Trying not to miss Grandpa, the Grandpa who would have looked after me and made me laugh and made everything bearable. Trying not to think about home and everything that had happened ... everything left behind ... Mischa—

I was wondering when you'd finally get round to me, imaginary Mischa said. *I mean, jeez, Clem, you could have put me a bit higher up the list, don't you think?*

'It wasn't in order of importance,' I said.

Sure. She looked at me sceptically over the round sunglasses she'd bought at the hippy stall on the market because the guy who worked there said they made her look like a Victorian vampire, which was exactly Mischa's look of choice.

'You know I miss you loads,' I said. 'All the time.'

Yeah, yeah, I know. She sat down next to me.

'It's like I have to pretend all the time that everything's fine. Or that it's going to be fine. Because if I don't, what's the point of anything? I mean, how do I even keep going, Misch? But nothing's fine. Nothing can ever be fine again.'

She leaned her head on my shoulder.

Sorry, babe.

I closed my eyes again and wished she was real.

Then I sat up, tense, listening.

There was a sound coming from outside. Rustling. Breathing?

I sat completely still.

The rustling had stopped. Just a squirrel probably. I stood up, relieved, moving to the door to see if the rain had stopped.

A dog barked, loud and abrupt, right outside the hut, so sudden that I jumped. I stopped completely still, hardly breathing, one foot half off the ground, willing the dog to run back to its owner. But it knew I was there and carried on barking, sniffing, scratching at the door.

And then there were footsteps and a male voice, further away than the dog but getting closer.

'What is it?' the voice said. 'Skadi? What have you found?'

And then the door opened and on the other side of it was Jonas.

I was so angry I forgot to be afraid. I *knew* he couldn't be trusted. He was spying on me. How dare he follow me here!

This was my secret place, mine and Billie's and Mum's. He had no right to be here.

'Is this what you do for fun then?' I spat at him. 'Spying on people just because they dare to break your stupid rules? Off you go then and report me to Mummy.'

He stepped back, hands up, the surprised smile that had appeared on his face when he saw I was the person behind the door quickly disappearing.

'No!' he said. 'Of course not. I'm not spying on you. I didn't know you were here. I'm disobeying the rules as much as you are just by being here.'

'Right. And you just happen to be here at my hut.'

'I didn't know it was you who'd been coming here. I knew someone had. I saw the cushions and candles and stuff. I like the paper birds. Did you make them?'

'You've been here before?' I felt outraged.

'I escape here,' he said. 'When I can't stand it at home any more.'

But it's mine! I wanted to say. *Mine and Billie's and Mum's.* But even in my anger I could hear how childish it would sound, so I said nothing. There was an awkward silence. I found myself wondering why he couldn't stand it at home.

'You don't trust me, do you?' he said at last.

'Trust you? After you threatened me on the green that time? When I know who your mum is?'

'Sorry,' he said. 'I wanted to apologize properly that night I brought Huw round but ...' He trailed off, presumably not wanting to say, *But you slammed the door in my face.* 'Has ... has Shaun said anything to you about me?'

'Oh, totally. We do nothing but sit around talking about you.'

He flushed. 'I didn't mean it like that.'

The rain was falling even heavier now, pattering on the leaves all around us. Jonas wasn't wearing a coat.

'Look,' he said, 'can I come in? Just till the rain passes? I'll explain it all to you properly and you can make your own mind up. If you want. Or, if you'd rather, I can just sit in silence and you can pretend I'm not there and talk to Skadi instead till it stops raining.'

At the sound of her name the dog came trotting over and gazed up at him hopefully. I looked at Jonas, dishevelled and dripping, and remembered his concern for Grandpa that night he'd found him and brought him back, how he'd not been embarrassed by Grandpa, or treated him like a crazy old guy for thinking his dead wife was alive, like some people would have done.

'Okay,' I said. 'But only because I like your dog.'

Skadi ran around the hut sniffing things and generally being adorable, which was just as well because without her it would have been a billion times more awkward than it already was. I passed Jonas one of the cushions and we both sat down. He rubbed at his wet hair with the sleeve of his sweater so that it stood up in spikes.

Cute, imaginary Mischa said.

Not the time, Misch. And anyway, no.

Okay. You keep telling yourself that if it makes you feel better, Clemmie.

'I've got chocolate,' Jonas said, taking a bar out of his backpack.

He has chocolate, Mischa said. *I mean, come ON.*

'Here.' Jonas broke off half the bar and held it out to me.

I wanted to refuse haughtily, but I couldn't remember the last time I'd eaten chocolate. Being related to the Queen Bee of the village clearly had its advantages. But maybe . . . maybe there were disadvantages too. After all, didn't I know as well as anyone that you didn't get to choose your mum?

'Thanks,' I said, trying to resist the urge to shove it all into my mouth in one go. Instead I set about breaking it into neat pieces. Skadi sat next to me and watched intently as I ate them one at a time, following each square of chocolate with her eyes until I'd eaten them all. Eventually she lay her head down on my lap and let me stroke her ears. The rain thrummed on the roof of the hut.

'So, go on then,' I said. 'Explain.'

He was silent.

'Or don't,' I said. 'It's up to you.'

'It's not that,' he said. 'I just don't know where to start.'

'That day on the green maybe? Where you and your family told me if I didn't get out of the village I'd be in trouble?'

'Okay. My mum is . . . well, you've met her. Has Shaun told you about her? About who she is, I mean?'

'A bit,' I said. 'Not much. Just that she's on the council or something.'

Jonas nodded. 'She's always been on the council, since I was a little kid. Back then, it was all just boring meetings

179

and putting leaflets through doors. But when the whole Toby Knight movement started, she got obsessive about it. It was around the time she and my dad split up, I don't know if that was part of it or what. They went for away-days and conventions and they had all these online forums. I don't know. It was like a cult. She was selected as the candidate to be MP in the last election. Her campaign got really nasty, smearing her opponents, that kind of thing. One of them even got arrested, but it never came to anything. He lost his job though because of the rumours. He'd been a teacher and no one wanted their kids in his class. I know the whole thing was her doing. She's made sure she's got all the right friends. She's always been good at that. The local police chief, local businesses, council bigwigs, all that. But when the election didn't happen, even though she's not the actual MP, she's kind of appointed herself as the person in charge. And everyone just assumes I agree with her.'

I thought about how it would feel to have a parent like that.

I thought of Jonas that day on the green. 'Well why wouldn't they think that, if you just go along with it?'

'I did just go along with it, for a while.' He looks embarrassed. 'I shouldn't have. But I was always sort of trying to win her approval I guess. When I was a kid she'd always make me feel like I was a bit ... like I wasn't good enough. Not the son she thought she'd have. You know? She wanted someone good at rugby and rowing, and good at being friends with all the right people like her, which I'm ... I'm really not. I just liked dogs and being in the woods and collecting caterpillars and whatever. Which she thinks is weird. I mean, I guess it is kind of weird.'

I wanted to say it was only a bit weird, and in a good way, but I didn't.

'Anyway, when it got more extreme, and I was a bit older and didn't care so much whether she approved of me or not, I'd argue with her. I mean, I had to. She was attacking second-home owners to build her popularity, attacking people who'd moved here from outside. She said people from the cities, especially those with 'different cultures', were changing the character of the village, they didn't have our values, they were a threat to our way of life, our kids. Except the ones who funded her campaign of course.'

'Wow,' I said. 'Okay. I can see why she thinks Toby Knight's so great.'

'And she's a control freak. Anyone who disagrees with her is made to feel ostracized by the rest of the village and there are usually some rumours started about them. When the shortages began, she used that as a way to get even more control. She started doing favours for her supporters – extra food, more medicine, that kind of thing. I couldn't pretend any more that she was doing it all for good reasons.'

'So how come you seemed to be all happy families when I met you on the green that day? How come you're a Community Guard if you're so different from your mum?'

He shrugged. 'In the end I decided that if she and everyone else thought I agreed with her, why not use that? I told her I'd been wrong, she'd been right. It was just immaturity, teenage rebellion. I blamed it on my dad leaving too – she's always more than happy to blame him for anything. That's when I started passing on information to Shaun.'

'What do you mean?'

Jonas looked at me, surprised. I looked away. His eyes were very blue.

'He hasn't told you anything at all?'

'About you? No. Just that I should trust you.'

'I suppose he thought it was safer for me if you didn't know. Maybe safer for you too.' He looked doubtful suddenly, as if maybe he shouldn't say any more.

'I don't need keeping safe,' I said. 'Shaun worries too much. And who am I going to tell? I think you can be pretty sure your secret's safe with me.'

'Okay,' Jonas said, and then hesitated as though he still wasn't sure he should be telling me. 'Shaun helps people. Secretly, I mean.'

'Helps who? How?'

'Whoever needs help. He gets them out of the villages and towns round here, even out of the country if they need to. Helps them get papers and stuff they need if they haven't got them. Organizes locally to try and stop my mum and her lot.'

I nodded slowly, feeling stupid for not having worked out some of what he was saying already for myself. It all made sense.

'I just pass on anything useful I happen to hear from my mum,' Jonas said. 'Plans. Decisions they make at meetings. I listen out and pass it on.'

'Wow,' I said. 'You're secretly betraying your own mum?'

He looked half-embarrassed, half-defiant. 'Maybe I should just stand up to her, confront her with what she's doing. But this way at least I'm doing something useful. If I just argue with her all the time about it what good does it do? She wouldn't take any notice and I wouldn't be able to help.'

I thought about this. If he could fool his own mum, he could equally be fooling me and Shaun. He could be passing information on Shaun back to Imogen. All this could just be an act.

Oh, please. You know he's one of the good guys really, Mischa said. *You just don't want to admit you were wrong.*

We thought Danny was a good guy, Misch.

Mischa went uncharacteristically quiet.

It could be an act.

But I found I didn't want it to be.

'Okay,' I said.

'Okay?' he said. 'You mean I passed the test? We're friends?'

'I wouldn't go that far,' I said. 'Me and Skadi are friends. Me and you are . . . not enemies.'

He smiled. 'I'll take that.'

I half-smiled back. 'I mean, you have no choice.'

'Are we not-enemies enough for me to come back here?'

I thought about it and realized as I did how quiet it was suddenly.

'Listen.'

He looked up sharply. 'What is it?'

'The rain's stopped,' I said. 'That means you can go.'

183

I watched them leave, Skadi trotting ahead. Jonas turned and waved.

'Skadi's welcome back any time,' I called after him. 'And if she brings you, I suppose that's fine too.'

He smiled and disappeared into the trees.

Afterwards, I sat in the hut, which seemed too quiet now. It smelt of wet dog and some other smell that was Jonas, not aftershave, just a trace of him in the air that almost made me wish the rain hadn't stopped quite so soon.

Pheromones, Mischa said.

'No one asked, Misch.'

You know – like animal sex chemicals that tell you whether you're sexually compatible with someone. Whether you're aroused by them.

'Please stop talking now,' I said.

She smiled her knowing smile. *Just saying, babe.*

I piled up the cushions in the corner and picked up the jam jar of dried bluebells. I'd warned Billie they'd fade as soon as they were picked but we couldn't resist. I explained that Grandpa told me once that the fact that they didn't last long made them even more beautiful. He used a Japanese word for it, but I couldn't remember what it was. The bluebells had gone from the woods now too, the hazy carpet of blue like fallen sky. I'd pressed some into the pages of my notebook for Billie, trying to trap them, make them permanent.

*

'Wabi-sabi,' Polly says.

'What?'

'The Japanese word. *The acceptance and appreciation of transience and imperfection.*'

'Oh, right,' I say. 'Yes. I'd forgotten.'

I tell Billie later how I was telling Polly about the bluebells and she'd known the word I couldn't remember.

'But I like the pressed bluebells,' Billie says. 'I want to keep them for ever.'

'Me too,' I say.

'But even more I wish they could stay alive for ever. Even after you've picked them.'

'Me too.'

I close my eyes and see us running through the blue cloud of them, arms outstretched, Billie calling out, 'This is what it's like to fly, Clem.'

*

The girl knew she must find the blood-red flower to save her sister but she did not know the witch had enchanted the forest so that no one could escape it without magical help. As she lay under the tree a robin flew down to her with something in his beak. She saw it was a tiny gold key, which he dropped it at her feet.

'A key?' the girl said. 'But what does it open?'

The robin looked at her intently, as though he wanted to tell her but couldn't.

'Thank you,' the girl said. She stood up, wondering which way to go. The robin flew to an oak tree a little further ahead and looked back. The girl realized he was waiting for her and so she followed. Flitting from tree to tree the robin flew ahead of her through the forest until the girl began to wonder whether he wasn't leading her anywhere at all and she was more lost than ever.

But just as this doubt began to form, the thicket of trees grew thinner and the girl found she was in the grounds of a great and strange palace, with towers and turrets that seemed to reach up into the clouds.

The robin looked at her again and chirped. This time he was telling her something, she was sure of it. Then he flew off into the trees.

'Don't go!' the girl called after the robin, but he was gone.

She walked up to the great wooden door and looked in vain for a keyhole small enough for the little golden key, but there was only a great iron door knocker, so the girl knocked on the door three times.

*

I was sitting in the garden, the shoebox marked SEREN in marker pen waiting in front of me on the patio table, still taped shut. Like every other time I'd thought about opening it since Shaun gave it to me, I hesitated. I wasn't sure why. What did I want to know about Mum? What did I not want to know? I wasn't sure. Perhaps it was better just to leave it, for now anyway. There was no rush.

Billie was trying to train Merlin, despite the fact that in dog years he must have been about a hundred and probably too old to learn new tricks. I watched her, an echo of when I was a kid and he was a puppy. Billie had always wanted us to have a dog. Walking to school or the shops with her always took twice as long as it should have done because she'd insist on stopping to pet every pampered pooch and mangy mutt we met on the way. But Dad said with everyone out of our house during the day it wouldn't be fair.

'Merlin, roll over!' Billie told him sternly while he trotted off to sniff at something on the lawn. She ran after him.

'Look, Merlin!' she said, lying down and rolling over in the long grass. 'Like this. See?'

Merlin licked her face and she wriggled and squeaked, just as I remembered doing myself.

'I'm going in to talk to Grandpa,' I called. 'You hungry, B? Want a snack or a drink?'

'No,' she called over. 'But Merlin says he needs some bacon.'

'I wasn't asking Merlin. Anyway, there isn't any bacon. And if there was, I'd definitely eat it all myself.'

'Mean.'

'Yep. Just call me Cruella.'

'I'd give all mine to Merlin. I'm going to show him some cartwheels now.' She skipped off to where he was barking at a fat pigeon.

I watched her a while longer as she played with Merlin and did handstands and cartwheels on the grass.

As I walked towards the patio doors, I heard Shaun talking

to someone who was too tall to be Grandpa. No one ever came into the house, Shaun made sure of that. I looked more closely and saw it was Jonas.

My heart flipped. I hadn't seen him since we'd waited for the rain to stop in the hut. Every time I went there now I secretly half-hoped he'd be there again.

I'm saying nothing, Mischa said.

It was a good thing he hadn't come back, I'd told myself. After all, I didn't really know I could trust him. Not really. But I still looked out for signs that he'd tried to find me there. I imagined he might have come by and left me a note saying he was hoping to see me again, or some chocolate, or ... And then yesterday I'd found a crane made out of paper that had been written on in pencil. I unfolded it carefully. It said:

Skadi says hi and why are you never here when she visits?

I knew it, Mischa had said. *And please don't pretend you're not smiling, because that would demean us both.*

Now I prepared myself to look casual and not particularly pleased to see him, but as I walked into the kitchen both he and Shaun looked round and I realized from their expressions that something was wrong.

'What is it?'

'We've got a bit of a problem,' Shaun said. 'Jonas has heard that they're going to start doing searches in the village.'

'Searches?'

'House to house,' Jonas said. 'For people who are here without permission.'

By then, we'd been there for weeks.

'Why?'

'They'll start with second homes and holiday rentals, and anyone they know who's had visitors. They're saying they'll reward anyone who reports seeing people they think are outsiders.'

'Right. When are they going to start the searches?' I asked.

'In a couple of days.'

'Look,' Shaun said to me. 'Don't panic. They might not come here.'

'You know they will,' I said. 'You told me yourself: Imogen was suspicious when she came round all those weeks ago to check I'd gone. And, like you said, she's always looking for ways to cause trouble for you.'

'We'll have to find somewhere to hide you,' Jonas said.

'Okay,' Shaun said. 'But I don't know where.'

'I do,' I said.

Shaun looked at me in surprise.

I saw Jonas realize. 'Oh,' he said. 'Yes. Of course. Good idea.'

Shaun looked from one of us to the other. 'Okay. Are you two going to let me in on the secret or what?'

'The forest,' I said.

I tried to pack our things quietly in the bedroom while Billie slept, but apparently I wasn't quiet enough.

'Do you like Jonas now?' Billie said in the dark.

'I guess. I mean, he's okay.'

It had been a risk for him to come and warn us about the searches, I knew that.

'Yes,' I said. 'I like him.'

'But do you *like* him like him?'

'You need to be asleep, Billie. It's late. We need to be out of here early tomorrow.'

'I can't wait to live in the forest.'

'I know.'

'Like Robin Hood. Or squirrels. Or witches.'

'Sleep,' I said.

'Okay. But can we come back and visit Merlin sometimes?'

'Close your eyes.'

'They are closed.'

'Well then . . . close your mouth.'

'It is closed.'

'It really isn't.'

'I mean mmm mmm mmm.'

'Okay. Night. I love you.'

'Mm mmm mmm mmm.'

I smiled.

'That meant I love you too,' Billie whispered in the dark.

'You sure you'll be okay?' Shaun said, anxiously looking round the hut, when he'd run out of excuses to stay. 'Definitely got everything you need?'

He'd brought a camping stove and a load of slightly

out-of-date tins of beans and soup, a tin opener, some Jammy Dodgers, porridge and a few eggs he'd won in a game of chess against a retired civil servant who kept chickens. There were also sleeping bags, blankets, pillows, a bucket and loo roll; Granny's fancy old picnic hamper with plates and cutlery and glasses; some matches, candles, a string of battery-operated fairy lights; a tube of sting and bite cream, loads of bottles of water, a pack of cards, a sharp knife and Grandpa's cricket bat. He leaned it against the wall next to where I'd laid out my sleeping bag. 'Just in case,' he said.

I'd brought my rucksack which I'd carefully re-packed with all our stuff from home, so that there was not a trace of us left at Grandpa's. I'd also brought the SEREN shoebox at the last minute, hidden under a blanket in a carrier bag so Shaun wouldn't ask about it.

Billie was already off in search of squirrels, unicorns and other forest creatures. She'd been sad to leave Merlin behind, despite my promises that we'd visit him often.

'You worry too much,' I said to Shaun. 'I mean, I can't say I'm a fan of the toilet arrangements, but other than that it's perfect. Like you said, no one comes into the woods at the moment anyway.'

'Come back to the house if you need to, but stay out of sight if you can till you know it's safe. If there's any reason why you can't come in, I'll put a warning in the window.'

'What warning?'

He thought. 'That red rose plant that's usually on the side. I'll put it in the window. You'll see that?'

I nodded.

'I'll come back and see you're all right tomorrow, okay?'

He gave me a bone-crushing hug.

Then he was gone, and we were alone in the forest.

The first night was kind of scary, though obviously I pretended to Shaun the next day it wasn't. The dark was dense and black, and everywhere there seemed to be rustling and scratching and scuttling. Why had Mischa made me watch all those old horror movies set in the woods? *Oh right, blame me*, she said, and for a second I was comforted by the memory of us watching them through our fingers with bowls of microwaved popcorn, screaming at every jump scare till Mischa's mum came in and said something annoyed-sounding in Polish. But the thought was only briefly comforting and in another moment I was gripped by a primal fear. As I listened for predators – tigers, serial killers, tarantulas – I could feel every bit of me go tense, ready to spring into action and . . . do something. Presumably involving Grandpa's cricket bat. Or screaming.

Until I remembered there was no one to hear me scream.

I hardly slept.

But as the days went by the forest became our home. We couldn't go back to Grandpa's. 'Best to wait till things calm down a bit,' Shaun said, and I agreed. In the searches, they'd found several 'unauthorized outsiders', he told me. Family of people from the village mainly, people like me who'd just come here to be safe. They'd been arrested and threatened with detention if they didn't leave. There had been a meeting

192

at the village hall and things had got pretty nasty, Shaun said, with some people arguing it was outrageous to treat innocent people like that, and others claiming that it was only fair, that there wasn't enough food to go round, that people who've done nothing wrong don't need to hide, and, anyway, that no one knew who these people were. Everyone was tense. Shaun said it was fine to visit as long as we were careful, but not to go back to stay, not yet. I didn't argue.

We'd wake early. Breakfast was usually porridge made with water and cooked on the gas stove. For the first weeks we had honey, which we rationed carefully. Shaun brought us raspberries from his garden. Occasionally he'd bring us more eggs and if we were really lucky some cheese or butter. 'Sorry I can't bring you more,' he said. But I didn't want him to. I didn't want to take his and Grandpa's rations.

After breakfast, Billie would say, 'I'm going to find squirrels today,' or 'I'm on a hunt for fairy circles,' or 'I'm going to visit my favourite tree.'

'The other trees will get jealous,' I told her as she skipped off, clutching Luna.

I told her about an article I'd seen online once about how trees can talk to each other and look after each other, and how they have memories and even heartbeats.

'I know,' she said, as if it was obvious.

To my surprise, despite the spiders and the night-time noises and the previously unthinkable toilet arrangements, I found I liked living in the forest.

Wow, Mischa said. *I did not see that coming. I thought*

we agreed we were the people least likely to survive the
apocalypse because we had no practical or relevant skills.
And now look at you, surviving in the wild! Next thing you
know, you'll be whittling and foraging and starting a fire with
sticks. You'll be skinning squirrels and drying their meat for
winter and making their fur into mittens.

Shaun visited when he could, in the afternoons when
Grandpa had a nap, but he never stayed long. Since the time
Grandpa had wandered off and got lost, we both worried about
him being on his own. We'd agreed that when he could he'd
stay overnight at Grandpa's. Eventually he pretty much moved
in so he could care for Grandpa all the time.

Some evenings Billie and I would walk through the forest to
Grandpa's, always checking that the rose wasn't in the window
before we went in. But it was never there. Billie would skip
ahead, desperate to see Merlin. As we got closer to Grandpa's
I'd call her back. In this part of the forest, closer to the village,
occasionally there were people around – joggers, couples
sneaking into the shadows, dog walkers – and we'd have to
hide behind trees until they were gone.

Sometimes Grandpa remembered who I was, sometimes
he didn't. I'd get him to talk about the old days, when I was a
kid or when he and Granny were young. He still remembered
things from back then vividly. He was always pleased to see
me. I told myself that was enough.

'Grandpa,' I said one night. 'There was a word you told
me when I was a kid. A Welsh word. You said it couldn't be
translated because there isn't a word for it in English. It sort

of means homesick, but it's more than that. Like longing for a home you can never go back to because it doesn't exist any more. I wish I could remember it.'

'*Hiraeth*,' Grandpa said immediately.

I looked at him, surprised. 'Yes! That was it.' I wrote it in my notebook in the candlelight when I got back to the hut that night.

It was hard to leave Grandpa. I always had a moment of panic that this might be the last time I'd see him. But the panic passed as I walked back through the woods with Billie at dusk, the damp, green, growing smell of everything all around us, the birds, the leaves, the trees watching over us.

Billie's favourite tree became the wishing tree. I told her there had been one in a story Grandpa had told me and that they were a real thing all over the world. Every day we went and sat under it and made a paper crane and put it in a branch of the tree and made a wish.

There was a robin who came to visit us every day. We'd feed him scraps and leftovers even though we barely had enough for ourselves. Every morning when I got up and went out of the hut he'd fly down. Every morning it made me smile.

Jonas visited too. Occasional, brief, slightly awkward visits at first, but as time went on he visited more often and for longer.

Hmmm, back again, Mischa said. *Someone's keen.*

He's just being nice, I said. *Helping Shaun out.*

Right, Mischa said. *Or maybe he just really, really likes trees.*

He brought me things I needed. I started writing them down in a list, so that when I wanted sanitary pads I didn't have to ask him face to face. Whatever I asked for he seemed to be able to get.

'Try asking for sticky toffee pudding and salt and vinegar crisps,' Billie suggested.

'That's too much, B.'

Ask him for a diamond necklace, Mischa said. *He'd find a way to do it for you, babe.*

During the day, he brought Skadi. She was his excuse for being out. At night he'd visit if the rest of his family weren't around or sneak out when they were in bed. Billie would be asleep by then. We'd build a fire and we'd sit and talk.

After a while he stopped talking about it. He didn't want to talk about it. I didn't want to know. Instead, we talked about life before, our friends, the bands we liked, what we wanted to do when life was normal again. We wanted to keep the real world out. The forest had its own time.

I found myself waiting for his visits.

'What month is it?' I said to Jonas one day.

'July,' he said. 'Why?'

'No reason.'

My birthday had passed and I hadn't known, hadn't even thought of it. It felt so strange to realize it. Even stranger to think of my birthday last year, the perfect picnic Dad had organized, in that other world.

Had he remembered my birthday this year? I knew he would have. He'd have been thinking of me, wherever he was.

'Hey,' Jonas said. 'Clem. Are you okay?'

I nodded because I couldn't speak.

He looked at me for a moment as if deciding whether to ask me what was wrong. I was grateful when he didn't. Skadi trotted over to me and laid her head on my lap.

Later, when Jonas was gone, I took the torch and walked through the forest. It was still warm. I sat under the wishing tree and took out my notebook. I thought of that morning, of Billie waking me with the notebook, of Dad, the picnic, the cake. Danny. Of the letter waiting for Claudia on the doormat at home.

I opened the notebook to a fresh page. I wrote, *Dear Dad*.

But I couldn't think what I would write to him, even if he could read it.

I tore the page out and in the dark I folded it into the shape of a bird.

Then I placed it next to me among the ancient roots of the tree.

I closed my eyes and thought of Dad and wished.

Time was different in the forest. We didn't measure it with clocks or calendars, but by colours: of berries, of leaves, of sky at the beginning and end of each day. We picked blackberries and ate them for every meal until we were sick of them. The trees turned yellow and orange and red. We crunched through the leaves and kicked them up, made piles of them to jump into. In the mornings, the outside of the hut was draped in cobwebs beaded with what looked like diamonds glittering in the chilly air. We collected conkers and acorns and their tiny cups, which Billie filled with drops of morning dew and left out to entice the woodland sprites she was sure were watching us.

I sometimes felt watched too. I'd hear a rustle in the undergrowth or see a flash of something in the corner of my eye that wasn't there. Not sprites. Something bigger. But just as imaginary, surely.

Shaun brought us extra clothes and blankets, sleeping bags he assured us were made for sleeping outside at the top of mountains. Jonas brought tins of coffee and rice pudding and custard that we could heat over the stove to keep us warm.

There hadn't been a frost yet but, still, the mornings and nights were cold and would only get colder.

Billie and I both caught colds. Billie's was just a sniffle; she was better in days. Mine wouldn't shift. It sat on my chest. I woke in the night coughing till I could hardly breathe. My whole body ached. Shaun was worried. He brought me fresh ginger to mix in boiled water and goose fat which he told me to rub on my chest at night. I told him I had, but I couldn't do it. It smelt dead.

'Do you think it'll be safe enough for us to move back to the village by the time it gets really cold?' I asked Shaun.

'I expect so,' he said, but his face told me the opposite.

'What if it's not?'

'We'll work something out,' he said, not meeting my eye.

When Billie and I were better we filled the tree with paper cranes as the real birds migrated. In the clearing near the hut, we'd see great Vs of them in the sky. We'd imagine where they were going and how long it would take to get there. We'd imagine flying away with them.

The box of Mum's stuff stood in the corner of the hut, unopened. I pretended to myself that I forgot it was there but I never did. It whispered to me, like Pandora's jar in the story Grandpa used to tell me. *Open me.*

Why didn't I?

I thought of all the times I'd tried to find her online, secretly googling her name. Not because I wanted to contact her, I told myself. I was just curious. Just to see a picture of her maybe or find out what she was doing. But there had been nothing. She was just an absence. I sometimes felt I'd dreamt her or invented her.

When I was a kid, I used to make up stories about why Mum had left. She'd won the lottery and gone to live on a private island where I'd soon be joining her. She was a spy on a secret mission. She was in witness protection and had been given a whole new identity. I even half-believed them sometimes. I invented her witness protection persona: Mitzi Sinclair. She had dyed blonde hair. She wore leather trousers and big earrings and dark red lipstick and worked in a fancy boutique. I liked Mitzi. Sometimes a part of me hoped I'd get to go and live with her one day.

But Mitzi wasn't real, of course. The truth was more mundane. One Saturday morning when I was five, Dad made me pancakes for breakfast and said he had something serious to tell me. I was prepared for the worst straight away, because the last time he had said that was when my guinea pig, Dotty, had died. So I thought instantly of Shadow, our beloved, bad-tempered cat. Surely fate couldn't be so cruel as to take her too?

But it was worse than the worst. This time the something serious was that Mum hadn't just gone away for a break to get well again, like last time. She'd gone away for ever.

I'd stared at Dad, trying to make sense of what he was telling me.

'Is she in heaven?' I asked at last. That was where Mischa's granny had gone when she went away for ever.

Dad was silent for a moment.

'No, Clem. Not in heaven.'

In fact, it turned out she was in Birmingham. She had taken her highest-heeled shoes and the silky party dress that made her look like a film star. She had not taken the photo of her holding me when I was a baby that was in a silver frame Granny had given her. It sat smiling at me from the mantelpiece for weeks afterwards until I accidentally knocked it onto the floor and then accidentally stamped on it. She'd gone to live a life where she could be the film-star version of herself and not the version in the photo with the snotty toddler. This new life could only exist without me, or even the memory of me. This much was clear to my five-year-old self.

She hadn't said anything to me or left me a note saying *Sorry*, or *It's not your fault*, or *One day you'll understand* or *I love you*.

The last day I saw her, the day before she left, became imprinted on my mind. It had been hot. I'd helped her to hang out washing on our balcony, handing her the plastic clothes pegs, but when she didn't take one I looked up and saw her leaning on the balcony rail looking away from the line of damp socks and limp knickers, away from our flat and out over the playground and the streets and the rooftops.

'Wouldn't it be lovely to swim in the sea?' she'd said, closing her eyes. 'Even just to paddle. I can't remember the last time I swam in the sea.'

I spent hours, weeks, years trying to decode that message, in class, in diaries, in the dark of night when I couldn't sleep. In the end I realized it just happened to be the last thing I remember her saying to me. And maybe she didn't say it at all. Maybe I just imagined it afterwards because of the stories Grandpa told me about beautiful women who were really creatures of the sea and couldn't live on land without wasting away. When you think about it, it's far more likely that the last words she said to me were something like 'Brush your teeth', forgotten because of their pitiful lack of hidden meanings.

Real or not, that memory of the washing line messed with my sense of geography for a while as I assumed that Birmingham was by the sea. I imagined Mum walking along the beach there, eating ice cream and fish and chips, swimming in the wide blue ocean. It felt like an extra betrayal when I discovered that Birmingham, the place she'd chosen to go, was so very landlocked. I suppose she just knew someone there. And she didn't stay there long anyway.

She didn't stay anywhere long, going by the mutterings I overheard between Grandpa and Dad. She travelled abroad, always on the move, settling somewhere for a while and then off again. Granny was the only person she was in touch with, and even that only occasionally. I looked up the places I heard them mention on the world map stuck on the kitchen wall – Thailand, Greece, Morocco – plotting the course she was following, trying to work out where she might go next so I'd be ready if it turned out to be back home. If there was mention of a specific town or city I googled images of it so I could see what she saw.

And then, at last, I stopped. I didn't want to see the world as she saw it. I didn't want to know where she was. There was no map that would explain to me the route she'd chosen, the journey that had taken her away from me. And I didn't want her to come back. Home was where she wasn't. It was where Dad and Billie were. And Claudia too.

I pictured Mum swimming out to sea, further and further away, smaller and smaller until she was a dot on the horizon and then . . .

gone.

*

More and more I found myself thinking of Jonas.

I felt light when I thought of him, in my head, in my heart.

When he visited I'd watch him as he talked in the flickering firelight and find myself wondering how the small scar above his lip would feel under my fingers, or against

202

my lips. I had to concentrate to stop myself reaching out and taking hold of his wrist, feeling the beat of his pulse beneath my fingertips.

I mean yes, that's slightly weird, Mischa said. *But that's just how physical attraction is, babe.*

Don't, I said.

Don't what?

Say 'physical attraction' to me ever again.

Okay, she said. *Would you prefer sexual desire?*

I would not.

Mischa laughed her dirtiest laugh. *Oh, I think you would, Clemmie.*

I caught myself imagining conversations with him ... as I washed our clothes in the basin Shaun had brought now it wasn't safe to visit the house so often. As I hung them out on the branches of trees where they would grow cold and fail to dry. When I boiled water over the gas stove. I thought of clever things I'd say to him that would make him laugh or think I was interesting.

At night, in the dark, I'd find I was remembering him looking at me, the intensity of it, so that I felt the heat of his gaze on my skin. I imagined him touching me, the response of my body to his touch.

Pure filth, Mischa said approvingly.

I ignored her.

I tried not to think about him.

The thought of him made me happy and I couldn't be happy. I didn't deserve to be happy.

I'd tell him to stop visiting. Next time.

Or the time after.

Still, I waited for him.

*

'Is that what you still feel?' Polly says. We're not in her office today because someone's in there fixing a leak in the ceiling. Instead, we're in a room with no windows that smells faintly of cheese and contains a piano, a bike with no front wheel and a hatstand.

'What?'

'That you don't deserve to be happy?'

I shake my head. I don't feel it. I *know* it.

'Am I allowed to play?' I say, nodding at the piano. I don't particularly want to, but it's better than answering questions.

'Sure,' Polly says, smiling. 'I didn't know you were a pianist.'

'I'm not,' I say. 'I mean, I can play a little bit. My grandpa taught me when I was a kid. We used to play duets together and he'd get the notes all wrong on purpose. I wasn't very good. My mum was really good, I think. Like, Grandpa said she could have been a professional player if she'd stuck with it.'

Polly looks interested. 'You remember her playing?'

'No,' I say. 'We didn't have a piano.'

I wonder now why that was, and if she minded.

I wonder if she has a piano wherever she is now.

I decide maybe I don't want to play the windowless-cheese-room piano after all.

Shaun arrived late one evening. When I heard him coming through the trees I'd hoped it might be Jonas as neither of them had been for a few days. But as soon as I saw Shaun I could see something was wrong.

Things were worse in the village. Much worse.

There'd been another wave of house searches and this time everyone they found had been arrested and detained, even kids. They were all relatives of people from the village, or friends, or friends of friends. People like us who'd been unsafe in their own homes, or who'd been threatened with deportation or arrest like Claudia. The people who'd been hiding them had been arrested and detained too, no matter who they were or how long they'd lived in the village. Some of those arrested were pregnant women, pensioners, people who were sick or disabled. Imogen Glass wanted to make an example of them, Shaun said, to show her strength and to show people they needed to be on her side if they knew what was good for them. He'd found out through his network that they'd been taken away to a disused army barracks a few miles away that was now being used as a detention centre. He knew someone who worked there, who passed him information, who said the camp was chaotic – so packed and dirty that people were getting sick.

I felt cold when he told me. Claudia could be in a place like that. Dad too.

'Why's she doing this?' I asked.

'She's getting edgy,' Shaun said. 'Knight's in trouble.

People I trust are telling me the army might split. Some of the senior military have turned on him.'

'But that's good, isn't it?'

'In the long term, I hope so, yes. But for now it means things are more dangerous. We could end up with two armies fighting each other.'

'You mean, like a civil war?'

'It may not come to that,' Shaun said. 'Things may get better not worse. But for now, you need to stay hidden.'

He didn't need to tell me. I wouldn't risk Grandpa ending up in a place like that, not because of me.

'How's Grandpa?'

Shaun smiled. 'He's fine. He'd be happier if you were there but I'll tell him you send your love. Talking of which, I'd better get back to him.' He got up to leave. 'That cough of yours sounds bad again.'

'I'm fine.'

He looked at me. 'No you're not. Your breathing sounds laboured. Does it hurt to breathe?'

'No,' I lied.

'I'm going to see if I can get you some antibiotics,' he said. 'I expect Jonas can get hold of some. He said to say sorry he hasn't been able to visit, by the way, but we've got to be more careful than ever with Imogen how she is at the moment. If she finds out about him ...'

'Sure,' I said quickly, and hoped he couldn't tell how much I minded.

*

The evenings stretched out long and dark without Jonas. I had nothing to do but sit and think. I would get out the SEREN box but I could never bring myself to open it. Then one night, when Billie was asleep, and I couldn't sleep because I was coughing so much, I took the box out by the fire.

Why was I so scared of opening it?

I'd let Mum go. I didn't need her any more. I didn't want to let her back in.

But it was natural to be curious. What harm could it do? Before I could think too much about it, I opened the box.

There wasn't much inside. Folded neatly was a baby's sleepsuit and a pair of baby shoes. I felt strange looking at them. There were some cards and postcards, which I read eagerly, but quickly realized they were all to Mum rather than from her. Mum remained as invisible as ever.

Under the postcards was a small black velvet ring box. Inside was a silver ring with a tiny green stone in it. I recognized it at once as Granny's engagement ring. I'd loved the ring as a child and loved hearing the story that went with it. I'd heard it many times, Grandpa loved telling it. How he'd spotted Granny taking out a copy of *The Mabinogion* at the library in Edinburgh and how he'd fallen instantly in love with her. And how it had turned out she was actually getting the book out for her American boyfriend who was studying a module on Celtic Literature because he had thought, wrongly, it sounded easy and how she was planning to go to California with him when she graduated. And how Grandpa had persuaded her to meet him on some spurious pretext at a café on the Grassmarket and, as a result of this meeting, the American boyfriend went back to California heartbroken, without completing his module in Celtic Literature and without Granny. And three years later Grandpa had taken her to that same café on the Grassmarket and given her an emerald ring that he'd started saving for the very night they first met there. Because emeralds were Cleopatra's favourites, he told her, and only a jewel good enough for the most beautiful queen that ever lived was good enough for Granny. And because they were magic, and legend said that if you put one under your tongue you could see the future, and the future that Granny would see if she tried that, he'd explained, was them, happily married with a load of kids and dogs and books and whatever. 'Three billion years old, the oldest emeralds are,' he'd said. *'Just think of all the years this one's been waiting to be put on your finger.'* It's a good line, you've got to admit. And it worked. Granny hadn't put the ring under her tongue. She had taken Grandpa's word for it. And six months later they were married.

I found a piece of string and looped the ring onto it then tied it round my neck. It was too precious to leave lying around the hut.

There was a photo in the box, of Mum with Grandpa. At first, I thought it was me. She must have been almost my age from the date Granny had written on the back. I hadn't realized I looked so much like her. She was standing with Grandpa, her head thrown back, laughing, and he was looking at her with that expression, the one I'd always thought was just for me. Before that, before Grandpa was mine, he was Mum's. I stared at the photo for a long time, trying to work out why it made me feel whatever it was I was feeling. Why I was crying. Then I folded it into the pages of my notebook.

The last thing in the box was a book of Grimms' fairy tales, which I saw from the inscription that Grandpa had given Mum for Christmas a long time ago.

I put everything back in the box except for the book. Whatever I'd hoped – or feared – I might find, it hadn't been there. I didn't want to examine too closely what that thing had been. Now I just felt disappointment and the familiar nagging anger that Mum remained as invisible and distant as ever.

The book was an old hardback. I opened it carefully and turned the pages, remembering Mum telling me these stories when I was very small, not from a book but her own versions of them. As I turned a page, a postcard fell from behind it. I picked it up and looked at it. There was a picture of a castle on a hill on the front. I turned it over and realized I recognized the writing as Mum's. It was an address in Edinburgh. Beneath it was simply written:

My address. Sx

I looked again at the postmark. It was from last year.

For the first time since Mum had left, I knew where she was.

She wasn't on the other side of the world with oceans between us, as I'd imagined.

She was in Scotland.

Somewhere I could get to.

Somewhere safe.

The next thing she knew, the girl found herself in the banqueting hall of the palace being welcomed as the guest of honour by the old king and queen.

'We've been waiting for you,' they said.

They gave the girl a fine gown to wear. Then there was food and dancing and, for a time, the girl forgot all about her sister and the island and the blood-red flower.

At the end of the evening, she fell into the softest bed she had ever slept in. That night she dreamt her sister came to her as the bird the colour of the blue summer's sky.

'Don't forget me, sister,' the bird said.

'I never would,' the girl replied.

But the next day the feasting and dancing started again, exactly as before, and, exactly as before, the girl forgot all about finding the blood-red flower. The days went on like this, and days turned to weeks, and weeks to months, until one night, instead of dreaming of her sister, she dreamt of the robin.

'Remember the key!' the robin said.

When the girl woke up, she looked in the pocket of the dress she had been wearing when she first arrived at the palace and found the tiny golden key. When she looked at it closely, she realized it was a key for winding a clock.

That evening, instead of joining in with the feasting and dancing, she searched the palace for a stopped clock.

*

Shaun didn't visit. Jonas didn't visit. At first I didn't worry but as the days went by I started to. What if Shaun had been arrested? What if Jonas had? What if something had happened to Grandpa?

My cough got worse, especially at night. Billie slept through it, but I lay drifting in and out of consciousness, waking dripping with sweat then shivering with cold till my teeth chattered. My breathing got more painful. I became so weak I could hardly stand.

'Are you okay, Clemmie?' Billie said. 'You look bad.'

'I'm okay,' I said, trying to catch my breath. 'Don't worry. I just need to sleep.'

More days and nights passed then that I remember only for being so hot or so cold, so heavy and in pain and fighting for every breath, and Billie saying, 'It's okay, Clem, I'll look after you,' and singing her made-up songs to me.

And then sometime later I thought I heard Shaun's voice, *Christ, Clem, can you hear me?* Taking my pulse. Giving me water and medicine that tasted so bad I tried to spit it out but he made me take it. Time drifted by, Shaun appearing, giving me medicine. Billie humming in the background or the sigh of her breath at night.

Until one morning I woke up and I could breathe again, I could even stand again and I walked slowly to the door of the hut and looked at the trees, bars of thin sunlight sloping through their branches, and it was so beautiful that I cried.

Because I knew we couldn't stay here.

*

A few days later I got up one morning and found the robin's little body, cold outside the hut. I was surprised by how upset I was. I didn't tell Billie. I scooped him up carefully and carried him to the wishing tree and cried as I buried him there. I made a wish in the frosty dawn, but I knew it couldn't come true.

Late that night when Billie was asleep I heard footsteps coming towards the hut. I tensed, waiting. Was it Shaun? It was later than he usually came.

'Clem?'

It was Jonas. I threw open the door and we stood grinning stupidly at each other. I'd missed him so much.

'You took your time,' I said. 'I nearly died since you were last here.'

'I know,' he said. 'I'm so sorry.'

I smiled. 'Don't be. I didn't want you to come. I mean, I did, but I knew it wasn't safe. And I didn't really nearly die. I just had a chest infection or something.'

'Shaun said it was pneumonia.'

'Well, whatever. I'm fine now as you can s—' I was overwhelmed by a badly timed coughing fit.

'Yes, so I see,' he said, but he was smiling now too. 'I can't stay long, but my mum's out at a meeting till late so I thought I'd take my chance.'

'I'm glad you did,' I said. I couldn't stop smiling.

'Come on,' he said.

'Where are we going?'

'Not far,' he said. 'Don't worry. Just to the clearing.'

*

It was a clear night and the sky seemed impossibly full of stars. We sat on a rug, huddled under blankets we'd brought from the hut, hugging our knees to keep warm, and looked up at them.

'I remember Grandpa bringing me stargazing out here when I was a little kid,' I said. 'I couldn't believe how many there were. In London, you can't see the stars properly because of all the artificial light.' I remembered the excitement of that night, my too-big coat with the hot-water bottle inside it, my gloved hand holding Grandpa's, the thrill of being allowed out long after my bedtime.

Jonas lay back on the blanket and looked up.

'It makes you feel a bit dizzy, doesn't it?'

I nodded. 'I remember Grandpa telling me that when you see a star, the light is millions of years old – the memory of a star rather than a star. And how if someone was looking at Earth from one of those stars, they'd see history. Like time travel. I couldn't get my head round it. I still can't.'

I lay back too. I could feel the warmth of Jonas next to me, and a kind of buzz where our hands were almost touching. I wondered if he could feel it too.

'I saw this picture of space where the stars all looked like confetti,' Jonas said. 'Hundreds and thousands of them in the dark. But it turned out they weren't stars, they were galaxies. Each speck of light was a whole galaxy.'

I turned my head and looked at him in the dark. 'I can't work out if that's amazing or terrifying.'

'Both,' he said.

'We're so small. It makes me feel like maybe we don't matter at all.'

He propped himself up on his elbow and looked at me. 'Maybe it makes us matter more,' he said. 'I mean, you're the only you and I'm the only me in all those billions of galaxies. The chances of us existing and being right here right now are so small. But here we are.'

Here we are. He looked at me, and it was as if I could feel us spinning through time and space, nothing holding us up, the sky beneath us as well as above us, just miles and miles and years and years of space all around us in all directions, and us hurtling through it. It felt extraordinary and terrifying. Without thinking, I reached out and held Jonas's hand as if it was all I had to keep me anchored, the only thing I could be sure of.

'I can't stay here, Jonas,' I said. I hadn't meant to say it, but it was true and I was going to have to say it sometime.

He stared at me. 'Why not?'

'Living in the hut, it was only ever meant to be a short-term thing. Till it was safe to go back to Grandpa's. But it's not safe. It might never be. It's putting you and Shaun and Grandpa at risk. You know I'm right. I've got to go.'

'Go where?'

I took a deep breath and made myself speak.

'I have a box of my mum's old stuff. It was in the house. I've had it for ages but I kept putting off looking at what was inside it. Anyway, in the end I did look. I wanted to find out more about her. And I found her address, Jonas. She's in Scotland.'

Jonas looked at me. 'You want to go to Scotland?'

'It's not a case of what I want, is it? Scotland would be safe.'

'If you can get there, maybe,' he said. 'But they've closed the border. If you get caught this side of the border you'll be detained. And even if you get across you could end up stuck in one of the refugee camps on the border.'

'But it's dangerous here. You know that. Loads of people have gone to Scotland since all this started. And my mum's there.'

He looked at me. 'Maybe you should go, if that's what you want to do. I'm sure Shaun could help you get there. He knows the right people to get you across the border.'

I felt stung at how 'okay' with it he sounded. I didn't want him to stop me but I thought he'd at least sound upset about the idea of me leaving.

'Fine,' I said. 'I'll go to the house and talk to Shaun about it tomorrow.'

'Okay. But be careful.'

He wasn't looking at me.

'It's late,' I said. 'We'd better be getting back.'

We walked back in silence through the dark of the forest.

'Okay then,' I said when we reached the hut. 'Bye.' I felt like I was going to cry. This was an ending, I knew it. It was really going to happen. I would leave and I probably wouldn't see Jonas again. I didn't want to mind as much as I did. Especially as he didn't seem to care. I turned away to go inside.

'Wait,' Jonas said.

'What?'

'I don't want you to go,' he said at last. 'I want you to stay.'

Despite everything, I felt a rush of happiness. He stepped towards me and our breath puffed out into the dark and mingled.

'But more than that I want you to be safe,' he said. 'So obviously I'm not going to try and stop you. More than anything I want you to be okay.'

'You could come too.' The words were out before I'd even thought them. I felt my face grow hot even in the cold night air. Why had I said it?

He was silent.

'Jonas?' I said at last. 'Sorry. I didn't mean to say that. I mean, obviously. This is your home. But you could come and visit, maybe when everything's more normal.'

I was gabbling.

'Maybe . . .' he said. 'Maybe I could come with you. '

'Really?'

'If you wanted me to.'

'I do,' I said.

He smiled.

I smiled back at him, feeling suddenly shy.

'I'll come back tomorrow,' he said. 'We'll talk about it once you've spoken to Shaun.'

'Okay.'

We stood a moment longer.

'I'd better go,' he said. 'I can't risk anyone noticing I'm gone.'

'I know.'

'Tomorrow,' he said, and then turned and walked off into the woods.

The next morning, I went talk to Shaun about my plan. I knew going to the house was risky, but we'd be careful. It was cold and clear, the shadows dusted white. Our toes tingled in our boots. Billie picked leaves, crisp and white-veined with frost. I smiled and thought about Jonas.

We walked cautiously through the back garden, Billie trailing behind. I looked up to see if anyone was in the kitchen.

The warning red rose plant was in the window.

I darted back.

'Quick, B. Hide,' I hissed.

There had been someone in the kitchen, I thought, but I wasn't sure. It had just been a silhouette. Could it have been Shaun? If it wasn't, would they have seen me?

We ran back through the trees, stumbling over tree roots, gasping for breath.

'What's happening?' Billie said. 'Is someone coming?'

'I don't know,' I said. 'We just need to get back to the hut as fast as we can. We'll be safe there. We just have to wait for Shaun or Jonas to come and tell us what's going on. Then we can make a plan. It'll be okay.'

But what if they didn't come? What if they couldn't?

'Let's hurry, B.'

We half-ran, then walked when our legs grew too tired,

through the trees, hand in hand. As we drew close to the hut we slowed, panting, relieved—

I stopped dead.

The door to the hut was open.

I'd definitely shut it when we left.

'Wait here,' I whispered to Billie. 'Behind this tree. Don't come out till I tell you it's safe. And stay completely quiet. Okay?' She nodded, putting a finger to her lips.

I crept slowly closer through the trees, watching, listening. There was no sign of anyone, no footsteps or voices, so maybe they'd gone, or maybe they were inside the hut. Maybe it was Shaun, come to tell me what was happening, and he'd just taken the path rather than going the long way.

I took cover behind a tree on the edge of the clearing, watching the hut. Should I risk going inside? Or should I wait and see if anything happened?

And then there was a bark from inside and out of the door bounded Skadi.

Relief washed over me as she ran towards me. It was Jonas. I hadn't dared hope he'd manage to get away so soon, or that he was as impatient to see me as I was to see him.

'Hey, Skadi!' I stepped out from behind the tree, smiling, and she jumped up, trying to lick my face as I bent down to stroke her. 'Good girl.'

'Skadi!' a sharp voice called from the hut. The dog trotted back obediently and I looked up to see Imogen Glass standing in the doorway.

I felt a flash of fear, but I stood up straight and looked her in the eye, determined not to show I was afraid.

Don't let that psycho scare you, babe, Mischa whispered.

Imogen walked towards me till she was standing a few feet away.

'So, you're the reason Jonas is such a diligent dog-walker these days,' she said. 'I should have guessed it would be a girl. He's so predictable.'

'What do you want?' I spoke loudly, as if I was in a play, to stop my voice from shaking. My mind was racing. Should I run? Fight? She was on her own. She couldn't force me to go with her.

'Straight to the point,' she said, smiling. 'I like that. Why waste time? What I want is I want you gone. I know what's been going on between you and Jonas and I won't allow it. I'm giving you twenty-four hours to leave.'

'I don't know what you're talking about.'

'Don't lie to me,' she snapped. 'Just do as I'm telling you.'

I made myself look her in the eye. 'Maybe I will. But not because you want me to.'

'You don't understand,' she said, as though she was explaining something to a small child. 'It's not a suggestion, it's an order. If you don't leave, you'll be arrested.'

'Are you sure you want me to go?' I said, trying to stop my voice shaking, 'Because if I leave maybe Jonas will come with me.'

She smiled, all perfect teeth. 'He won't leave.'

'Are you sure about that?'

She frowned. 'Of course, I could arrest you right now but frankly I don't want my son getting caught up in any of this. I just want you gone. I don't care where, or how. I'll make sure you don't get stopped as long as you are gone within twenty-four hours, without Jonas.'

'Maybe that's up to Jonas,' I said.

Imogen paused. 'Clem,' she said, as though we were friends having a chat, 'what do you think would happen to your grandfather if Shaun wasn't able to look after him? What will happen if Shaun is found to have been engaging in illegal activity of some kind, let's say, and gets himself arrested? Or if something unfortunate should happen that means he has to leave the village? It's amazing how quickly rumours spread in our small community, and everyone knows Shaun's always been something of a troublemaker, never really one of us.'

'Shaun's worth a hundred of you,' I said.

'Sweet,' she said. 'But as I say, if something were to happen to Shaun, would poor Huw be able to look after himself? I doubt it. And with things how they are there's no guarantee he'd be able to access the care he needs as his condition worsens. Unless of course he had someone powerful in the community to advocate for him, to ensure he gets the best possible care. Which is, I'm sure, what you would want for him.'

'You'd actually do that?' My voice was choked with anger. 'You'd actually threaten my grandpa and use that against me to get what you want?'

'There's no need to get upset,' Imogen said. 'I'm not

threatening anyone. I'm just saying, I can help Huw. Or not. So, do we understand one another?'

I looked at her, with her perfect hair and expensive clothes, her absolute conviction that she was right.

'Oh, I understand you,' I said. 'Jonas does too. You can stop him from coming with me, but you can't make him into someone he's not.'

As soon as I'd said it I wanted to take the words back. I didn't want to get Jonas into any more trouble than he was already in. And if he had to stay, wasn't it better that Imogen thought he really was still on her side?

She walked towards me till we were face to face. She was taut with anger.

'You don't know my son,' she said. 'Not really. Not like I do.'

And she turned and walked off through the trees, Skadi trotting after her.

'Go back to the hut and stay there,' I said to Billie. 'Don't go outside, okay? I won't be long.'

She looked at me, eyes wide.

'It's okay,' I said. 'Everything's going to be okay.'

I ran through the trees, blinded by tears, not caring about the branches of the trees, the thorns that ripped at my clothes. I tripped and fell into brambles, got up, kept running.

Shaun looked up as I burst into the kitchen, alarm on his face.

'Clem! What are you doing here? Didn't you see the warning?' He came closer. 'What's happened to you? Are you okay? You're bleeding.'

I told him about Imogen's visit, her threats and ultimatum, while he dabbed at my face and hands with cotton wool. 'I don't know how she knew,' I said, trying to keep my voice steady.

Shaun's face was grim. 'There was trouble,' he said. 'Last night.'

'What trouble?'

'The meeting turned nasty. Imogen and her sidekicks were whipping everyone up, telling them they had to defend themselves and their families against outsiders taking what was theirs. *Did they want their kids to starve?* That sort of thing. I happen to know there's more food than they're letting on. The Army's been delivering emergency supplies. But she just wants people scared so she can control them. And angry. Some people had gone to argue against her, disrupt the meeting. It all kicked off. There was shouting and fighting and then some of them were arrested and the police dispersed the meeting. People were meant to go home, but some of them went to the pub and at closing time they staggered up to the top of the village, chanting and shouting, and started yelling and chucking rocks at the holiday homes up there where some of the city folk have been staying. Next thing, two of the houses were on fire.'

'Oh my God,' I said. 'Was anyone in the houses?'

Shaun nodded.

'Are they okay?'

He shook his head. 'No one knows. Several people were taken away in ambulances.'

I didn't know what to say. I could hardly take in what he was telling me.

'Anyway,' he said. 'That's not all. It turns out, in all the shouting and yelling at the village hall, someone said to Imogen that if she was looking for people acting suspiciously, maybe she should start looking closer to home.'

I stared at Shaun. 'Jonas?'

He nodded. 'Someone had seen him out in the woods a few times. You never could keep a secret round here. Jonas wouldn't tell her anything though. But my name came up too, as it does when there's trouble. So she was round here earlier, demanding I tell her everything, making threats. I didn't tell her anything but she already knew enough.'

'She didn't say anything to Grandpa?' I couldn't bear the thought of him being upset or scared.

'No,' he said. 'She was all fake smiles to him. But once it was just us, she made a few veiled threats about what she could do if she chose to.' Shaun shook his head in disgust.

'She did the same to me.'

'I'm sorry, Clem. I want to tell you she's all talk and it all means nothing. But I know Imogen. She'll do it all right. We have to get you out of here.'

I look at him. 'The thing is, I'd already decided I was going to leave.'

He stared at me. 'What do you mean? Why?'

'I told Jonas last night. I've been thinking about it for a few days now. Even before Imogen, I knew it wasn't safe to stay. I can't keep putting Grandpa in danger. Or you, or Jonas.'

'But where will you go?'

'I've got a plan.'

I told him about my idea of going to Mum's, how I'd found her address in the shoebox, how I knew it was the right thing to do. I told him about Jonas saying he wanted to come with me, but now Imogen had put a stop to that.

He was silent for a long time, thinking.

'Are you sure? About Seren, I mean. She's not ... I don't mean any offence but she's not always been the most reliable sort.'

'I know she hasn't,' I said. 'But she is my mum. She's not going to turn me away.'

'What if she's moved?'

'She'd have let Grandpa know.'

Shaun looked doubtful and I felt a flash of anger.

'Look, Shaun. I've decided. You can help me or not. But I'm going.' I didn't want to ask myself whether part of the reason this plan seemed so right was because finally, after all these years of Mum being invisible, I'd found her and I wasn't going to miss this chance of seeing her.

'It's not like there aren't problems in Scotland too, you know,' he warned. 'Things haven't been easy for people up there either these last few years. And there's so many arriving up there now, it's not like they're all welcoming refugees with open arms.'

'I know that, Shaun,' I said. 'I'm not stupid. But it's safe. Safer than here. And my mum's there.'

'Okay,' he said at last. 'I know people who'll be able to get you across the border. And they'll be able to help you out if ... if there's any problem with your mum.'

'There won't be.'

He looked at me, making up his mind.

'Okay,' he said finally. 'I'll make contact with them now. If you're serious about this we need to do it now.'

It was real suddenly. Not an idea. Not a crazy plan. It was actually going to happen.

'Okay,' I said, trying not to let him see that I was scared. 'Thanks.'

'We'll leave first thing tomorrow. I'll take you north.'

'What about Grandpa?' I said.

'Don't worry. I'll find someone to stay with him till I'm back.' He looked at me. 'You'd better say goodbye to him now.'

'Now? Can't I come back tomorrow?'

'We can't risk you coming to the house again, Clem. Not the way things are in the village now. If someone saw you . . .'

My eyes filled with tears and I brushed them away angrily. 'You'll talk to him about me, won't you? Make sure he doesn't forget me? Make sure he knows I'll come back when it's safe?'

Shaun put his arm round me. 'I will,' he said. 'Every day. He won't forget you. I promise.'

Grandpa was sitting with a blanket over his knees listening to the radio, Merlin at his side, half-smiling. As I walked towards him, I told myself it didn't matter if he knew who I was today, in this moment. Merlin's tail thumped feebly against the sofa as I drew close. Grandpa looked up and saw me.

'Clem,' he said, as though I was the answer to a question. I tried to reply but the words wouldn't come.

Was Shaun right? Would Grandpa remember me when I'd gone? Would he look for me? Or would I become the child he told stories to, or the baby lying under the tree while Mum sang to me, or an unnamed ghost who flickered in and out of rooms and dreams? All of those, perhaps. But I suppose that's what we are when we're not with people, a collection of moments, real and imagined. Stories.

Ghosts.

I sat down next to him and took his hand. 'I've got to go away tomorrow, Grandpa.'

'Go away?' Grandpa said. 'You've only just arrived.'

I nodded. 'I'm going to miss you so much.'

'We'll miss you too, *cariad*,' he said. 'But we'll see you again soon. Where is it you're going?'

'To Scotland. Edinburgh, actually.' I tried to sound excited, like it was a holiday. An adventure. I wondered if he remembered Mum was there. In Grandpa's world, Mum might be at school or asleep in her cot or not have been born yet.

'Edinburgh!' he said, delighted. 'How lovely! Where I met your granny. Where I proposed to her.'

'I know.' I smiled, trying to imagine him young and handsome, sweeping Granny off her feet. Then I remembered the ring. I still had it round my neck on the string.

'I found Granny's engagement ring,' I told him, pulling it out from under my clothes. 'In a box. I put it round my neck to keep it safe.' I started to undo it to give to him.

'No, you keep it,' Grandpa said. 'Maybe it'll keep you safe.'

'Thank you, Grandpa.' I hugged him so he wouldn't see my tears.

I saw the house as Grandpa saw it, glimpsing Granny through the kitchen window, Mum looking out of the window of the bedroom that had been hers, out to the forest and beyond it to the wide world. I'd be one of the ghosts in the house once I was gone, a presence in other rooms, glimpsed through windows. I found the thought comforting and true. A bit of me would always be here while Grandpa was. And even after that, perhaps, in the forest, the trees would remember me – would remember me in hundreds of years, when the rest of us were long gone.

That night, after we'd packed our things and Billie was asleep, I sat outside the hut by the remains of the fire and hugged my knees. The fire was nearly out now. I felt so lonely suddenly it took my breath away. The embers blurred. I wanted to see Jonas. I wanted to tell him I was sorry that I'd made life difficult for him and that I wished we'd had longer together. That I wished I'd told him how I felt about him. Why hadn't I? Mischa would have. God, I missed Mischa. And I missed Dad too. I missed Grandpa, how he was before. I missed Claudia, even though she'd make me write a list or do a breathing exercise. She'd have made everything okay. I even missed Danny. The old Danny, before all this.

Tomorrow we would leave. I'd arranged to meet Shaun on a farm track on the road out of the village, the way we'd walked here all those months ago. It didn't seem real. Going to see my mum. All these years I've imagined finding her, speaking to her, meeting her. Now it was going to happen and I didn't know how I felt. Scared? Yes. Maybe more scared of that than of the dangers of the journey. Shaun would look after me and if he trusted the people who'd get me across the border, they'd look after me too. But I also felt something else. Curiosity? Yes. Excitement? I didn't know. I closed my eyes.

The forest noises were all around me. Even now they soothed me, although I was bone weary and my body ached and I still couldn't quite catch my breath, though I hadn't told Shaun or Jonas. I was part of the forest. It felt impossible that I'd leave. Perhaps I'd start growing roots. In Grandpa's myths and fairy tales, people were always turning into trees, or else trees turned out to be people in disguise. I liked the idea of being a tree, of having roots and leaves, of being so old that everything would seem small and fleeting and part of a cycle that you'd seen before and would see again.

I needed to sleep.

I stood up and threw the washing-up water on the smouldering remains of the fire so that it hissed and smoked. Inside, Billie was fast asleep on her back with her arms up on either side of her head like when she was a baby. She always looked younger when she was asleep. I lay down next to her.

'Sleep tight, B.'

The sound of the wind in the trees surrounded me for the last time, lulling me to sleep.

*

The girl looked all over the palace but nowhere could she find a single clock. It was as though time didn't exist within its walls.

Eventually, while she was wandering the corridors, she noticed a tapestry hanging on the wall that showed a robin with a key in its mouth. The girl pulled back the tapestry and behind it was a small wooden door. She pushed it open and found she was at the bottom of a steep spiral staircase. She climbed the stairs and came out at the top into a tiny room. Standing in the middle of the room was a golden clock whose hands had stopped at ten past three who knows how long ago.

The girl saw there was a small keyhole at the bottom of the clock's face, near the number six. She took the little key, fitted it into the hole and found it was a perfect match. She turned the key three times. As soon as the clock began to tick again it was as if a spell was broken.

The girl knew she must leave.

She hurried downstairs to find the king and queen to thank them for letting her stay. But when she reached the banqueting hall she found there was no feast, no music, no dancing. The palace was empty ... and had been for centuries. The great banqueting table was covered in dust, there were holes in the roof, the windows were broken. She saw a portrait on the wall she hadn't noticed before. When she brushed the cobwebs aside and peered at it closely she saw it was the king and queen, only much older, and she realized they must have died many years before.

The girl cried because she had loved them and they had been so kind to her. Then she saw something shining on the table in the place where the queen had sat. It was the only thing not covered in dust: a ring set with a green stone, the same one the queen was wearing in the portrait. The girl was as certain as she'd ever been that it had been left for her. She slipped it on her finger and knew immediately that the ring would take her where she had to go.

*

I woke so early it was barely light. Shaun had given me the alarm clock from the spare room. It wasn't broken after all. It just needed winding. Time was moving on. I didn't want it to.

I made a coffee and sat outside the hut one last time before waking Billie, cradling the mug in my hands.

I felt Granny's ring on its chain next to my heart.

It was time to go.

The sun was rising as we made our way through the trees, back the way we'd come that first night. The light cut through the almost bare branches of the trees. I felt empty and scared. My whole body ached. But still, the forest was beautiful, the light and shadow of it, its new morning scent.

When we got to the edge of the forest, we went back along the field we'd walked through to get here but then instead of heading for the road to the station we carried on further, across more fields, until we came to a farm track. My nerves were rising. What if Shaun wasn't there like we'd arranged?

But after we'd turned down the track, gone over the cattle grid and reached the farm gate, I saw the van waiting.

Shaun got out and glanced quickly both ways.

'Very punctual,' he said once he was sure no one else was around, smiling and opening the back of the van so that I couldn't be seen from the road. 'Right. I apologize it's not exactly luxury travel, but safety first and all that.'

There were assorted pieces of furniture and crates in the back of the van covered in tarpaulins and rough old blankets.

'I know,' he said apologetically, seeing my face. 'But I've put water in there. And biscuits. You'll be okay ... Keep the door open a bit,' he added, seeing my panic. 'Unless we get stopped, obviously.'

'And if we do? If they search the van properly?'

'They won't. I'm the world's most convincing liar.'

'True,' I said.

'Anyway, I've worked out the safest route. We'll avoid most of the checkpoints. We can even stop at a services once we're further north.'

He went off to check something in the cab and I helped Billie into a crate.

'It'll be fine, B.'

'I know,' she said. 'I'm not scared. It's just Luna. She doesn't like small spaces.'

'Me neither,' I said. 'But it's not for too long.'

I stood by the van, putting off getting in. I wanted to run back. I didn't want to leave.

'Okay,' Shaun said. 'We'd better get going.'

'Shaun,' I said, trying not to let my voice crack, 'you will tell Jonas, won't you . . . I mean, just make sure he knows I . . .'

I looked around one last time, breathed it in, the sweet morning air, the dazzle of the morning sky, the dark line of trees at the edge of the forest—

'Bloody hell!' said Shaun. 'Who the fuck's that?'

I spun round in alarm, ready to run or hide—

Then I realized he was smiling.

'Whatever that message was you were trying to give me for Jonas, you can tell him yourself.' He pointed down the track, laughing.

At Jonas.

Jonas, bright red in the face, on a pink child's bike with a basket on the front covered in plastic flowers, riding as fast as he could, his knees up practically to his ears.

'Jonas!' I ran towards him.

'Nice wheels, mate,' Shaun said.

Jonas climbed off the bike and let it fall to the ground, then bent over with his hands on his knees trying to catch his breath.

'My sister's old bike,' he said, panting. 'It was the only way I could get here. Shaun got a message to me but I didn't think I'd make it. My mum's got me under lock and key. I had to climb out of my bedroom window. This was the only available transport.'

I hugged him.

'I want to come with you,' he said. 'You know I would . . .'

He stopped, unable to speak. I put my hand up to his face.

'I know,' I said. 'I know you would.'

'I know my mum too well. She's not joking when she says she'd make sure you paid for it.'

'Not just me,' I said. 'Grandpa and Shaun too.'

'I'll look out for them,' he said. 'I'll do everything I can for them. And when this is all over we'll see each other again. I know we will.'

He kissed me, there in the middle of the farm track, the sharp wind carrying the smell of the cow dung all around us, and I wondered how it was possible to feel so happy and so sad and so guilty and so scared all at the same time. And then I stopped wondering because all I could think about was Jonas.

About bloody time, Mischa said.

Eventually Shaun said awkwardly, 'Sorry to interrupt, you two, but we really need to go.'

I held on to Jonas. I didn't want to let him go.

'You're shivering.' Jonas took off his scarf and put it round my neck, the warmth of him against my skin.

I wished I'd listened to Mischa and we'd got to this bit sooner. All those weeks we'd had together and I hadn't told him how I felt, hadn't even admitted it to myself. And now, whatever he said, neither of us actually knew whether we'd see each other again.

But maybe, a voice in my head said, that's because you deserve to be on your own.

We only got stopped at one checkpoint, near Birmingham.

We curled ourselves up in our crate, the blanket pulled over us, barely breathing in the dark, listening to muffled voices.

233

'It's okay, B,' I whispered. 'It'll be fine.'

'How do you know?' she said.

My fingernails dug into my palms.

'I just do,' and I knew she was giving me a scathing look in the dark.

Please don't let them check the back of the van. Please don't let me have a coughing fit. Please, please let it all be okay.

I strained to hear what Shaun was saying. They were checking his papers and it was taking for ever. Shaun being Shaun was trying to engage them in conversation but it sounded like they weren't having any of it.

Then a voice said, 'Hang on, don't I know you?'

There was a pause.

'I don't think so,' Shaun said at last.

'Didn't you used to be a boxer?'

I breathed out.

'I did, as it goes,' Shaun said, and I could tell from his voice it was going to be okay.

It turned out, Shaun was slightly famous. I mean, not really, but for a while he had been a name in the boxing world. So he got them talking about that and they waved us through. He even gave them an autograph.

'Bloody hell,' he called back once we were safe. 'Did you hear that? You're being chauffeur-driven by an A-list celeb.'

He thought it was hilarious.

I thought it was hilarious.

It was strange to find I could still laugh, even then.

*

I wish Shaun was here now.

And Jonas.

I put Jonas's scarf around my neck, lean my face into it, as if I can breathe him in.

I will see them again. I will.

*

'Sorry,' Shaun called back. 'I've gone wrong somewhere. Bloody satnav. Just need to check the map. Might as well stretch your legs anyway while we're here.'

I clambered out of the stale dark of the van, blinking into the late-afternoon light. Billie had fallen asleep and was curled up under a blanket. The air was colder than I expected, fresh and sweet. We were parked in a layby. Away off in front of us were mountains, dark against the pink glow of the sky where the sun was setting, the higher peaks pale with snow.

'Wow.'

'Not a bad view, eh?'

Shaun poured a cup of steaming tea from a flask and handed it to me. We both stood silent for a while, cupping our hands round the warmth of our tin cups. I took a sip of the tea, dark and sweet and comforting. I was grateful for it. My throat was sore and my head was aching.

Shaun went off to 'answer a call of nature' and try and get a phone signal and I stood looking at the mountains and thinking about how Grandpa had told me once that even the very top of the tallest peak was once under the sea. There was a sound close by and when I looked round Billie was next to me, rumpled and still half-asleep.

'Hey, B.'

'I'm thirsty,' she said. I got out a bottle of water from the van and handed it to her. As she drank, she began to wake up properly.

'Wow,' she said. 'Mountains.'

'I know. Pretty cool, huh?'

'Look at the kestrel!' she said. I followed to where she was pointing and saw it: some kind of bird of prey hanging in the air before diving down out of sight to catch some unsuspecting creature hiding in the grass. I shivered.

'I'm cold,' Billie said. 'I'm getting back in the van.'

Shaun came back. 'Not far now,' he said.

I just stood and looked out at the mountains.

'I wish . . .'

I stopped.

What I wished was that Grandpa was here to see this. The mountains were so big, so old. I felt tiny, like a little kid. I wanted Grandpa to tell me stories about the giants who lived in the mountains and the sacred stones that used to be people and were cursed by witches or gods. I just wanted him to be here. I wanted him to be how he used to be. I wanted to be a little kid again. I couldn't say any of it.

And I wished that Dad could be here too, and Claudia. I imagined us here on holiday, me and Billie moaning about being made to go on long walks, Dad ordering pints and pies in pubs where the walls all leaned at gravity-defying angles, Claudia finding towns with second-hand bookshops and cheesemongers, just happy that we were all together.

I felt so far away from Dad now. We were in different worlds. What would he say to me about all of this, my plan to go to Scotland, to go to Mum? I hadn't let myself think about it properly till now, probably because I worried he would say it was a stupid idea. Every mile we'd driven had taken me further away from him.

I wished it hurt less as time passed.

'I know,' Shaun said and he put his arm round me and I knew he did know.

After about another half-hour we stopped again. This time when the doors of the van opened and we climbed out I saw we were outside a big white pebble-dashed house. There were no other houses anywhere, just farm buildings, a stone barn, some wooden sheds.

'You wait here.' Shaun went up to the front door, which was so big and heavy it looked as though it had been built to keep out mountain trolls. Billie ran off to chat to the sheep who were nibbling at the grass nearby.

A man, maybe in his thirties, with dark hair and a beard opened the door, but only far enough to see who it was, ready to get rid of them and close it again as quickly as possible, like you do when it's somebody trying to sell you something or preach to you about being saved.

Shaun spoke to him, gesturing towards us and the van and

the bearded guy looked over, said something and closed the door. Was something wrong? Shaun didn't turn round, so I couldn't see the expression on his face. Then the bearded guy opened the door again and there was someone else with him, a black woman with grey hair. They talked some more and then Shaun beckoned me over.

'This is Clem,' he said. 'Clem, meet Cass. She's going to get you to Scotland. You'll stay here tonight and then they'll drive you over the border.'

'Hi,' I said. 'Thanks.'

Cass smiled. 'Come on in. Have something to eat, you must be hungry. And tired.'

'I'll bring your bag up, then I'll head off,' Shaun said. 'If I step on it, I might be back by midnight.'

He must have seen a look of panic cross my face. I'd hoped Shaun might stay overnight but I also wanted him to get back to Grandpa.

'Hey,' he said. 'Don't look like that. These are good people. They'll get you over the border. And if there's any problem when you get there, they'll help you.'

'I know,' I said.

Another goodbye. He wrapped me in a massive bear hug.

'Take care you,' he said. 'Don't do anything I wouldn't do, eh?'

'Look after Grandpa,' I said.

'You know I will,' he said. 'Hey, come on. Don't be upset. We'll meet again. I know these things.'

I just felt small and scared and bone weary. My head ached and my throat scratched.

But then we were inside and there were people, cigarette smoke, hot tea in chipped mugs. I sat at the kitchen table with an undrunk cup of tea and tried not to look awkward or shy or show that I was so tired that everything around me seemed to be happening at a slight delay. The relief of being there didn't take away the fact that being around strangers felt weird, unnerving. My fingers made imaginary paper cranes under the table, sent them fluttering invisibly around us. Billie wandered off to the other side of the room to watch cartoons with a younger kid and pet a ginger cat that was stretched rug-like next to a radiator.

The woman called Cass seemed to be in charge.

'You'll stay here tonight,' she said. 'And then first thing tomorrow we'll leave. There'll be four others travelling too. You'll go in the back of the van. There are packing crates for you to hide in till we get through the checkpoints.'

'Thanks,' I said woozily.

'You look tired,' she said. 'You should rest. It'll be another early start tomorrow.'

She led us up creaking stairs to an attic room and left us. Pushed against the walls of the room, dimly lit by a bare bulb, were stacks of dusty books, tatty framed posters of plays that had taken place decades before, cobwebbed cardboard boxes, a chair with a wickerwork seat, gaping and split. In a square of space between the low sloping roof and the curtain, just big enough to lie down in, were blankets, sleeping bags, a couple of ancient, flattened pillows.

I spread out the blankets as best I could. I ached with

cold. In the shadowy space, Billie looked ready to fall asleep on her feet.

'This'll be okay for us, won't it, B? Quite comfy really.' She lay down to try it out.

'It smells weird,' she said. 'Kind of like . . .'

But it was probably best not to think about what it kind of smelt like.

'Do you think there are mice?' she asked.

I shuddered.

'I like mice,' Billie said sleepily.

'Well, at least we've got Luna.' I put the small, fluffy toy owl next to the pillow. 'She'll protect us.'

'Luna doesn't eat mice. She's a vegetarian owl.'

'Course she is. I'll just have to kill them with my bare hands then.'

'Clem!' she said. 'You wouldn't!'

'You know I wouldn't. I'd be on top of that massive box, screaming. Except it's probably full of spiders.'

Billie smiled, eyelids heavy.

'You're silly.'

'That's me.'

I lay down next to her, my limbs so heavy I thought I'd never get up again.

I rested my head back on the pillow and stared up through the dark to the skylight in the ceiling. No stars.

'But that's wrong,' Billie said. 'There are stars. You just can't see them.'

*

I woke to the sound of knocking on my door.

Had I overslept? Was I late for school?

'Clem? It's Cass. Can I come in?'

'Yes,' I tried to say, but my throat was so sore and swollen I could hardly speak. Cass's face swam in front of me. It was still dark and I didn't seem to be able to focus my eyes.

'Clem,' she said. 'Are you okay? You look sick.'

I felt Billie stir at my side.

'I'm fine,' I lied.

'Change of plan,' Cass said. I realized through the haze of sleep that she was speaking urgently. 'We need to leave now.'

'What?'

I stood up, although my limbs seemed heavier than usual and my head spun.

'Some of our people got arrested trying to cross last night,' she said. 'We think we may be compromised. We need to get out of here.'

'But where to?'

'The coast,' she said. 'You'll go by sea. It's quick.'

But is it safe? I wanted to ask but realized that would be stupid. Nothing was safe.

*

'And that was what happened?' Polly says. 'You came by boat?'

I nod. I don't want to remember it.

I close my eyes.

*

241

I see glimpses.

Rough hands, shoving us aboard.

Shouting.

A woman crying: she wants to get on this boat with her partner but they tell her no. No more room. Get in the other boat. She won't go.

'Leave her,' one of the men says. 'It's her choice.'

Then one of them takes my rucksack and someone else's and throws them back onto the beach and then pulls the woman onto the boat.

'No!' All the things Dad carefully packed for us. Our paper birds. My notebook. All gone. I try to get up, to jump out, but we're too tightly packed and my head spins so much I nearly black out and they can't hear me. 'I need that!'

'They'll put them on the other boat,' a woman next to me says, but I know she just wants me not to make a fuss.

'Make sure your life jacket is done up properly,' I croak to Billie, my throat stinging and raw. Mine is too big but I pull the strap as tight as I can.

We're crammed in together, too many for this small boat, people packed all around me, pressing too intimately.

'Think of being on the Tube,' I say to Billie. 'It's kind of like that really.'

I see under my closed, hot eyelids a crammed carriage, feel the heat, my slipping fingers clinging to a rail already damp with someone else's sweat. Sometimes, clattering through the dusty tunnels, you'd remember, just for a second, the weight above you of all the dark, underground, unseen things, the sewers and wires and pipes and bones and the foundations of buildings, and you wouldn't want to think of how it was all pressing down on you and in around you. But even that seemed a million times safer than this journey, this floating, untethered but unable to move, into the night, being held precariously above all those other, unseen things in the dark of the sea.

Everyone's quiet, edgy. The woman next to me looks like she's praying, her lips moving silently. Billie holds my hand.

I close my eyes. My eyelids feel hot and sore.

The boat vibrates loudly.

We start to move.

Now it's cold. It's dark. The sky is dark, no stars. The sea is dark.

'We should sleep,' I say to Billie, knowing it's impossible.

The smell – of other people, the strange stale smell of the boat, the salt wind, seaweed, a petrol aroma – catches in my throat. The thrum of the engine vibrates through me. My head throbs with it.

Panic rises, and nausea. My eyes won't focus so I squeeze them shut tight.

'Where's Grandpa?' I say to Billie.

'He's over there,' she says.

Now we're floating in blackness, the engines silent, the crash of the waves all around.

'What's happening?' I say, panic rising. 'What's happening?'

'*Shhhh*,' the man next to us hisses. '*Shut up.*'

'It's the patrols,' a woman says. 'They've cut the engines so they don't hear us. We're drifting.'

We're drifting.

Impossible and possible are not what I thought.

I sleep, or slip in and out of something like sleep, at first in blank, black scraps then in disjointed, unnerving visions like old movie reels.

Grandpa says, 'You should have put coins in your mouth, to pay the boatman.'

Of course. How could I have forgotten that this was the way to get safely across the river to the underworld? There is a coin in my mouth, growing bigger and bigger so that I can't speak—

I wake up properly, briefly. It's bitterly cold and the waves are tipping the boat sickeningly. The men are swearing. The other people are silent. They hold each other, except for the people with no one to hold. Some are vomiting, over the side, on each other. The stink of it is unbearable. I sink back into black.

'There! Patrol boats! *Shit*—'

The men are shouting, panicking.

Through the blur of night, I see searchlights.

You're supposed to go towards the light, get out of the dark, I think.

But this light is dangerous.

There is screaming, scrambling, nails—

The sea becomes the sky—

A boot in my face—

The shock of the icy sea knocks the air from my lungs and then I'm under the water, my shout bubbling to nothing and my breath turning to thick liquid salt, stopping up my throat and nose—

Then air for a split second gulped in and then – gone thrashing kicking trying to grab something but there's nothing and then up to the surface but there's something there above me pushing me down down—

Breath held, held, growing inside me till it will burst through my ribs—

I'm a good swimmer. Yes. Did my lifesaving with Danny way back, rubber brick, pyjamas—

Trying to swim up but I don't even know which way is up because everything's dark like in hospital, after, those murky underwater days, weeks—

But that was a dream. Wasn't it? Or is this the dream and I just have to let go ...

Billie!

Where is she?

I thrash wildly, try to call out to her – but pain bursts through my chest every part of it—

And now something grips me, something strong, a selkie, a shark, a sea monster, and I'm being pulled up or maybe pulled down, down, into the deep. And the sea is in my nose and my throat and my lungs and my belly, it is filling me with salt and cold and dark until it is part of me until I'm part of it ...

Until I am the sea.

And Billie's voice in the dark says

Don't

let

go—

*

Coughing, gagging, salt water and bile spilled from me, my breath came in agonizing gasps.

Eyelids fluttered open. I half-saw the blurred faces of strangers.

I fainted at school once. It was sports day and it was the hottest day.

'Lucky,' Mischa said later. 'I've always wanted to faint. It's so dramatic. *And* you didn't have to run in front of everyone.'

It didn't feel lucky. It felt confusing more than anything. I'd been standing, head throbbing, feeling a bit out of it, and then I'd woken up lying in the shade of the stand, with the PE teacher staring into my face and clamping a cold compress to my head, Mischa next to her looking anxious.

This memory didn't belong here.

They were speaking but I couldn't hear.

Should I know who they were?

Where was I?

Where was Billie?

My throat closed. I couldn't speak. Everything spun. Shivering.

Cold and dark.

Cold.

Dark.

Deeper, deeper, back into the welcoming dark.

*

After many weeks and months, the ring with the green stone led the girl to a village by the sea.

'I need to find the island,' she said, 'where the blood-red flower grows. Can you tell me how to get there?'

'The island only appears at the full moon,' the villagers told her. 'When it does, you can only get there if the boatman will take you.'

'How do I find the boatman?' she asked.

'He'll find you,' they told her.

So, on the night of the full moon, the girl waited on the shore, looking out to sea. She spied a black dot in the distance that she thought might be a great sea bird or a seal. But as it got closer she saw it was a small boat being rowed through the waves by a man in a blindfold.

'Will you take me to the island where the blood-red flower grows?' the girl called.

The boatman said, 'I will take you, but in return you must give me the thing most precious to you.'

'I only have this ring,' she said. She didn't want to give it to him but she knew she must if it meant she would see her sister again.

'That is not the thing most precious to you,' the boatman replied.

The girl despaired as she had nothing else to give him.

Then she remembered the blue feather. She took it from her pocket and handed it to the boatman.

'My sister is most precious to me,' she said. 'And this is part of her.'

The boatman nodded and helped her into the boat and they set out across the stormy sea to the island.

*

I woke in a light room with thick whitewashed stone walls and a small window. I was in a soft bed under a thick eiderdown. On the bedside table next to me was a jug of water and a glass, a small vase with tiny purple flowers in it. On the wall opposite was a fireplace and on the mantelpiece was a pale blue candle, several stones with holes in them; above it, the skull of an animal, a sheep maybe. The room smelt of fresh herbs.

Billie sat on the end of my bed.

'Clem!' she said. 'You're awake again.'

I tried to speak but found I couldn't.

Billie smiled. 'It's nice here.' Then she ran off and after a while I heard her outside, singing.

I tried to sit up to pour myself some water but it took a while. I was weak and everything hurt. Eventually I managed it but felt out of breath and flopped back down on the pillow once I'd had a few gulps.

'Hello?' I called. There was silence. But it felt like a calm silence rather than a threatening one.

You know that doesn't make sense, right? Mischa said. *You*

*might have been abducted or something. Or maybe you're
dead and this is all like heaven or purgatory or whatever.*

Her voice sounded far away.

'It doesn't make sense, but it's true,' I said. I felt safe.

Mmmkaay, Mischa said. *If you say so.*

I realized suddenly that I really needed to find the bathroom.
My head spun and throbbed as I stood up, my feet cold on the
flagged floor. I swayed for a moment before my legs gave way
and I found myself sitting on the bed again.

A woman who could have been any age between fifty and
eighty came in. She had long white hair and very blue eyes
and I knew at once that she would make me better. The room
felt different with her in it, calmer. She had a kind of strength
about her that I couldn't describe or make sense of. I felt like
she knew me.

'Oh no you don't,' she said, grasping my arm as I wobbled.
'You're not strong enough to walk on your own.'

She told me her name was Bridie as she helped me to the
bathroom, thankfully just next door, and I convinced her that I'd
be fine to go in on my own, though she wouldn't let me lock the
door in case I fell. I didn't, but I was glad to know she was there.
Everything felt hazy and my body didn't seem to belong to me.

Once she'd helped me slowly back into bed, she left me
again and came back with warm milk and honey.

'Drink this and then rest,' she said. 'Even just those few
steps will have tired you out.'

I lay back on the pillows. She was right. I could hardly
stay awake.

249

Billie, I thought as my eyes closed.

'Don't you worry about a thing.' Bridie's voice, calm and soothing. 'Just sleep.'

For a few more days I slept and woke in the sunlit room. The pale blue candle was always burning and the scent of herbs was always in the air. Sometimes Billie was there, drawing or writing or folding birds. Sometimes she'd tell me a story or say, 'The goats are so cute, with their weirdy eyes and little stubby horns,' or 'You've *got* to see the chickens!' I told her I could hear the goats bleating sometimes if the wind blew the right way, and the rooster crowing in the mornings, but I'd thought maybe I was dreaming them because I was asleep most of the time.

'You look a bit better now,' she said. 'A bit more like Clem.'

'Who did I look like before?'

'A ghost,' she said.

At some point after that, I woke up and for the first time felt ravenously hungry. A few minutes later Bridie appeared with a bowl of something yellow that I wasn't sure about.

'Baked egg custard,' she said. 'For a day or two. Till you're stronger.'

I scooped up a cautious half-spoonful. It was the most delicious thing I'd ever eaten.

Whenever I woke up she brought food: egg custards, bowls of creamy mashed potato, porridge with brown sugar, eggs with dark orange yolks, warm crusty bread with yellow butter. It was all like the taste version of seeing things in colour for the first time. I couldn't decide whether it was because I was so hungry and had been hungry for a long time, or because I'd nearly died, or because the food just actually tasted better than any food I'd ever eaten.

Or because she's a witch, Mischa said.

'I think she is,' I said. 'The good kind though, not one who's fattening me up to eat me.'

She's a real witch, Clem, not a storybook one. Mischa knew what she was talking about when it came to witchcraft. *Also, she could be microdosing you with mushrooms? Just saying. It would explain a lot.* I honestly didn't care whether it was psychedelics or witchcraft or organic cooking that was making me feel better.

Soon I felt strong enough to get up and walk beyond the bathroom for the first time. My room was on the ground floor and at the end of a corridor that opened out into a sitting room with stairs leading up to the next floor. A door led through to the kitchen, where Bridie was sitting at a scrubbed wooden table peeling potatoes.

'Hello,' she said, as if she'd been expecting me.

I sat down at the table.

'How long have I been here?'

'A while now,' she said.

'Like days? Or weeks?'

She nodded.

'What happened?' I asked. 'I mean, I can't really remember.'

She told me there had been two boats. The boat I was on capsized. Seven people had drowned.

'And you've been looking after me? What happened to the others?'

'They're being looked after too, those that needed it.'

'Here?'

'Not here, no. I knew I could get you better, here on the island. It's taken time though and it'll take a lot more.'

I shook my head. 'Thank you. I really appreciate everything you've done. But we can't stay much longer. We've got to get to Edinburgh.'

She shook her head. 'You were ill before you were in the sea, weren't you?'

I nodded.

She put her hand to my forehead. It felt cool and soothing.

'Sit there,' she said.

She went to a cupboard and took out various jars and tins and ground something up with a pestle and mortar.

'Did the other boat land here safely?' I asked.

'Yes.'

'I think my rucksack might have been on it,' I said. 'I mean, I don't know. It might have been left behind or just carried out to sea. But it had all my stuff in.'

'It will be at the church then,' Bridie said. 'Everything that gets washed up, it ends up there. In case anyone ever comes looking for it.'

She rested her hand gently over my heart. 'You are sick, in there,' she said. 'Until that's healed, you won't be properly well.' She turned to stir the saucepan she was heating over the range and I was glad because I could feel that tears were going to spill from my eyes and I was too weak to stop them.

'All that joy and energy,' Bridie said. 'A strong spirit. You mustn't worry about her, you know.' She turned and poured the liquid from the pan through a strainer and into a heavy mug.

'Easy to say, I know,' she said. 'And impossible when you love her so much. Anyway, drink this,' she said.

I carried the hot mug back to my room and sank back into bed, the tears still sliding down my cheeks. My breathing was still laboured and I ached all over. I drank the tea, which tasted spicy and sweet and slept.

Late the next day, I woke up and found my rucksack leaning against the end of my bed. It felt miraculous, as if Bridie had magically brought it into being. But I knew it wasn't that. It was just chance. Ugly, random, indifferent chance. My rucksack was here, smelling faintly of salt water but otherwise unmarked. The woman who had insisted on taking a place on our boat might now be under the sea.

When I went outside at last, I realized it was winter. The wind whipped my hair and my eyes stung. The air tasted of salt and rain that would soon fall. I bent into the wind and walked away from the whitewashed cottage, aiming for a tall, grey standing stone at the other end of the island.

It looks kind of like a person, don't you think? Mischa said. *Do you reckon Bridie turned some guy into stone back in the day?*

I was getting stronger. Billie walked next to me, encouraging me. 'You can do it, Clem. Hold my hand. Don't let go.' Then

253

she'd spot something interesting and skip off to take a closer look or run ahead with her arms outstretched as if she was about to fly away.

The first time I tried to reach the standing stone I only got about a quarter of the way. I wanted to cry. I couldn't believe I was still so weak. But I wasn't going to give up.

The second and third times I made it halfway. The fourth time, I really thought I was going to do it, but my legs gave way and Bridie had to come and help me back.

The fifth day, the sun was shining. The sound of the sea all around seemed to carry me along. I made it to the standing stone. It was lined and pitted, mottled with patches of moss. I leaned against it, breathing deeply, lungs aching, and looked out to sea, miles and miles of it, white-tipped, fierce. I felt dizzy and light as a feather, blown along on the wind. I turned and started the walk back towards the cottage. Each breath was painful and my legs felt heavy with the effort of the steps but I kept my eye on Bridie, who stood at the door watching me. When I reached her, I leaned against the wall and was too tired to speak.

But my mind was made up. We would leave tomorrow.

On the morning we left Bridie gave me one of her stones with a hole in it.

'A hag stone,' she said. 'Loop it through that cord round your neck with your ring. That way I'll know you're safe.'

I did as she said.

'Go now or you'll miss the tide.'

She walked with us down to the causeway that joined the island to the mainland for part of the day when the tide was low. A paid-for taxi would be waiting for us on the other side, she said.

'Thank you, Bridie,' I said. 'For everything.'

I hugged her and breathed in the calm of her that was almost like a scent. Then I walked across the causeway, Billie just in front of me, the sea all around us, not wanting to look back in case Bridie and the island weren't there any more.

*

As the girl stepped ashore, she found the plant growing just as she had seen it in her dream, but it was not yet flowering. She knew it would not flower until midwinter, which was not for three nights. She waited in the cold.

On the first night the plant grew a bud.

On the second night the bud grew fuller and fatter.

On the third night it began to snow. The girl pulled her cloak around her, frozen to her bones, but she would not fall asleep.

As she heard the bells from across the sea ring out for midnight, the bud opened out into a beautiful flower. But it was not blood red, it was as white as the snow that fell around it. The girl wept. This was not what her dream had told her. This flower would not save her sister. Then she had a thought. With a small knife she carried in her pocket she cut her finger and let the blood fall onto the snow under which grew the roots of the plant.

One, two, three drops of blood in the white snow.
And as the blood fell so the flower bloomed blood red.

*

The man waiting for us in a silver Ford Galaxy with a sticker in the window saying MY OTHER CAR'S A PORSCHE made it clear he didn't want to be giving us a lift at all. He didn't introduce himself just said, 'In the back. And I've just had it valeted so you'd better not get mud on it.' He was sullen and silent for the whole journey, listening to loud music with a tinny beat that felt as though it was piercing my head. Billie sat next to me in the back seat and sang little made-up songs to Luna, who sat on her lap. It soothed me. I dozed.

'Okay, out,' the man said. 'You can get the tram from here.'

I started awake and looked around. I had no idea where we were, but we clearly weren't going to be taken any further, so I climbed out and hauled the rucksack after me. The man drove off almost before I'd slammed the door shut.

My brain was slow and it took a while to work out which tram to get. Once we were on, it was so loud and full of people I felt overwhelmed. It was so long since I'd been in a city, a normal city where people were living normal lives. Here were Christmas shoppers and tourists and people on their lunch breaks, noise, tourists, the sound of traffic and music blaring from cars and shops, the smell of chips and people's perfume and mulled wine. It was too much. I'd been somewhere where time passed differently. Stepping back into the real world I felt I might crumble into dust, like in Grandpa's stories.

Grandpa had told me Mum's address was near the centre of the city. I didn't know if I'd recognize it but I could hardly miss the castle on the hill from Mum's postcard. We got off the tram, found a map of the city centre by the tram stop and began to walk.

My head throbbed and my legs shook as we turned into the street that had been written on the postcard. I paused to catch my breath, then we began walking again.

The road was wide and the buildings several storeys high, with tall windows and wide flights of steps leading up to front doors and down to basements. Some of the doors we passed looked grand, paint fresh and brass shining, others were peeling and tarnished. I wondered which kind Mum's would be.

We must be getting close now. I counted down the numbers till we reached the one written on the postcard. Number fifty-two.

'This is it,' I said.

The blood beat in my head. The air seemed to flicker a little as though invisible things moved in it. The door at number fifty-two was painted black, the woodwork cracked.

Had I remembered the address right?

Yes, I knew I had. I had stared at that address, pressed it into my memory. The place where Mum was, where I would see her again.

I looked at the row of buzzers, searching for the handwriting I'd hoped as a kid I'd see on the envelopes of birthday and Christmas cards, the writing on the postcard. But by the buzzer for flat B was nothing, the space left blank. Everything was swimming a bit, in and out. My palms were prickling and sweaty but the rest of me felt ice cold.

What did I have to lose?

I tried to remember the little speech I'd been muttering to myself.

Oh, hello, I'm sorry—

No. No apology.

Oh, hello, I know this will be a surprise but—

Oh, hi. I hope this isn't too much of a shock but—

Oh, shut up, Clem. It doesn't matter how you say it. She either loves you or she doesn't. There's no magic order of words you can use that's going to change that. Still, though. I felt sick.

'Go on,' Billie said.

Go on, Dad and Grandpa and Shaun said. I felt Granny's emerald ring under my jumper, its millions of years pressed against my skin. If I put it under my tongue, I could see the future.

Mischa rolled her eyes.

Okay, yes, alternatively I could just push the damn buzzer and get to the future.

I pressed the square metal button, the vibration of it loud and grating, then stood, shivering, wondering, waiting. Waiting to find out whether I'd recognize her voice, whether she'd recognize mine, whether she would see how much I looked like she used to.

Waiting to find out whether she loved me.

'You're shivering,' Billie said. She took my hand. I felt faint. What if she was out?

I hadn't thought of that, stupidly. I'd thought she'd just be there, waiting for me. We'd have to sit and wait. But as I was about to press the buzzer again a voice came through on the intercom.

'Hello?'

The voice was a bit distorted but I thought it was familiar, maybe. It sounded bright and friendly, not like people's voices usually do if they're not expecting you, where you know they're just waiting for a reason to tell you to get lost. Maybe she was waiting for someone else and would be disappointed it was me.

'Hello?' I said. 'Is that . . .'

I couldn't say it. I couldn't say, *Is that you, Mum?*

I tried to remember the speech. *I know this will come as a shock but—*

But what?

In the end I just said, 'It's Clem.'

There was a silence. Billie looked up at me and squeezed my hand.

'Oh, and Billie. My sister.'

'Clem?' the voice said. It had changed. It was soft, almost a whisper. 'Clem, is it you?'

'It's me,' I said, glad it was just an intercom and not a videophone so she couldn't see what a state I looked. I wondered how she pictured me. Not the mess of greasy hair and stale clothes, the shivering, clammy-skinned wreck on her doorstep, I guessed.

'My God,' she said, her voice low. 'My God. Wait there, Clem. Wait there. I'm coming down.'

The minute or so she took seemed like a lifetime, like my lifetime since she'd left, waiting to see her. My heart – that had beat inside her before I ever saw the world, before anyone but her knew I existed – bumped against my ribs. I felt I was swaying, or maybe the world was.

The door opened.

Behind it was a woman, older but not so changed that I didn't recognize her, her face a picture of wonder as she took us in.

'Clem,' she said, in the way people do when they've known you for ever. 'Just look at you.'

She stepped forward and held out her hands to me. I thought for a second she was going to shake mine but she took hold of my arm and pulled me to her and held my face in her hands as she studied every freckle and eyelash, and tears spilled down her cheeks as she threw her arms around me—

*

Polly watches me.

'That's not what happened though, is it?'

I look around at the office, the grey-streaked windows, the row of spindly cactuses on the sill, the piles of leaflets about assorted mental health issues on Polly's desk.

'I guess not,' I say, refusing to meet her gaze. 'Or I wouldn't be here. I remember imagining it though. Before.

'I dream it sometimes, I think. Sometimes my dreams feel

more real than this. Do you ever have that? Where you can't remember if something's a dream or real. Some people think your dreams are your real life and everything else is a dream. And how would you know?'

I'm talking and talking, to avoid saying anything.

'Anyway,' I say. 'You asked for my story. That is my story. Stories don't have to be true.'

Polly doesn't speak, she just lets me ramble until I run out of words.

Then there's silence. Polly waits.

I sigh. 'You know what really happened.'

'Yes,' she says, gently. 'But not in your words. Tell me.'

*

I pressed the square metal button, the vibration of it loud and grating, then stood, shivering, wondering, waiting. Waiting to find out whether I'd recognize her voice, whether she'd recognize mine, whether she would see how much I looked like she used to.

Waiting to find out whether she loved me.

How long had passed? Time often distorted itself now, and my fever had begun to creep back around the edges of my consciousness. Had it been seconds or minutes since I pressed the buzzer?

Not hours, or it would be dark by now. I pressed it again.

Nothing.

I felt faint. I'd thought she'd just be there, waiting for me. But why would she be?

I'd have to sit and wait till she came home. Which was worse, much worse. Telling her over the intercom would have meant I wouldn't have to see her face as she realized who I was. Accosting her on her doorstep, my hair lank and greasy, my clothes stale and grimy ... I shrank into myself at the thought of it.

But what else could I do?

It was dark now. Eventually someone, a longish-haired man with round glasses and expensive trainers, walked up the steps to number fifty-two.

'Excuse me.'

He looked round at me, surprised and wary, ready to tell me he didn't have any change. 'Do you know the woman who lives in flat B?'

He frowned.

'Flat B? It's empty.'

I stared at him. The world shifted around us.

'What?'

'Yeah. She moved out a few months ago. Maybe more actually.'

I tried to take in what he was saying.

'Do you know where she's gone?'

He shook his head. 'Sorry. Only found out she'd gone when the landlord came round asking questions. Think she owed rent. He reckoned she'd gone abroad. He wasn't best pleased.'

I had no idea what to say or do.

'I really need to find her,' I said eventually.

'Sorry, I can't help,' the round-glasses guy said.

I thanked him anyway.

'Are you okay?' he said. 'You look a bit pale.'

'We'll be fine. But we'd better get going before it gets dark.'

He looked uncertain.

'Are you sure you're all right? You seem ...'

I nodded, my head fuzzy and throbbing. 'No. Fine. Really.'

'Okay, well, if you say so,' he said. 'I'm sure you'll track her down eventually. Do you know her well?'

'No,' I said. 'I don't know her at all.'

The road seemed longer going back. It seemed to stretch ahead and the buildings crowded in on either side. My skin burned despite the knife-edge wind that cut through my thin coat and jumper. The rucksack felt as though it was full of rocks, dragging me down with every step.

'I don't know what to do,' I said. 'What should I do?'

Billie said nothing. Her face seemed to hover nearer and then fade as my head throbbed. I had to close my eyes.

'Sorry,' I said. 'Sorry, B. It'll be okay. I just need to ...'

I needed to lie down. I felt like lying down there in the road.

Find a pharmacy, Clem. You need paracetamol. Water. Eat something if you can.

Who had said that? I looked around. Was it Mum? No. It was Claudia's voice.

'Okay,' I said. 'Thanks, Claudia. Come on, B.'

I pushed my leaden legs on up the road, back towards the city centre, the great castle looming over it all like on Mum's postcard. There was a Christmas market ahead, thronging with people. Tinny carols came from loudspeakers, Christmas lights hung above us, twinkling, blurring, hurting my eyes.

The ground felt spongy, pulling my feet down, like walking in mud wearing wellies. There was a Superdrug a little further on. When I got inside, the overhead lights hurt my eyes. I stood in front of a display of lipsticks, transfixed. The tubes glittered like jewels. Mischa swatched colours on our hands. But no, that wasn't right. Mischa wasn't here. Where was she? She went to get fries. I tried not to panic but I wanted to call out for her.

Cooler colours for you, babe, Mischa said. *But not too blue or you'll look like a corpse, and not in a hot vampire way. No offence. Plummy tones, that's what you want . . . Here, Damson Jam – that's more you.*

'I thought you'd gone, Misch,' I said.

You don't get rid of me that easy.

I picked up the purple shiny tube and drew a line on my hand. It looked like a cut.

'What do you think, B?'

'Are you okay?' A bleach-blonde shop assistant was looking at me doubtfully.

'Yes thanks, we're fine,' I mumbled. 'I am going to pay for it, don't worry.'

I bought the lipstick along with a box of paracetamol. It was only when I got back outside I realized I'd forgotten to get any water. I sat on a bench and forced myself to swallow the tablets down, grimacing at the taste and the pain of my swollen throat.

It'll be tonsillitis, Clem. You know you always get it when you're run down. You probably need antibiotics.

264

'It's just a sore throat, Claudia. Don't fuss,' I said.

Billie was looking at me, her eyes big.

'It's okay,' I said. 'I just need to think. I just need to . . .'

What did I need to do? I didn't know. I had no phone. I had barely any money. I couldn't go to the police. Without Mum I had no reason to be here. Would they send us to a camp, a detention centre? Would they send us back to London?

Perhaps we were safer just staying here. If my head would just stop hurting, if everyone's voices could just stop so I could work out what was real and what wasn't—

I closed my eyes, waiting for the pain to ease. My eyelids felt tight and hot.

Billie was singing quietly.

Away in a manger, no crib for a bed.

I felt her head resting against my arm.

I think I fell asleep.

When I woke up the light had changed. It wasn't dark yet but it would be soon. The lights seemed brighter, the castle and the hills darker. I was numb with cold but somehow still hurt everywhere. I stood up like an old person, every bone and muscle stiff and painful.

'We need to walk . . . I know, I know, but it's too cold to sit here.'

The city moved and blurred around me as I walked through it. The spiced smell of mulled wine, the noise of the shoppers talking and laughing, the screams of people flying above us on a fairground ride, the lights – it all felt too loud but faraway, all spinning, dissolving, unreal.

The castle had moved now. It wasn't behind me any more

but almost in front of me, its points reaching up into the orange-pink sky. We were walking on cobbles, there were people sitting outside bars and restaurants and I was sure suddenly that one of these places, just up the hill, was Granny and Grandpa's café, the one where they'd met, the one where he'd given her the emerald ring. I pulled the chain out from under my jumper and held the ring in my hand.

'It led me here!' I said to Grandpa. 'The ring. It brought me here.'

'I know,' he said.

But it couldn't be Grandpa. It must have been Billie.

But Billie was silent.

'I'm sorry,' I said. 'You're tired. Just wait. I just want to look ...'

I walked towards the tables outside the café and watched. Groups of students laughing, couples holding hands. And a woman watching me.

I didn't know her but I felt like I did. She felt the same, I think. Have you ever had that, even though the person's a complete stranger? Grandpa says when that happens it's because somewhere in the multiverse you do know each other and you're catching an echo of it. I don't know if I believe it, or even if he does, but I hope it's true.

I walked a bit closer to her. I could tell she didn't want me to, but she also did want me to. She was kind really, I could tell, but she didn't want to admit it.

I tried to tell her, about Grandpa and Granny and the ring, but the words wouldn't come out right. She looked sad and I thought I was making her sadder, so I'd better go.

And then I turned back to Billie and everything went strange and bright. I was flying, not high up in the sky but above people's heads looking down, reaching down to Billie.

And then everything tipped. The cobbles hit my face.

I fell into the dark.

*

'What?' I say.

Polly is smiling. 'Not many people describe my sister as kind. She's not a natural do-gooder.' Her smile fades. 'You reminded her of her daughter, I think.'

I nod. 'Is her daughter dead?'

Polly looked at me. 'I wasn't sure whether to tell you in case it freaked you out. How did you know?'

I shrug. I know because I know. I know about seeing ghosts.

'So, that's it,' I say. 'Then I woke up in the hospital and then I met you and we came here. I've told you the whole story.'

Polly watches me. 'The whole story, yes,' she says at last. 'But not the whole truth.'

I say nothing.

*

'Not many return from the island,' the boatman said. *'You will find things have changed when you arrive back in your own land.'*

The boatman's blindfold was gone now. One of his eyes was bright and blue, but where the other should have been there was a cracked mirror.

'Look into my seeing eye and tell me what you see,' he said.

The girl looked in the mirror and saw the face of an old woman. For the girl did not know that time passed differently on the island of the blood-red flower. A hundred midwinters and midsummers had passed while the girl had waited on the island for the flower to bloom. If she had not been carrying with her the blood-red flower, she would have become nothing more than dust blown on the wind the moment her foot touched the land. But the powerful magic of the flower protected her. She touched it to her lips and in the boatman's mirror eye she saw her reflection grow younger until she looked like herself again.

They reached the shore and the girl climbed out of the boat. Her foot touched the ground and she did not become dust blowing on the wind. She turned to thank the boatman but both he and his boat were gone.

Carrying the flower like a precious jewel, the girl travelled day and night and night and day all the way to the forest. This time, when she reached the darkest part deep among the trees, the flower broke the witch's enchantment so the girl did not get lost.

Before long she came to the wall of rose thorns that surrounded the witch's castle. She touched the flower to the thorns and instantly they sprang back and made a path for her into the castle.

*

I'm sitting in the corner of the TV room on my own when a girl I've seen around but never spoken to comes running in.

'Are you Clem?' she says, breathless. 'There's a phone call for you.'

I look at her, not understanding, though her English is good; it's my brain that's slow. She gestures impatiently with her hand held to her face: *phone*.

'Downstairs. For you.'

'For me?'

'Your mother.' She smiles as I gawp at her and takes my hand. 'Yes! Your mother!'

But I sit, unable to move, and stare at her, trying to take in her words.

My mother. On the phone.

My *mother*?

'You must come, now.'

My brain tries to catch up, slower than my feet, as I let myself be pulled along the corridor to the top of the stairs.

Mum. On the phone. Waiting to speak to me. Now.

What will she say?

What will *I* say?

'Wait,' I say. 'Stop. I just need to . . .' I hold on to the stair rail, dizzy suddenly, a little sick.

I cling to the bannister and try to catch my breath and my thoughts.

What can I say to her, to my mother who left me, who I now need to save me? What words will I possibly find?

I know you probably don't love me but please can you help me anyway? Because I haven't got anyone else.

Or:

I hate you.

Or:

Did you swim in the sea like you wanted?

'Come,' the girl says, anxious. 'Or she may be gone.'

'Yep,' I say. 'That'd be about right.'

I go downstairs, I stop outside the door of the office and I take a deep breath.

Everything has that too-real feeling, like when you're at the optician's, everything blurry, and they slot a lens in and suddenly everything is clear. I feel my heart beating. I'll say hello. That's all I need to do. The rest is up to her.

I walk into the office and Polly's there, holding the phone out to me, smiling and nodding encouragement. I hesitate and then take it from her.

'Hello?' I say. It comes out croaky, not calm and grown up, and just a tiny bit bored like I'd heard it in my head.

And then there's silence.

And then a voice says, 'Hello?'

And with a shock of familiarity, I realize her voice is one I know.

Not the voice of a stranger, as I'd expected.

Distant from myself, I think: *Does this mean I remember her? Or do I know her voice because she's part of me, I'm part of her?* And I notice, from my distant viewpoint, that I'm pleased.

270

I don't mean to be. I don't want to be. But I am pleased that her voice is familiar because it means we know each other, really know each other, and so mine will be familiar to her too.

And then, all in a slowed fragment of a second, I know that's wrong.

That's not why her voice is familiar.

'Hello? Clem? Is that you?' the voice says again, and even though the line is terrible, I can hear this voice is shaking with the effort of not cracking. 'Can you hear me, love? Are you there?'

And everything, in that elastic fraction of a moment, seems to disintegrate. It falls apart and I fall with it. I close my eyes, and when I open them the world has put itself back together in a completely different shape.

And I'm so overwhelmed with relief and disbelief and with guilt and fear and with something else that I'd forgotten I could feel, that everything blurs and I have to lean against the wall by the desk to keep from falling.

'Claudia,' I say, my voice sounding far away from where I am.

'Clem!'

'Claudia, oh my God.'

And I'm crying. Not pretty crying, like on films. Scary-sounding crying that sounds nothing like mine, not even much like a person's.

'Oh, Clem,' Claudia's voice says, 'Clem, it's okay. It's okay. I've found you.'

'Billie,' I manage to say. 'Billie . . . She—'

'I know,' she says, and her voice is cracking now. 'Oh, Clem.'
She can't speak. She sobs.

I have never heard Claudia cry like this. I have never heard anyone cry like this.

And it's my fault. I promised I would take care of Billie for her.

'I'm so sorry,' I say but it's not enough, nothing can ever be enough, but I can't stop saying it. 'I'm so sorry, Claudia, I'm so sorry—'

'No,' she says. 'No, no, no. Don't be sorry.'

'It was my fault.'

'Never say that. Never, *never* say it. Never think it, Clem.'

'But—'

'No. It's not true. I know it's not true. None of this is your fault.'

I try to breathe, gulping in air.

'I thought you'd hate me.'

'Oh, Clem. How could you think that?'

I feel weak with relief and then with fear.

'Dad . . .' I say, not wanting to hope. 'Do you know what's happened to him? I've heard nothing all this time.'

There is a pause.

'He was arrested, Clem, that's all I know. A few months ago. I don't know where he is now. But we will find him, I promise.'

My whirling brain starts to slow and settle. There are so many things I need to ask her.

'Where are you?' I realize I'm imagining her back in our kitchen, phone balanced between her ear and shoulder as she makes coffee or types on her laptop or hunts for some missing item of Billie's school uniform. But that's impossible, of course. That life is gone.

'I'm in Ireland,' she says. 'It's a long story. But I can live here, Clem, until it's safe to go home. And so can you. It'll take a while to sort out but we can be together.'

I tried to take it in. 'Could we? Are you sure?'

'I'm sure. Look, I've got to go but I'll call you tomorrow, okay?'

I don't want her to go. I want to keep her with me.

She is part of me. I am part of her. The careful not-mother-daughter almost-love we had before is gone. We're bound now by something more than that, something greater even than love.

I step out of the office, dazed. Polly sees my tears. She hugs me.

'Claudia,' I say at last. 'It was Claudia.'

'Yes.'

'I thought it was my biological mum.'

'You thought ...?' She puts her hand to her mouth as she understands. 'I'm so sorry, Clem ... You're okay?'

I realize she means do I mind that it wasn't Seren, that she is still as disappeared as she ever was, as absent when I needed her as she has been all my life. Well, do I mind? I pause to consider it and, yes, I do, a bit. Of course I do. But it's nothing new, that hurt. An old scar, not a wound. And I find it doesn't really matter now. Hearing Claudia's voice, I felt safe for the first time in a long, long time. And something else too. I felt love. More than I could ever feel for Seren.

'Claudia's alive!' I say, and I feel the tears come again. 'I'm going to see her.'

Polly smiles. 'Yes,' she says. 'Soon.'

'She knows. And she doesn't ...' I was going to say, *She doesn't hate me*, but I stop myself.

Somehow, the way Polly looks at me, it's like I said it anyway.

'Clem,' she says, 'can I ask you a question?'

I look at her. I know what that question will be.

It is time for me to let go.

'Yes,' I say. 'You can ask me.'

I wait. We've both been waiting for this moment, for this question, and its answer, to be spoken out loud. We've waited ever since we met.

'Where is Billie?' Polly asks at last.

Her words make the air strange and alive, like the moment before lightning.

Where is Billie?

Is she outside with the others?

Is she making up some nonsense song? Talking to her friends in a made-up mix of Arabic/English/Hungarian with lots of handwaving and actions like charades at Christmas?

No.

Is she sleeping? Perhaps she's asleep. I have hoped this before.

The words won't come. I close my eyes.

It's the day I left London.

I'm saying to Dad: *I can't go. I can't leave without her. It was supposed to be both of us.*

And Dad says: *You're not leaving her, Clem! She's with you. She'll always be with you. You know that. But you have to go. I need you to. I need you to be okay. Do it for me. Do it for Billie.*

That is the truth.

She *is* with me.

I see her across the room now, nose pressed to the window, looking out at the cat on the flat roof opposite, laughing; saying, 'Eww, Clem, look at the kitty-cat! He's licking his bum. I still love him though.'

And she's outside, in her red raincoat, waving at me with the new friends she's made, because she always makes new friends wherever she is, sticking her tongue out and telling them all to do the same in various languages, real and invented.

And she's in one of the rooms downstairs too, along the corridor, but I can still see her, carefully folding a paper crane from coloured paper, her tongue sticking out in concentration.

It's true. But it's also a story.

'Will you tell me what happened to Billie?' Polly says.

Will I? Can I?

once there was a girl who

I'd rather leave it unfinished.

But every story has an ending.

LOST

Unable to find your way. Not knowing where you are or how to get to where you want to go. That which has been mislaid, taken away or cannot be recovered. Without hope.

U p the steps from the shadowy Underground station into the sharp, silver light, the hum and chatter and shout of the crowd, the smell of frying onions and cigarette smoke.

'I didn't realize there'd be so many people,' says Mischa.

Oxford Street bathed in sunshine.

'You hold too tight,' Billie whines. 'Your nails dig in.'

'See you in a minute.' Mischa calling over her shoulder, turning and walking away. 'I'll bring you some fries, B.'

Dad's voice on the phone, the garbled message. We need to get away.

'Can I speak to him?' Billie says.

Shouts and screams and a wave of people, running, pushing, crushing.

'Billie!' She stumbles. I grab her, try to lift her up as best I can.

'Are you okay?' I gasp. 'Can you breathe okay?'

She nods with wide eyes.

'Run,' the woman in the purple puffa jacket says.

If we can just get to a shop doorway out of the tide of people—

'Come on, Billie, we have to—'

I look down and somehow—

'Billie!'

Jesus.

'Billie?'

Somehow, she's gone.

'BILLIE!' I yell. I look all around. I want to run, but in which direction? I could be running away from her.

'BILLIE!' I scream, blind and paralysed with panic. Oh, God. Please. 'Billie!'

She can't have gone far. She can't have. She was there a second ago. I was holding her hand.

'Billie!' I can't breathe.

And then—

And then . . .

Then someone grabs hold of me and drags me along.

'You need to get out of here. Fast.' A man about Dad's age.

'My sister! I've lost my little sister.' I'm sobbing and gasping.

'Shit.' He looks back at me, reflecting my horror, and then looks around, scanning the chaos of running people, fallen bodies. 'Look, someone will help her. She's a little kid. Someone will get her out of here and then you can find her, after.'

'But what if they don't? What if—'

And suddenly, there's screaming and another sound. A crack. Another crack.

I look at the man, not understanding. Is someone setting off fireworks?

'Plastic bullets,' he says.

Bullets?

'They're only plastic bullets. They hurt you but they don't kill.'

And then there's the crack of another shot and a tall guy, middle-aged, in a parka, drops to the ground a few metres away.

I stare, unable to understand what I'm seeing. A dark patch spreads across the ground beneath him.

My insides heave.

'Shit!' The man grabs me and pulls me with him and we run. All the time I'm screaming for Billie but she's not anywhere.

I see a child running but they're too tall for Billie. I see another in a red coat, hood up like Billie's, being carried on the back of an adult and my heart leaps, but no, that kid is pale-skinned and blonde. Not Billie.

'Billie . . .' I try to shout but it comes out as a gasp. I can't run. I can't breathe. I stand, dizzy, looking around me through the fog of tear gas spreading back behind us the way we've come, people swarming everywhere, grey shapes around me like ghosts. Another shot rings out nearby and I'm pulled into a shop doorway where other people are crouched.

I try to run but someone is holding me back.

'Stay down!'

The crowd has thinned, fractured from a mass into people running, staggering, calling names.

'My sister,' I say again, though I hardly have any breath left and struggle to form the words, and I shake off the hands holding me back and run, calling, calling. *Billie—*

And then I see something lying on the ground.

It's a child's toy, an owl. I bend to pick it up. My hands are shaking. There is blood on them. I look up and I know what I'm going to see.

She's lying in the road, a few metres away, but I know it's her even through the smoke. Her hair, her clothes. Everything else fades. There is nothing else. I run towards her. One of her trainers has come off and lies abandoned in the road next to her.

'Billie!'

There's shouting somewhere nearby and at a distance—

'*Get down—*'

'*No—*'

Someone's hand is grabbing my arm but I shake it off and then I've reached her small body, lying in the road as if she's asleep.

'Billie! Billie, it's me. Wake up, Billie.'

Then there's another *crack crack* and searing pain in my shoulder and the ground slams hard against my back. I'm staring at the bluest sky, dazzling above me, not a single cloud anywhere. My body is heavy and far away, the pain the only part of me that feels real. I concentrate on where my arm must be and force it to move. I feel across the tarmac for Billie's hand. I find it and clasp it in mine.

'Don't let go,' I try to say. 'Billie, don't let go.'

But her hand is limp.

Billie. Don't let go.

But the words won't come and the colour is draining from the sky.

I'll tell you a story, Billie ... I try to say, but it's no good.

I see a bird, I think, flying far above us, far, far away. I want to tell Billie that I'm wishing on the bird and that means it will be okay, but I can't speak. I just try to fix my eyes on the bird – only now I can't see it —

Now I can't see anything.

Don't let go, I say in my head.

Don't let go.

Don't—

*

There's a voice somewhere. A woman's voice. But it's muffled, echoing, like I'm hearing it underwater.

It's saying words I don't understand. Am I in a foreign country?

I try to listen closely and some of the words seem almost familiar.

I hear my name.

A face appears far above me, a blue mask over the mouth. It floats. It blurs and warps.

Something is very wrong, but I don't know what. I can't remember what. There's pain. I can't breathe. I'm drowning.

I look around for Billie. She won't drown. She can swim like a fish, like a mermaid. Perhaps she'll save me if she just takes hold of my hand and doesn't let go. But I can't see her and so I am drowning.

I try to move, try to get the attention of the woman, whoever she is, up there floating above the water.

'It's okay,' the voice says.

I force my eyes open again although everything is hazy and too bright and my eyelids are so heavy.

'Mum?' I say, or try to, but it bubbles away into the waves. I can see her more clearly now, in her silky, film-star dress, with the tiny buttons all the way up the back, the mask gone. But then she blurs again and her eyes grow bigger and darker, her shining dress turning to sleek fur as I sink deeper and she fades into shadow.

'Her BP's spiking,' Mum says.

'Clem!' Someone else is there. 'Clem, can you hear me?'

A hand on my arm. Dad.

'Can't you do something?' he says. He sounds scared. 'Please do something.'

'I can't, Dad. I can't do anything. I'm sorry. I can't do anything.'

But maybe the current is too strong and my voice floats away, out to the deepest sea where no light reaches. I fight against the pull of it.

'It's okay, Clem,' Mum says. But she's changed. She isn't Mum now. She takes off her mask and is someone else altogether.

'Oh, it's not you,' and I wonder whether Mum has always been someone else.

'Hush. You sleep now, Clem,' the not-Mum says. Her voice is soothing. 'That's it.'

I give myself up to the current and it pulls me under, into the darkness, away from them.

'You've been here three weeks,' Dad says, sitting on my hospital bed, holding my hand. 'More.' He has bruised-looking rings under his eyes and greyish stubble. He is thin. Out of the window I can see it's raining.

'No,' I say.

'They brought you to St Thomas's. After ... Do you remember?'

I remember flashes. Someone carrying me and running, leaning over low, shielding me with their body. A person running in front of us, I could see their legs upside down as my head lolled back; they were holding something white and red-stained up towards the sky, which was below us. There were no birds to wish on in that fallen sky. On the paving stones, above us, blood, a shoe, abandoned placards. And then an ambulance, the driver arguing with someone in army uniform, shouting at them. Sirens. And then screaming. Me, screaming and—

'Billie?' I say. 'Billie. Where is she?'

Dad's eyes flicker away from mine. Time has shifted. His stubble is now a beard. Sunlight streams through the window.

'Clem ...' He takes both my hands and looks right at me again.

'No.'

'Billie's here. No, I mean, she's in this hospital. A few floors up. She's in a coma. She's . . .' He can't speak.

I shake my head and take my hands away from his.

'She's very ill, Clem,' he says at last. 'They say . . .'

His voice falters.

'They're wrong,' I say.

'They say she's dying. That she's gone already really.'

'She's not.'

'I'm sorry,' he says. He is crying. He covers his face with his hands.

I close my eyes.

They tell me I'm not yet strong enough to see Billie but I tell them that if they don't let me I'll take out all the needles and tubes and go up there anyway, and then if I collapse and die it will all be their fault. They're busy, understaffed. They can't watch me all the time. The consultant says wearily, 'Well, under the circumstances, I suppose . . .' and so they let me go up to see her.

Dad takes me in a wheelchair. I'm still attached to a drip, which has to be wheeled along with us, and its wheels are like the sort on a supermarket trolley that all try to go in the opposite directions from each other and us. The whole thing would have been funny once but now I can't imagine what laughing feels like.

We get the lift up. I look at us in the endless lift mirrors, the thin, grey man and the pale girl in a hospital gown, sprouting tubes and metal, repeating and repeating into infinity. I don't recognize us.

Billie is lying in a hospital bed like mine and when I see her I smile and although my voice catches in my throat I call out to her, because the doctors are wrong. She's not dying! She's Billie, sleeping, looking like she always looks when she's sleeping – okay, yes, with lots of tubes and pumps and drips and monitors, but otherwise just as though I've finished telling her a story and she's drifted off to sleep.

I make Dad wheel me right up to her, close enough to reach out and hold her hand. It feels small and right in mine.

I shouldn't have let go. I don't understand how I let go.

'Billie,' I say. 'I'm here.'

And although she doesn't reply I know she knows.

'Don't let go,' I whisper.

I sit on the edge of Billie's bed, as I do every day, waiting to catch my breath after the short walk from the lift, watching her face.

I wonder where she is. Far, far away. I remember how it felt, being under the water, seeing not-Mum through the water. Billie is deeper than that. She is in the depths near the seabed, I think, where the fish glow because it's darker than night down there. She can't see me. But I think she can hear me. They say maybe she can, the nurses – they say, 'Go on, Clem – talk to her. Go on. It might help.'

I take a deep breath and I try to find the right thing to say.

'It's me,' I say, heart thudding. 'Billie, it's me. Clem.'

Then silence, except for hospital noise. *Beep, hiss, thud.* I have nothing to tell her.

'There's a man on my ward who snores like a pig,' I say. 'And there's a woman who cries. Especially at night. Nice and quiet here though. We're a lot of floors up. Really high. We're looking out over the river.'

The Thames is silver-grey today, like the sky. It's always surprising when you see it from above, the way it loops and bends, twists of satiny ribbon dropped across a toy city.

'You can see the London Eye,' I tell Billie. It's not turning though: it's like a stopped clock, which seems right. The glass pods are all empty. No tourists now. No day-trippers.

Everything is quiet. There are no buses today. No traffic on the bridge. No queues for the London Eye or the Aquarium. No joggers, no buskers. Everything is still, slick with rain. No passenger boats either, only a police boat – or army maybe. A boat with armed officers onboard anyway. The breath seems to stick in my throat as I watch it patrolling up and down, cutting through the dark water in a straight line. The police boats are like cats, seemingly lazy and indifferent, advancing slowly, but in reality watching, always on the alert and ready to pounce. Shadow, our old cat would sit for ages in the garden, patiently watching the birds flying back and forth to their nest. And then he'd rattle in through the cat flap and deliver limp, fluffy-feathered baby birds at our feet, tiny burst cushions, all the life gone. The patrol boat passes right in front of me, so I can see each uniformed figure, each hand, each weapon. I press the glass with my hands to convince myself that it's really there and then lean my forehead against it because it's cool and close my eyes again.

The silence presses in, suffocating, and I need to break it.

'Remember Shadow?' I say. 'Remember how he used to lie on your head and purr during the night.'

Billie never fully forgave him for the baby birds, despite loving him intensely. When he met his own demise, under the wheels of a Tesco delivery van, she cried. But after we'd covered over the shoebox containing his remains she stamped down the earth forcefully with a wellied foot and said, 'The birds will be safe now.'

I turn around to Billie.

She's still exactly as she was: expressionless, calm, far, far away.

If I could only find the right thing to say, the right story to tell, perhaps I can bring her back.

'Clem?'

Billie's voice.

I fight to get to her, force my eyes open, push myself up through the dark to reach her. It should be hard to sleep on the too-loud, too-bright ward but one of the pills or tubes sees to that and blurs the time I'm awake.

When I open my eyes, I see Billie standing there in her nightie, holding Luna, just like that night after Claudia left, just like I will see her many times on many nights to come, when I will wake in the dark and hear her say my name.

'B?' I say, hazy with sleep and painkillers. 'Can't sleep? Come on. In you get.'

She just smiles.

'I'll tell you a story,' she says.

And she does, a story that makes me laugh and cry and reach out to hold her hand. But by the time she finishes it I find it's gone from my mind completely, like words written in wet sand washed away by a wave.

'Now go to sleep,' she says.

I slip into blank emptiness.

When I wake up, she is gone. The bed is cold.

Dad's there. He is crying.

'Clem,' he says. 'Oh, Clem.'

'No,' I say, my voice sticking in my throat. 'I just saw her. She was here.'

'I'm sorry.'

No.

I close my eyes.

This is the ending.

Once there was a girl who died.

*

As the girl ran into the castle, the sound of birdsong grew louder and louder. She found a courtyard, with a fountain at its centre and flowers growing about it. There stood the witch, still as young and beautiful as ever. All around her were hundreds upon hundreds of golden birdcages. They hung from every branch of every tree, and in every cage was a bird singing its own sweet, sad song. The girl knew she must destroy the witch before she could find her sister and free all the other birds.

The witch sprang towards her. At once the girl took the blood-red flower and touched the witch with it. As soon as the red petals touched the witch's skin she began to wither like a rotten apple, shrivelling and crumpling, then collapsing into dust.

The instant the witch was dead, her enchantment was broken. The golden cages all sprang open and the birds flew out. For a moment the girl saw them all as the children they had been before the witch had cast her spell on them, saw their eager faces, heard an echo of their chatter, the joyful sound of their laughter.

But the moment was brief, for had it not been for the witch's enchantment the children would all have died long ago.

And so, as the girl watched, the bird-children all rose up, birds once more, in a rainbow of wings and birdsong, until they faded into nothing. One bird flew towards the girl, and she knew it was her sister. The little creature was weak, barely able to fly, so the girl cradled her gently in her hand as the bird sang her beautiful, sad song.

'You must fly away with the others,' the girl said, choked with tears.

But the bird would not leave. She sang on, the music growing fainter and fainter, until at last her song and her breath stopped.

The girl wept bitterly. Her search had all been for nothing. She carried the bird to the tree where she had first dreamt of the blood-red flower and buried her there. Then she lay down and cried until she slept. She dreamt her sister was sitting next to her.

'You buried my bones beneath the wishing tree,' the sister said, 'and so now, whenever you sleep with my feather beneath your pillow, I will come to you.'

When the girl woke, she heard birdsong in the branches of the tree above her and a single blue feather drifted down as the bird flew away.

The girl picked up the feather, as blue as the summer's sky, and knew her sister would always be with her.

*

The last thing I pack is my notebook. I close the rucksack and bend to lift it onto my back.

Downstairs, Polly is waiting for me. She hugs me.

'This is for you,' she says, holding out a tiny spider plant. 'Or maybe for your stepmum with the green fingers.'

'Hey,' I say. 'Your spider plant had babies. Congrats.'

She smiles modestly.

'Oh,' I say, 'this is for you.' I hand her a paper crane, folded out of a flyer from the rack in the foyer about sexually transmitted diseases. 'Sorry, it was the only thing I could find.'

'I'll treasure it always,' she says.

'Thanks,' I say. 'I always thought I hated shrinks but you're okay.'

'I'm not exactly a shrink, but thanks anyway. I'll miss you, Clem. Let me know how you're getting on, will you?'

'I will,' I say, because you have to, don't you? But then I think, maybe I actually will keep in touch with Polly. Because when she says, 'I'll miss you, Clem,' I can see she really means it. And I realize I might even miss her too. She didn't have to do what she did. I bet the pay's rubbish and Polly's smart. She could get an easier job in a proper office with a fancy coffee machine and a gym and a healthcare plan. But instead she sits in a cupboard full of plants she's killed and helps people like me. So maybe I will send her a postcard, one day. I turn and walk to the door.

'Oh!' I turn back to her suddenly, just as I'm about to walk out. 'Can you tell your posh sister thanks too? Tell her she *is* kind, even if she doesn't think she is. And tell her my sister Billie agreed with her: stories should have happy endings.'

Polly smiles. 'And what about you, Clem? Do you think stories should have happy endings?'

I turn again to the door. Through its glass I can see the world outside, waiting for me to step into it.

'I guess we'll find out.'

HOPE

The feeling of wanting something to happen or be true. A person or thing that may help or save someone. An optimistic belief that something good may happen.

We live by the sea now, Claudia and I.

When I first saw her, at the airport – months ago now – it was hard to believe it was really her. I walked through the doors and there were all the people waiting with signs with other people's names on and I couldn't see her, and I started to panic, thinking maybe something had happened to her or maybe she couldn't face seeing me after all because of Billie, or maybe I'd just imagined the whole thing. Panic is always there now, just under my skin, between every heartbeat.

And then a big guy from a taxi firm holding up a sign moved out of the way and there was Claudia just standing there waiting, looking sharpened and thinner but really just the same, and her face when she saw me made me feel like I'd made it home at last.

At first, we didn't talk much about what happened to us.

She'd been moved from the detention centre in Kent to a camp somewhere in Wales. She didn't tell me too much about what it was like, except that it was bad. I remembered what

Shaun had told me about the camp near the village. There were so many people there, Claudia said, that the guards were overwhelmed. Some were just kids themselves really, some were even kind. Eventually, when food and medication was in such short supply that people were dying, there was a riot. The guards couldn't stop it. They didn't even want to, Claudia said. They were as hungry and sick as everyone else. And she'd escaped and made it across the sea to Ireland.

Toby Knight's days are numbered, Claudia says. He's no longer in control. It's only a matter of time before he goes. I don't want to hope, but if life has taught me anything it's that Claudia is always right.

We haven't found Dad yet.

We will, Claudia says. It'll just take time.

Every day she makes a new list, and every day she gets closer to finding him. As soon as she was safe, she tracked down other people in his resistance network. Most of them had either been arrested or were in hiding, but if you're an item on Claudia's list it's only a matter of time before you get ticked off. Some were unwilling to talk to her. They didn't know whether they could trust her or whether they were being set up. But eventually she found out that Dad was arrested at a house in Chatham and she thinks he was taken to a prisoner camp somewhere north of Newcastle. After that, she hasn't found any trace of him. She says if he'd died there, we'd know. I think she says this because she has to believe it. But she says some people who were in that camp escaped and made it to Scotland, so maybe we were closer together than I knew.

I still make paper cranes, every day, filling our tiny house with them. One day they will bring him home. When they do, I'll tell him I know he blames himself for what happened to Billie and that he shouldn't. I couldn't say it when I left and I wish I had. I'll tell him how he kept me alive, all those months. He told me I had to keep going, for him. And I did, even when I felt like I couldn't.

Claudia and I are lucky. Can this really be true, when the worst thing we could imagine has happened to us?

We know it can, even when we don't feel it.

We're lucky to be alive. Lucky to have a home, and food, a place to live and people around us – friends now – who have taken us in and looked out for us and been kind to us even though they didn't know us or owe us anything, kind just because we needed their help.

Others haven't been so lucky, we remind ourselves. Still, some days it is unbearable.

Most of all we are lucky to have each other, though even this isn't always easy. We drift as if carried by the tide, in and out, closer together, farther apart.

Never too far though. We are together. I love Claudia in a way that I will never love anyone else. She was the person who found me, who never gave up on me, who kept me safe. We are each other's. Nothing can change that.

But we are hollowed out.

We try not to wait: for Dad; for things to get better; for our old selves. When it's safe, we will go home, but our old life will not be waiting for us there. This is our life for now and we must live it.

I study, more than I used to. I signed up for a drama group to keep Claudia happy because she said it was important to join things. I haven't actually been yet. But last week I went to the cinema with some girls from college. Claudia works some locum shifts at the local hospital. She does yoga and goes on long walks by the sea. She works with other refugee families, helping them to find people they've lost or helping them to settle.

We planted an apple tree for Billie in a pot so we can take it with us when we leave. We sing it Billie's favourite songs to help it to grow. In the spring it will flower with white and pink blossom. In the autumn, if we sing enough, perhaps it will give us fruit.

We have started to make plans. It's harder than you'd think, looking ahead, so we're starting small. Nothing big. Day trips, that kind of thing. If the landlord lets us, we'll paint the front door cherry red.

We are even happy, sometimes.

I realized after a while I'd stopped waiting for Mum too. All those years I waited for her. I thought she was my story, but she wasn't, any more than I was hers. She doesn't want to be found. I don't need to look any more. I have Claudia. I have Dad and Billie, even though they're not here.

I still worry about Grandpa. For weeks after I got here it was impossible to get news from the village. Then one day a message popped up on my laptop screen when I was doing my homework. *Hello, stranger! You missing us yet? Huw sends all his love.* I cried.

Shaun messages when he can now, when the internet isn't blocked. Things are better, he says, though food is still rationed. And no one will forget what happened. Feuds run down generations in this village, he says, but then what's new?

Jonas escaped the village and his mum. Shaun says he thinks he's in France. He says he knows he'll get in touch with me when he can. I hope he's right.

I think he's right.

I allow myself to hope that much at least.

One day a miracle happened. My phone rang. Till then, my phone never rang unless it was Claudia asking me to pick up some oat milk on the way home from college or whatever. This was a number I didn't recognize. I ignored it, thinking it must be a wrong number or a cold caller. But then, once it stopped, I started to panic. Polly has my number; it could have been her. Maybe it was someone with news about Dad. I called the number back, feeling so sick I could hardly speak.

There was a crackling noise at the other end of the line.

'I think you just called me?' I said quickly.

'Well why didn't you bloody answer then, babe?'

After the protest her mum had booked them straight on a flight to Poland. They left that evening. 'We were lucky,' she said. 'If she'd left it a few more days we'd never have got there.' They'd lived for a year with Mischa's family on their farm in the middle of nowhere. There was no internet and no phone signal except at the top of this one specific hill. There was no anything except for pigs and 'extremely judgy' relatives, according to Mischa, who admittedly has been known to exaggerate. After not very long, her mum remembered why she'd left for England in the first place: her family drove her crazy. The countryside drove her crazy. Even the pigs drove her crazy. Her mum made Mischa promise not to use social media because she was sure she would say something stupid and get herself arrested. Mischa ignored her but she kept her identity very secret. She looked for me but I'd disappeared. Eventually, when the borders were reopened, they decided to go back to London, even though the advice was not to because the political situation was still unstable and no one knew whether it would be safe. The weird thing was that once she was home, Mischa found she missed Poland, which she realized was beautiful now she was no longer there. And she missed her family who she realized were loving and funny and generous, though still kind of judgy. And she missed the *pierogi* made by her *babcia* who she missed most of all, even though she was borderline tyrannical in Mischa's opinion. Anyway, when she arrived back at the flat, she found my note with Grandpa's number and after trying a million different versions of the number I'd written, which was wrong, she'd finally got through to Shaun.

He told her about Billie. I was glad I didn't have to. But talking to Mischa about Billie was a relief, somehow. We remembered. We cried. We laughed too.

We talked about Danny. Mischa hadn't seen him, didn't know

what happened to him. She said she wasn't sure she wanted to find out. I reminded her of that time he bought the pencil case for Billie. She said, 'Clem, don't. My mascara's enough of a mess already. Oh, why can't everything just be how it was?'

We talked until my phone battery was about to die.

'I've had conversations with you this whole time,' I told her. 'All the time you weren't there I still talked to you. I didn't even know if you were alive. I should have trusted Wendy. She said she could feel your vibrations.'

'Of course she could. My vibrations are hard to miss, babe.'

I asked Claudia one day if she remembered the word for Billie's spinning toy with the little pictures inside. It was a zoetrope. I liked the strangeness of the word. I looked it up, like Grandpa would have, but online instead of in a dictionary with a magnifying glass. It's from the Greek, apparently. It means 'life turning'.

On the windowsill of my bedroom is a bird folded from gold paper. Sometimes I think of Sakura, how she gave Billie the gift of a paper crane because she didn't want her to be sad, and how our trail of birds leads all the way back to her act of kindness for the friend she loved. I hold the fragile bird in my hands and wish for Sakura to be alive, to be well, to be happy. Next to the paper crane are a blue feather, a photograph, a cracked mirror.

I tell Claudia how Grandpa told me stories after Mum left. And about how after Claudia was arrested I told versions of them to Billie. I show her the notebook, though I can hardly bear to look at it. She reads, and her tears fall on the pages.

If this was a fairy tale, I think, where her tears fall on the petals pressed between the pages a flower would grow. And when the petals of the flower unfurled, inside would be a tiny, extraordinary girl, and the girl would grow and grow until she was tall and strong and clever, fizzing with ideas and love and curiosity.

But this is a story. It is my story. I can make anything I like happen.

Do I believe in happy endings?

Where Claudia's tears fall a flower does not grow. There will be no extraordinary girl, now, except in our dreams and in unexpected echoes.

Claudia closes the notebook gently.

It is late. It is nearly the end.

Is this a happy ending? No. But it is a beginning, as all endings are.

*

It's a steep walk up to the top of the cliff from where we live. It's cold at this time of the morning, even in summer, but I'm hot with effort by the time I get to the top.

I feel calm and strong. I think of Bridie and touch the hag stone nestled against Granny's emerald ring, which still hangs round my neck, on a chain now instead of twine, thanks to Claudia.

It's my birthday, again.

I woke early and my first thoughts were of Billie, of Dad, of my fifteenth birthday in the park. Of Billie putting Smarties on the cake, and Danny playing football with the kids. I hope I didn't imagine that Danny. I wonder where he is now.

For once, I was up before Claudia. Mischa had already messaged me with seven lipstick-kiss emojis:

> **HAPPY BIRTHDAY LOVE YOU**

Up on the cliff I sit and look out at the sea for a while. I take a picture of it and send it to Mischa. A message comes back straight away.

> **Okay now ur just showing off!**

I type:

> **Wish you were here.**

She sends me back a photo of the car park outside the flats. It's raining.

> **Me too, babe.**

I put my phone in my bag. I take out the notebook. I look through its pages, at the stories I wrote for Billie, at the little messages she wrote for me all that time ago, before she even gave it to me.

On a page near the end of the book she has drawn a picture of her and me with wings. Underneath she's written:

This is us flying

I stand as near to the cliff edge as I dare, the sea crashing below me.

I remember: Billie's smile, her frown, the way she stuck her tongue out when she was concentrating. But she wouldn't look like that now, not exactly. How would she have changed already? Who would she have grown up to be? And who would I have become in the version of my future with Billie still in it? All those possibilities, those dreams, those stories. They can never happen, but they're part of me anyway.

once there was a girl who

Billie was the story that kept me going, that got me here.

Stories are hope, even the sad ones.

The story ends. The hope doesn't.

'She'll always be with you,' Dad said. He was right.

I take out the first paper crane Billie and I ever made from where it's folded into the pages of the notebook and I throw it out into the salt-sharp air as the sun rises over the sea.

I make a wish.

I see it soar.

I hear its song.

I will always hear its song.

Then I sit and take out my pen. I turn to the last page of the notebook. It's still blank. And I write:

Once there was a girl who lived.

Acknowledgements

The Things We Leave Behind was written over a long and rather difficult time, and I am immensely grateful for the patience and support of my publisher and in particular my editor, Amina Youssef. Amina took over the editing of this book halfway through, at a point when I was despairing that I would ever be able to finish it or make it work, and her calm, clear-sighted approach made it all seem manageable. She has improved the book at every stage with her insight and guidance.

I'm also hugely grateful to Jane Griffiths, my editor when I first started writing this story, who believed in the idea and contributed so much to its development.

Enormous thanks as ever to my wonderful agent Catherine Clarke for her belief in my work, her patience, her support and her general wisdom. I feel very lucky indeed to have Catherine as my agent.

I'm grateful to Steve Voake, Lu Hersey, David Hofmeyr, Chris Vick, Finbar Hawkins and Mel Darbon for their always excellent ideas and suggestions in the editing process, as well as their general positivity and support.

Thanks to my dear friends Jenny and Maria who have been my unpaid therapists throughout the writing of this book.

Finally, and most importantly, huge love and thanks to my family, David, Marianne, Joe and Ewan, who have lived with the writing of this book for what feels like for ever and put up with the various hardships of living with a writer who is finding it very difficult to write. They have also all in various ways directly contributed to the story. And, as always, thanks to my mum and dad for their love and support.

© Lou Abercrombie

Clare Furniss grew up in London and moved to Birmingham in her teens. After brief stints as a waitress, shop assistant and working at the Shakespeare Centre Library, she studied at Cambridge University and worked for several years in political media relations. She now lives in Bath and has completed an MA in Writing for Young People at Bath Spa University. Clare's novels have been shortlisted for numerous awards including the Branford Boase, CILIP Carnegie and *The Bookseller* YA Book Prize. You can follow her on Twitter @clarefurniss and find out more information on her website www.clarefurniss.com

READ ALL OF
CLARE FURNISS' BOOKS ...

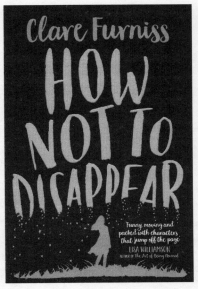